"A richly imagined, spellbinding romantic fantasy . . . atmospheric, absorbing, infused with dark magic, gripping intrigue, and mesmerizing sensuality. I'm totally hooked and I can't wait for more!"
—*New York Times* bestselling author Lara Adrian

"Excitement, adventure, royal intrigue, and a what-if scenario that could change the world. Terri Brisbin weaves them together with the masterful touch that has become her trademark."
—*New York Times* bestselling author Maggie Shayne

"An intriguing story filled with romantic tension."
—Fresh Fiction

"An amazing premise for a paranormal series . . . you gotta read it."
—Debbie's Book Bag

"Brisbin begins her romantic fantasy series in style . . . plenty of danger and romance."
—*RT Reviews*

**FURTHER PRAISE FOR
TERRI BRISBIN AND HER NOVELS**

"A carefully crafted plot spiced with a realistic measure of deadly intrigue and a richly detailed, fascinating medieval setting."
—*Chicago Tribune*

Also by Terri Brisbin

RISING FIRE
RAGING SEA

BLAZING EARTH

A NOVEL OF THE STONE CIRCLES

Terri Brisbin

A SIGNET ECLIPSE BOOK

SIGNET ECLIPSE
Published by New American Library,
an imprint of Penguin Random House LLC
375 Hudson Street, New York, New York 10014

This book is an original publication of New American Library.

First Printing, April 2016

Copyright © Theresa S. Brisbin, 2016
Excerpt from *Rising Fire* © Theresa S. Brisbin, 2015

Signet Eclipse and the Signet Eclipse colophon are trademarks of Penguin Random
House LLC.

For more information about Penguin Random House, visit penguin.com.

ISBN 978-0-451-46912-0

Printed in the United States of America
10 9 8 7 6 5 4 3 2 1

Penguin
Random
House

There's a very special group of women who are important to me in so many ways. We began as part of an RWA chapter retreat and now continue the Hermit tradition each fall in Charleston, South Carolina. We spend a week together, writing and talking and brainstorming and, sometimes, just being there for one another. These women have been a godsend to me in so many ways over the last couple of years and while I wrote this series. So Janice, Madeline, Gabrielle, Kim, Blythe, Robin, Bev, Ann, Amanda, Keena, Bernie, Deb, Sabrina, Ellen, and Neroli—this one is for you . . . all!
And to Jen Schmidt and Lyn Wagner, without whom I could never have written this series—thanks!

THE LEGEND

Centuries ago

Cernunnos, god of the earth and growing things, gathered with the others within the stone circle, waiting for Chaela's answer to their demands. Her destruction must stop. Her hunger for power and control must cease. Though he suspected she would refuse, he hoped that she would surprise him . . . and their brothers and sisters. The fate of humanity and this world awaited her next actions. But then her words, screamed into the air around them and into their minds, decided her wretched fate.

For a moment, he regretted what they must do to rein in her foolhardy aims. Only for a moment, for she rose into the sky, transforming into her favored shape and unleashing her destructions on the humans there, around them. As fire flooded the land, the henge, and the people, Taranis, the god of the sky and storm, nodded to him and Cernunnos knew their path.

The six of them—Cernunnos, Belenus, Nantosuelta,

Taranis, Sucellus, and Epona—began weaving the spell that would imprison their sister forever. The sounds began as but a whisper, gaining volume and strength as each one added his or her voice to it. This ritual would surround her and nullify her powers. The song they created would bind her in silence and imprison her in the empty abyss, away from humanity and away from this world. When the human priest added his voice, chanting human words to the ethereal melody, Chaela screamed out.

Her evil intent clear, she inhaled deeply, ready to finish the destruction she'd begun. They could wait no longer to take this painful action and sent their own breaths across the landscape there, surrounding the stone circle and drawing Chaela into its center. High above them, she struggled against their growing, combined power over her. Though they could each feel her struggle, her power and her words were swaddled within the cocoon they created around her.

"Cháela," Belenus, the god of healing and order, called out to her. "Cease this and you will be allowed to live." A truce. He, they, offered a way out of this confrontation.

"Fools!" she roared back, struggling to make her voice serve her will. "I cannot be destroyed!"

She was correct—they were elemental powers, flung into existence at the beginning of time, and could not be destroyed. But that did not mean they could not control her. . . .

"You can be defeated, Chaela," Sucellus, the god of war, warned her. "You will be imprisoned in the endless pit and never return. Your name will be forbidden and forgotten."

When she did not capitulate, Cernunnos gathered his power over the earth and plants and began to craft the prison that would hold her. At a thought, the earth in the center of the circle buckled and roared. He forced a deep crater into the earth's surface, an abyss that went on and on beneath it, toward its core.

Then he imbued the walls of it with power, whispering the words in his mind and guiding the soil to do his bidding. Soon, the endless pit was prepared and awaited its prisoner. Taranis's winds then brought her over it and pushed her into the earth, holding her while the final step was taken.

This step, a necessary but terrible one, for it called for a supreme sacrifice, would seal her out of this human world. A human male who carried Chaela's blood and power over fire stepped into the circle and joined them in the ritual, adding his voice to theirs. Her screams pierced the spell and made this human world shake on its foundation.

She knew now.

And she feared.

Taranis forced her farther down into the blackness, thrusting her deep into the chamber that existed within and outside this world. Their words sung and whispered would now seal it, and spilling the blood of Chaela's human son on the barrier would keep her there forever.

The man walked to the edge then and, with a nod, threw himself off the edge, soaring out over the abyss. Sucellus created a spear of iron and threw it at the man, impaling him, piercing his heart and spilling his blood into the pit.

Cernunnos and the other gods honored the sacrifice, freely made, with their words, and completed the ritual that sealed Chaela away. With but a thought, the earth flowed over the pit, hiding its location. Belenus, the god of order and healing, caused a blessed silence over the area as the chamber closed and disappeared. The stones in the circle shrank and returned to their usual size and positions and everything was right with the world.

Glancing at the others, Cernunnos could see the cost that they had paid for their actions. They would never be the same again, for they had raised their powers against one of their own. The worst part was knowing that they'd barely succeeded in this. It had taken all of their powers combined against Chaela's to conquer her, and then only a blood sacrifice brought victory to them. Now, at least, the human world and its inhabitants were safe and would remain so.

Forever.

Knowing that humans could continue without their help, they planned to leave this world. In spite of their triumph this day, they decided to instill their powers in their own human bloodlines to keep watch . . . always.

Warriors of destiny, not war. A race of men and women who could rise, if ever needed, and keep this evil at bay.

But, with the gods' course of actions this day, these warriors would never need to do more than keep watch. They would never need to rise up against evil.

Never.

PROLOGUE

S he, the unspeakable beast, rose on black-and-red wings and filled his vision of the sky. She tilted her head back and roared her joy. The sound of it turned his blood cold, but what Corann saw next caused his legs to give out and his heart to pound against the walls of his chest.

A dragon!

The goddess was a dragon.

She roared once more and spewed columns of fire into the air. Then she lowered her head and aimed her weapon on those who yet fought her human soldiers around the circle. With great bursts of flame and heat, she decimated them, leaving ashes in her wake.

And then only he stood between her and the rest of the Warriors of Destiny. He must stop her. Somehow he must stop her or their gods-given mission to protect all of humanity would end here and now.

Corann closed his eyes and began to chant. He knew not the words, only the melody, so he began with that. Words, he trusted, would follow. The screams around him faded as he focused his mind, heart, and soul on the protective spell he wove.

It was the hot air blowing in his face that distracted him from his task. Opening his eyes, he stared into the unholy gaze of the goddess Chaela. All his beliefs, all his faith, failed him in that moment and the only thing he could do was stand, shocked and terrified, as he watched the dragon inhale a deep breath.

And exhale. . . .

Corann jumped from his pallet, the scream still escaping from deep within him. Sweat poured down his head and body and he could not stop shaking. The other men sharing his tent all peered, wide-eyed and shocked, at him as he tried to regain control of himself and his terror.

Touching his chest, he knew he was not burned. He was alive.

It was a dream. Or was it a vision of some future or some past? Corann left the tent and walked into the woods. Disturbed by what he had seen, he wandered deeper into the trees seeking peace and guidance. If he was to lead these people, if they depended on him, he must understand what he had seen.

Hours passed and he did not find what he was searching for. When the sun rose, Corann did not understand what he'd seen or what it all meant. And that was when the real fear struck him.

For if he could not cast a spell or face the evil one when the time came, everyone would die. As the leader of the priests, he was responsible for protecting the others. It mattered not that he had just taken on this position. It mattered not that his abilities were nothing like what his mentor Marcus's had been.

None of that mattered when they all came face-to-face with evil.

Gods help them all.

BLAZING EARTH

The Faithful are Lost and the Lost have Faith.
The Bringer of Life cares for the Caretaker
and the One who Loses all will gain the most.

CHAPTER 1

The Lands of Lord Geoffrey of Amesbury
Plain of Sarum, southwest England

Tolan thrust his hands into the earth and crumbled the dry chunks of dirt between his palms. Closing his eyes, he used his other senses to determine the problem here. The pungent smell of decay wafted through the air as he continued to disturb the layers of dirt before him. But worse, a sign of dead earth, there were no creatures in it.

No worms. No insects. None of the usual inhabitants of healthy, growing soil. No life at all. Crops would never grow in this. He opened his eyes, tilted his head, and met the gaze of Lord Geoffrey's steward.

"'Tis dead," he said, withdrawing his hands from the soil and brushing them off. Standing, he waved his arm across the area, pointing to the rest of the large field. "Nothing will grow here."

"What can be done, Tolan?" Bordan asked as he twisted his hands together and frowned. "Lord Geoffrey wants to expand the production of crops in this area of his lands. He does not wish to hear that it is not possible."

Tolan shook his head and shrugged. Though he knew the problem, it was not something he could explain or describe to the steward. Bordan, indeed the lord himself, would not understand Tolan's link to these lands. To the land.

"Can you not mix one of your concoctions and add it to the soil? It has worked in the past." The man grew anxious and sweaty in spite of the cool air around them. "Lord Geoffrey . . ."

Lord Geoffrey brooked no failure among those who served him. Nor among those he dealt with or owned. Neither nobleman nor serf would naysay the lord and come away unscathed. Bordan, gods help him, would be the one to deliver this bad news, so Tolan understood his growing fear. Lord Geoffrey often punished the bearer of the news as well as those who were a cause for it.

"I will speak to him, Bordan. Let me check other places on the field and see what can be done."

"He arrives at Amesbury Castle on the morrow, Tolan. Come then."

The words sounded like an order given, so Tolan nodded and did not try to argue. He watched as the steward waved for his horse and rode off at a fast pace. The man had many tasks to see to if his lord was coming home on the morrow. Tolan glanced up at the sun high in the sky and knew his hours were limited as well.

Winter tried to keep its hold over the land and air

even as the soil yet held to the sluggish sleep of the cold season. The wakening of spring was close, so close that Tolan could feel the tingling sensation of its approach in his own skin.

As he did every year. His body felt the impending changes that would awaken to life or put the growing things to sleep before they happened. Once he reached manhood, this mindfulness of the earth had begun and it had grown stronger with each passing year. From awareness to something . . . more over the last several years, something that seemed to guide or encourage the plants to grow.

It had not been just him—his father and grandfathers before him all seemed to have this connection to the earth. Decades and generations of men committed to stewardship of the land, and their commitment had been successful through years of lean or plenty. Their results had been noticed, and the lords who held these lands over time always called on his family to oversee their estates.

His father and grandfather before him had served Lord Geoffrey's family since this lord's ancestors had been given the lands in reward for service to their king generations ago. And, as Tolan glanced across the distance at his own son working there, he knew the practice would continue for many more. 'Twas simply the way of things.

Walking to the shed where he kept supplies and seed, Tolan retrieved a small sack of useless powder he'd made for just this purpose and took it back to the field. Calling for a small cart, he and two of the workers filled the back of it with soil from the dead field. Making certain he was witnessed, Tolan poured the powder over the soil and mixed it with his hands.

"Spread this evenly over the field," he directed.

With his arms crossed over his chest, he watched as the men did as he'd ordered. It took some time and the sun was sliding down toward the west by the time they finished. He dismissed them and all the workers to seek their evening meal and rest and waited for the moon to rise.

In the silence of the gloaming, Tolan walked the perimeter of the field and when night fell, he was ready. Kneeling in the center, heedless to the growing cold, he removed his garments and plunged his hands and arms once more into the soil, spreading his fingers as widely as he could. He raised his face to the sky, closed his eyes, and whispered the prayers handed down to him by his father and grandfather before him.

"O mother of old. O mother of plenty. Send your life into this land, into this place, and grant abundance where there is none. Cernunnos, bring your fertility to this soil and bless it with life. As my fathers before have cried out to you for your favor, so do I."

He repeated the words over and over until they blurred into a single, chanting sound. He dug deeper and deeper into the soil until he could go no farther and his face lay on the surface and his body was in contact with the ground. Tolan lost himself to the chant and continued on and on and on until something touched his hands deep in the ground. Then the area around his body grew warmer and warmer, sending bursts of heat into his skin and through him.

When the heat lessened, he wiggled his fingers to loosen the soil now tightly packed around them. Easing back to his knees, he withdrew his arms from the ground and hissed in pain as his forearm scraped along the edge of the hole in the soil. Lifting it, he noticed an area of reddened skin there. Tolan brushed the dirt from his skin and pulled his breeches on. Standing still for several minutes, he offered up a new prayer now—one of thanks for the gift they'd given him and for answering his call for help with this field.

It would take some days for the results of his ritual to work—or not, depending on the whims and blessings of the mother and Cernunnos. However, he would be able to report to Lord Geoffrey that he'd taken measures to improve the chances of bringing the field back from barren to growing.

His stomach growled then, as it did each time he performed this or the other rituals, and he laughed aloud at the mundane occurrence. He had called down the god's power and all his body wanted was food.

Once he acknowledged that hunger, a new awareness surged through him that he'd not experienced before, making the irritation on his arm ache again. As he walked toward his cottage on the edge of the fields near the village, Tolan realized that this was indeed something new, something different. Mayhap it meant the god was pleased and would grant his request to bring life back to the field? Or was it another level of the gift he and the males in his family carried in their blood? All he could do was wait and watch the field for signs of the god's blessing or rejection of his plea. In the past it could take many days or even weeks, but Tolan suspected the answer would come more quickly this time.

Lifting the latch on his door, Tolan opened it to find his son and the girl he paid to see to the upkeep of the house and cook his meals huddled closely together whispering. They jumped apart and darted careful glances his way but said nothing. The tension that now filled the room around them told Tolan several things.

Blythe was a comely young woman and his son had noticed. His son was a boy no longer but growing into manhood. These two would be acting on their attraction soon, if they had not already crossed that line.

"Good even, Blythe," Tolan said with a nod. "Something smells wonderful." His stomach growled loudly, adding to his compliment. The girl smiled and went to the hearth to serve the meal. "Kirwyn, have you washed?"

Tolan stepped to the door and pulled it open. A bucket of water, kept there for that purpose, waited and both of them used it. Tolan took advantage of the moment for his warning. Better to speak of his concern than to ignore the signs and lament it later.

"Have a care, Kirwyn," he said, placing his hand on his ever-growing son. "She comes from a good family and is not to be toyed with. If you have needs—" He did not get the words out before Kirwyn interrupted him.

"I love her, Father," he whispered with the vehemence of youth and first love in his voice.

"And does Blythe share your feelings, son?"

"Aye. We will pledge to each other as soon as her parents give their permission."

Tolan felt a stab of guilt—he'd been paying more attention to the fields and not enough to his son and his son's temperament.

"Do you not seek mine, Kirwyn? And the lord's?" Tolan shifted to face his son. "Lord Geoffrey controls much of our lives, and your choice of wife, when it is time, will be one of the things he must permit."

His son looked as though he would argue, but he took a breath and let it out. "I would do nothing to anger Lord Geoffrey," he said.

"Good. When the time comes for such a request, and if you both feel the same way, I will add my voice to it."

Kirwyn smiled then and nodded. As his son glanced past him, Tolan knew he was smiling at young Blythe. "Until then, have a care and do nothing to ruin her reputation or yours." When Kirwyn nodded, Tolan smacked him on the back and nudged him toward the door. "Let us not allow Blythe's good food to grow cold."

Kirwyn entered ahead of him and Tolan silently observed their interactions throughout the meal. From the tentative glances and avoidance of touching, he thought this was simply infatuation. Both had much growing up to do before they would be ready to consider marriage. Even though Tolan had not been much older when he first spied Kirwyn's mother, Corliss, he did not pursue her in earnest until their sixteenth year. Kirwyn had time until then . . . however, not as much as Tolan would have hoped.

Tolan saw the girl to her parents' cottage on the other side of the village and wondered what Lord Geoffrey's reaction to a marriage between the two families would be. Sometimes the lord seemed very logical and concerned for his villeins' contentedness. But more recently, he'd been preoccupied with some great endeavor that took him from the area for weeks at a time. Fields, herds, and other critical aspects of their lives seemed unimportant right now.

A new interest drew Tolan's attentions and efforts. A shiver tore through his body then, shaking him to his very core. Somehow he knew that whatever was happening involved him, but he did not know how or why.

The area on his arm changed then, turning a brighter red and burning. Tolan must have scraped it along something in the ground and now it looked infected. That would be something new, for he rarely if ever became ill or suffered from injuries while he tended the land.

First, he would go to the stream and wash the dirt from his body. That should take care of the injury. And if it did not, he would see Elethea on the morrow.

This strange patch of skin was just the excuse he needed to seek out the village healer and her ministrations. His flesh hardened and rose at the thought of the woman known for her healing touch. Tolan, however, thought on her *other* touches as he finished his tasks for the day. Touches meant not to soothe but to inflame. Caresses meant to entice and not diminish interest. Kisses meant to stoke the fire of passion between them and not to ease the growing heat they shared.

Aye, a visit to the village healer was just what he needed for what ailed him.

The journey had been worse than he'd expected. Even knowing that those who carried the power of the sea and storm in their blood were set against him, Hugh de Gifford had no idea how bad it would be. The angry seas turned to becalmed ones, leaving his ships adrift in the waters north of Orkney. Days passed and he heard the grumbling that his men dared not make too loud. He'd called out to the goddess, begging for her help, even offered several sacrifices to appease her, but the only answer he received was the raucous laughter of the gulls as they flew overhead.

However, the blood of those before him, generations of firebloods descended from Chaela herself, would not allow him to sulk or be turned from his life's mission. Too much had been given in service to the goddess since the beginning of his family to be stopped by this. Too much paid and too much lost. This defeat was simply another test of his resolve and his faith in their quest. There were still two more circles to be found, which meant there were two gateways that gave him another chance to prove his worthiness as the human consort to the goddess who would rule the earth once her enemies were destroyed.

More than a sennight had passed when something changed. The grip of the sea on his ships slackened and their sails filled with wind. Deciding to head toward his lands in Normandy before trying to sail to the south of England, Hugh allowed himself a measure of hope for the first time in many days.

Mayhap Soren and Ran, the stormblood and waterblood from Orkney, could only keep him at bay while they were on the sea? Had they reached the southern shores already? Content in the knowledge that he had someone in place there, not only among their people, but also waiting for their arrival, Hugh smiled and gave the orders to seek the coast of Normandy. A few days to gather more men, more supplies and ready themselves for battle could not be a bad thing.

Indeed not.

CHAPTER 2

Elethea stepped outside the small cottage and stood up straight for the first time in hours. Pushing her kerchief off, she wiped the sweat from her brow with the back of her sleeve. Her hair lay matted against her head, so she loosened the tie holding it and shook it free. A breeze rustled through the nearby trees and lifted strands of her hair as it passed by her.

Pressing both fists into the small of her back, she stretched the overused, tense muscles for several minutes, enjoying both the pressure of her hands there and the cooler air here outside.

The babe was alive and well, but it had been a battle. Over the last two days, Linne had struggled to give birth to her very large son. To make it worse, the babe had been turned the wrong way around, so it took brute force and effort to guide him into the birth canal. Wee Medwyn's mother would most likely never forgive him or his huge father, Rolfe, for the hours of pain she'd suffered.

Well, that was one of the things Linne had yelled out during her pains, along with cursing poor Rolfe's parentage and his other attributes. The words brought a smile to Thea's face now, for most women did the same thing during childbirth. And the pain and those harsh words usually faded at the babe's first smile . . . or burp. She'd seen it happen countless times.

From the happy murmurings she could hear inside, she thought everyone might be well enough and already on the path to forgiving and forgiveness. A pang of bittersweet envy filled her heart then at the sounds—the soft words being exchanged by husband and wife. She allowed it for a moment and used the time to ease out the tangles in her hair before gathering it once more into a braid.

Stuffing her kerchief in a pocket, Thea knocked on the door and pushed it open a bit, peering in at the new family. Rolfe's mother would arrive in the morn to help Linne out with the babe and other tasks, so they would be in the hands of a good woman.

"I am leaving now," she said in a soft voice. "Summon me if you have need, at any hour, Linne."

The woman nodded. "My thanks, Elethea," she said without pausing as she rubbed the babe's head. "I could not have done this without you."

"Rest as you can this night. I will check in on you on the morrow," Thea promised.

She needed to escape. The feelings of loss and guilt and emptiness assailed her worst at times like this.

No words could fill the empty space within her, and no power on earth could give her a child. She could only content herself in knowing that she had helped many babes safely into this world.

Thea gathered up her supplies and put them in her basket, quietly moving around the room. When the babe whimpered, her knees nearly buckled. When Linne soothed him with sweet words and touches, her soul cried out in pain. She hurried her last steps and left quickly, pulling the door closed on Rolfe's words.

"Our thanks. . . ."

Her steps were rushed and quick as she made her way from their cottage in the darkness, along the path that led to the edge of village toward the woods. Only the moon's light illuminated her way and soon she plunged into the thicket. Following the flickers of light as they touched the ripples of the water, she slowed her pace and walked along the stream. There was a small pool that gathered near the turn of the stream, and she sought it now.

She'd spent many hours at the pool, allowing its calm current to ease her raged soul. Especially after helping with a birth. More especially when the delivery was not successful. For all her abilities and her seeming gift for healing, sometimes people died.

Babies died.

Those were the worst and each time it chipped away a bit of her heart, leaving her almost as damaged as when she lost her own. . . .

She had reached the pool just as the heat struck her, forcing her to her knees as it burst forth, from inside her. It had happened like this many times before, but this, this time it felt stronger and deeper than any she'd known. Like the piercing heat of a roaring fire, it spread through her, making her sweat anew and sending tremors through her body.

Reaching down, she tugged her kerchief from her pocket and dipped it in the cold water. The first swipe of it across her brow cooled some of the heat, but it returned. Waves of heat poured through her body. She put the cloth back in the water and repeated the soothing action several times before stopping, not bothering to wring the cold water from it. Then, as quickly as it had struck, it left, leaving her chilled and shaking.

Shivers tore through her body then, and the wet kerchief that had offered relief now caused pain. She tossed it to the ground and wrapped her arms around herself, trying to stop the shaking. Hers had little effect, but the large, strong, masculine arms that surrounded her had more.

"Thea, what are you doing here?" Tolan lifted her to her feet, never releasing her from his embrace. "Are you ill?"

She could not be ill, for the first thing she noticed was that he wore nothing but his breeches. His chest was bare, wet, and hard as he held her close. She closed her eyes for but a moment in an attempt to absorb some of his strength. Then she lifted her head and turned in his arms.

"Nay, not ill," she said, not yet able to meet his gaze.

"Ah," he whispered, touching his lips to her forehead. "Another birth? Or a death?" Stunned by his awareness, she frowned and looked into his dark brown eyes.

"A birth," she said, searching his face.

How had he known this part of her? She thought that no one noticed the price she paid each time. Worse, what else had he noticed about her life?

"And all is well? Now?" So close that his breath touched her face, he held her securely against his chest, almost as though he feared the worst.

"The babe is well, though the birth started out with much difficulty. I thought I might lose both of them." Thea leaned her forehead against his skin, inhaling the scent of him, allowing his strong arms to hold her.

A companionable silence surrounded them, and the sounds of the night creatures echoed in the forest. When the shivering stopped and she felt more at ease, she lifted her head and released her hold on him. A hold she had not even realized she'd had. Sliding her hands from under his belt at his back, she stepped back. A mistake, for it granted her a better look at Tolan, the overseer of Lord Geoffrey's lands.

He was taller than most men who lived and worked here, his dark hair touching his shoulders, shoulders strengthened through working with the land. Lean and muscled, his body held no softness. Every part of him was strong and sculpted. She shivered once more, but this had nothing to do with being chilled and everything to do with her intimate knowledge of every inch of his body.

"Have you eaten?" he asked, meeting her gaze and

smiling at what he saw there. She knew he recognized the hunger in her eyes that matched that in his own. And it was not for food.

"I have had little this day," she admitted, smiling at him for the first time. "Surely you have eaten your supper?"

The night had fallen some time ago and she knew that he had a girl to make his and his son's meals. He held out his hand to her. "Come. There is plenty in the pot and 'tis still warm. Even some bread and cheese."

"I wanted to wash," she said, glancing at the water.

"The water is frigid here, Thea. I will warm some for your use."

Thea knew that warming the water would lead to him helping her bathe. And that would lead to other pleasurable things. But her exhaustion was bone-deep and she doubted anything could rouse her body and keep her awake this night. She took his hand and allowed him to lead her back down the path to the village to his cottage even knowing 'twould do him no good.

They paused at his home to get the promised food before walking on to hers. While she ate, he built up the fire in the hearth and heated water for her use, all without uttering a word. Then she felt him at her back as he pulled her to stand. Thea's first thought was that she was too exhausted for anything but sleep, but even she was surprised when her body sought not sleep but more of his caresses.

Once she was clean, his touch became something else, something more insistent and enticing. Arousing and invigorating. With few demands of his own and with an unexpected patience and generosity, Tolan tended to her through the night.

His touch and attentions eased her worries and the tension that followed her for days after seeing to a birth or death. His mouth and hands awakened the joy from deep within her and allowed her body to rejuvenate and refresh itself. His words soothed the fragility that haunted her yet and made her feel alive and living. All things she'd never expected to find with any man after her husband had died. She fell asleep smiling at that realization.

But the next morn, when she woke in her own bed and he was gone, she swore she would never underestimate his determination again.

When Thea rose and dressed, readying for another busy day in her life here, she noticed it. A patch of skin, on her forearm, was red and raised there. Almost like a burn, but she knew she had not done that. Pulling her sleeve up to take a closer look, she thought it did not look like a usual burn. Or infection. Or abrasion. Yet there it was. She found the jar of unguent she used for such things and dabbed some on the area. With her sleeve back in place, she went about her tasks and saw to those she needed to tend.

It was much later that she realized she'd underestimated the strange mark and what it would do, just as she had underestimated Tolan.

Geoffrey of Amesbury was a worried man.

He pushed his helm off his head and let it drop,

knowing the man who followed along behind his every step would catch it. Sliding the mail hood back, he let the chill air cool his head and neck. Hours of riding and searching this day had found him nothing.

Not a sign or symbol on any of the standing stones here. Or those that had fallen or been knocked down. Geoffrey had himself searched even when his men reported there were none. Now, exhausted and frustrated, he accepted a skin of wine and drank deeply from it.

"My lord?"

"What is it?" Geoffrey peered out over the land before him, not bothering to face the soldier.

"There are more of those strange mounds to the west," the soldier offered. "We have not searched those yet."

Without hesitation, Geoffrey knocked the man to the ground with the back of his hand. Since he had been with these men, searching these lands for the last fortnight, he knew what had or had not been examined. And he knew that the markings he sought must be on stones and not in the ground. That this soldier thought to advise him was unacceptable. Geoffrey strode off toward the tallest of the stones before him here.

Walking into the center of the several concentric rings, he knew this place held power. He could feel it there, beneath his feet, as it moved into his body and sent small sparks of some energy into his skin. He squinted into the sun as it set in the west and waited for more.

Nothing.

He knew then that this was not the place that Hugh de Gifford sought. Geoffrey slid his hand inside his tunic and withdrew the parchment he'd received from his distant cousin just days ago. Though something prevented Hugh from reaching England, this missive had arrived and given him orders and knowledge, sketches even, of what to look for on his lands.

For some reason not disclosed, de Gifford believed that the circle of power lay here, in this area, on Geoffrey's lands. Whether or not his belief was based on the many strange mounds and stones and other artifacts, Geoffrey knew not. He only knew he must find it, for there were warriors on their way to destroy it.

He turned to find his men standing just outside the stones, in watchful readiness for his next command. Calling out an order to set up camp, he faced the sun again and wondered what would happen when Hugh arrived and he'd not found the circle yet. Tremors shot through him at the thought of failing this man. Well, de Gifford was more than a mere man—there was a power in him that defied explanation. Geoffrey had seen that power used and would never want to be its target.

He could return to his keep and the comforts it offered, but his time to find the stones was dwindling and he could not afford to let his desire for comfort interfere with his duty. Hugh said there were signs and so he knew there were. All Geoffrey had to do was find them.

And find them now.

CHAPTER 3

The two guards standing over the gates to Amesbury Castle nodded and waved Tolan inside. He guided his horse along the well-worn path, up the slight hill to the stark stone building in the center of the large yard. The design and coloring of this keep made it blend into the landscape around it, almost as though it had been done apurpose to hide it from sight.

As he glanced back out through the gates, the other prominent building in the area—the Amesbury Abbey—glistened in the sun. At the edges of the town, it caught the best light and seemed to call visitors to it as the flickering sun captured their attention. Visitors and pilgrims came aplenty to it, seeking repentance or favor. Even the king's daughter was there, answering the call of God or her father's orders. Rumors swirled that the king's mother would join her there soon. A blessed place, that.

A chill raced through him then, turning his attention back to the dark and dreary castle in which Lord

Geoffrey lived. He'd noticed the feeling before, indeed, on many visits here. Not one of evil so much as a lacking of good. As though the black and gray stones resisted the light even as the man ruling over this keep and these lands resisted the good around him.

Though Geoffrey had not been overtly a bad lord to serve, Tolan always waited for him to show his true nature. Thinking on that as he left his mount with a waiting stable boy and entered the keep, he wondered at his observation. Mayhap he was wrong? Geoffrey tended to his lands and his people as he should, but there was something else that Tolan could feel and yet not describe. A sense of something dark deep within him.

"Here he is, my lord." Bordan's impatient and panicking voice echoed across the large but empty chamber of the great hall. Tolan quickened his pace to reach the front of the room.

"My lord," he said, bowing his head. "I came at your call." Crossing his arms over his chest, he tried not to let his surprise show as he looked on Lord Geoffrey.

A haunted expression sat in the nobleman's gaze, and his coloring was pale and nearly gray. And some nervous movements accompanied the change in appearance, for he kept running his hand over his face and shaking his head. A touch of the palsy? Or some other affliction? It was new, for Tolan had not seen it before Geoffrey departed on this latest excursion of his.

"The field?" Lord Geoffrey demanded without pretense. "Will it take seed now?"

Tolan nodded. "I have seen to it," he said. "It will be ready for the second planting in a few weeks."

Tolan had not checked it this morn, but he had no doubt it would be. His faith in the Old Ones or their methods had not failed him yet. A nod was Lord Geoffrey's only answer as the nobleman turned away to address Bordan on some other matter. This behavior was strange. The lord went on about his business, never taking notice of Tolan, until Tolan finally spoke up on his own.

"My lord? If there is nothing else, I will go back to my duties?" Tolan began to nod and step back, but was stopped by a sharp command.

"Stay!" Lord Geoffrey called out, without turning to face him. "We leave at noon."

"Leave, my lord?" Tolan said. "Do you leave so soon after returning, then?" He must have misheard the words.

"Gather what you need, Tolan. We will be on the road for several days. Tell Langston to see to things until we return." Langston, of Norman descent, was assigned to help Tolan with his work on Lord Geoffrey's lands, but the man was nothing more than a worthless spy. Keeping him busy with meaningless tasks kept the man out of things he should not be involved in, but he was no one to be put in charge of . . . anything growing.

"My lord . . ."

"I have need of your expertise with the lands around Amesbury, Tolan. You and your family have lived here for generations and I—"

"My lord, I can accompany you. My family has lived here as long as Tolan's," Bordan began. The big man began to sweat as he spoke and pressed his case to their lord, never recognizing the growing anger and frustration on Geoffrey's face.

But Tolan did and so accepted what must be the inevitable result of this order. "I understand, my lord," he said, bowing lower now.

An angry nobleman was not someone he wanted to face down or set on the villagers or others under his hand, so Tolan had acquiesced. Even though the feeling of dread filled him now with Geoffrey's reference to the generations before him there.

"We will meet you in the village, Tolan. And bring along whatever tools or accoutrements you need."

"My lord, what will we be doing?"

Bordan gasped at Tolan's question and looked as though he would strike out at him, but Tolan needed to understand what this journey was about and how to hide his true gift from others.

"Bring along whatever you need to test the soil. To find obstructions beneath the surface. I am searching for hidden st . . ."

Lord Geoffrey stopped and glanced around them, over both of his shoulders and back to the doorway as though someone might be listening. That was not what made Tolan nervous. What made his skin crawl and his stomach heave was the word that the nobleman hesitated on.

St . . .

Stones.

Hidden stones.

Tolan fought to keep his reaction off his face. He knew the stories and the legends about these lands, passed down from a time when the pagans held sway and the Christians had not yet arrived. The stories about those who built and carved the huge circles of stones that lay across the Salisbury Plain for miles in all directions. None of those were hidden, though some lay partially out of sight due to the overgrowth of weeds and other plants.

He also knew about the other stones, the ones rarely known or spoken about. He knew their origin and their purpose and he knew, most importantly, of his duty to them. He clenched his jaw, trying to regain his control before he said something he should not. Pulling in a deep breath and easing it out, he nodded at Lord Geoffrey. "Very well, my lord. I will gather my tools and be ready."

His agreement seemed to break Lord Geoffrey's consternation and the man nodded and waved him off now. Tolan turned to go, knowing he must make other arrangements before he could leave and that there was little time. It took all his control not to break his pace and run from the keep back to his house. He urged his horse to move faster than he would usually and Tolan refused to stop even when several of those known to him called out as he rode by.

His first stop, though, was at the cottage of Githa and Durwan and arrange for them to see to Kirwyn while he was gone. Though a young man, Kirwyn could care for himself in most situations, but Tolan

would be more at ease if he knew someone was looking after his son. Once Githa had been told, he went to
see Thea. As was her custom, she was not at home but
out visiting with those who needed her attention.

He laughed then as thoughts of her and the night
they'd shared made his body begin to react in a way
that he had neither the time nor the possibility of acting on now. But he would seek her out on his return
and they would speak. There were many matters they
needed to discuss and he would not allow her to push
his questions and concerns away. Tolan gathered up
a tunic and a few other supplies and searched for Kirwyn in the fields.

When he reached the fields, Tolan sought out some
tools from the storage building there. With his only
intention to pacify Lord Geoffrey in this, he gathered
a hoe and a measuring stick and a spade. He had no
idea of what the lord would ask him to do, but these
simple tools would handle many possible situations.
After securing them to his horse, he rode to the field
that was being worked this day to find Kirwyn.

His son stood in the midst of the other young men
working there, but he seemed so much older than
them. Kirwyn would have Tolan's height and breadth,
but he carried his mother's fairer coloring. Tolan
prayed that the boy had inherited the same strong
connection to the earth and its power as he himself
had. Soon, on the next anniversary of his birth, Kirwyn would be of age to assume his place amongst the
generations of Tolan's family to tend the earth and
guard its secrets. Waving him over, he prepared for

the battle between father and headstrong son that had been the way of things between them for some time.

"I must accompany Lord Geoffrey on a journey, Kirwyn. We leave shortly," he said. The mulish expression appeared in less than a moment, for his son knew what would follow next. "Githa and Durwan will see to you while I am gone."

"Father, I can—" Kirwyn started.

"This is not about your ability to care for yourself, son," Tolan interrupted, reaching out and placing his hand on his son's shoulder. "This is so that I know you will be well. My only requirement is that you eat supper with them and sleep in their cottage. I still expect you to oversee ours and to tend to your duties here."

"And Blythe?"

"Ah, please tell her we will need her not to cook for us. I do not know when I will return but will try to send word, Kirwyn." Tolan purposely issued no decrees about not seeing the girl, knowing they would be ignored. He noticed the hopeful expression in the boy's eyes. "But have a care, as I said."

Kirwyn nodded and smiled. "What is this about, Father?" he asked in a low voice. Others were close enough to overhear anything spoken too loudly.

"I know not. Lord Geoffrey ordered me to accompany him and so I do. Langston is in charge of the fields while I am gone."

Kirwyn grimaced.

"Aye, I know. So, give him counsel as you can."

"Me? He will not listen to me," his son scoffed.

"He will if it means he will do less work."

Kirwyn nodded and smiled knowingly. Langston's laziness was widely known among those working the fields, even if the lord knew it not. The arrival of men on horseback stopped any other exchanges. Tolan patted his son's shoulder and nodded to him.

"Tolan, is this your son?" Lord Geoffrey called to him. Urging his horse closer, the lord scrutinized his son's face. "How many years does he have?"

"Aye, my lord. This is Kirwyn. He has ten and five years." Tolan put his arm around Kirwyn's shoulders and brought him closer.

"He does not have your look about him."

The words startled Tolan. Glancing at his son's face and then at Lord Geoffrey, he shrugged it off. Or tried to, for a deep sense of danger swirled in his gut, making it difficult to ignore what he wanted to believe was a simple comment.

"His coloring favors his mother, my lord," Tolan explained.

"His mother?"

"My late wife, my lord. Corliss. She died of a fever four years ago." A strange expression passed over the nobleman's face and disappeared in an instant before he spoke again.

"And you have not married again? You need more sons, Tolan, to work the land with you. We will speak of this on our return." Lord Geoffrey motioned with his hand at one of the men, who nodded. The man was charged with keeping track of the lord's business and concerns and was rarely anywhere but at Geoffrey's side.

"We ride," Lord Geoffrey called out without further conversation.

Tolan hugged Kirwyn and mounted up, following the group along the road, out of the village, and away from the fields. They traveled farther into the lands and properties owned by Lord Geoffrey and away from those controlled by the abbey and a few minor noblemen. Though he never said so, Geoffrey had a clear destination in mind and an urgency about the journey and task.

They traveled for miles, going south, around the abbey and then toward Salisbury and its great cathedral. They passed by Old Sarum and the huge hill fort still in use by the king's bishop. An awareness shot through Tolan as they approached the place where the earth had been pushed up into a bank surrounding the protected land within the circle. Built in olden times and covered with the remnants of the original cathedral, this land held power.

Although a score of men rode in this group, it was a hushed and silent journey through those first hours and first days. For Tolan, who rarely left Lord Geoffrey's land, it was interesting. The soil of the Salisbury Plain felt very different from that of the fields and hills of his own lands, too. His hummed with some living force that he had not found anywhere else.

Their journey moved along at a painfully slow pace as they stopped at various hills and mounds and stones along their path. At first, Lord Geoffrey disclosed nothing about his search and since they were journeying farther and farther away from any familiar places, Tolan offered no comments and practiced his patience. His thoughts were filled with all the tasks he should be completing back home.

When the orders were given to ride north, his unease grew.

On the sixth day of their journey, as they approached the more familiar large circle of stones nearer to the west of Amesbury, Geoffrey called for them to stop and make camp. A sense of nervous anticipation filled Tolan and he found himself holding his breath every time the nobleman uttered a word. And when the sun dropped behind the mountains to the west and Lord Geoffrey approached him alone, Tolan waited to learn the reason behind the journey.

"My lord," Tolan said, standing as the man grew nearer to his own place by the fire. "How can I be of service?"

"Sit." Geoffrey motioned back to the rock on which he'd been sitting. "Leave us," he said to the others who yet sat too close by. After those few wandered off to other places, Lord Geoffrey sat down. "What do you know of these stones, Tolan? Did your family pass down stories about them?"

"I know little, my lord. No one knows their origin or why they sit in such strange circles." Tolan shrugged, relieved that his questions involved *this* group of stones and not another. "Some say they were brought here by the ancient magician Merlin," he said, chuckling. "But I know not the truth of it."

Lord Geoffrey stared at him then, as though trying to discern whether or not to say more. When the man let out a rough breath, Tolan knew he had decided to do that.

"I must find a ring of stones in this area," he began, leaning in closer. "None of the others must know more than that." His gaze narrowed and he stopped speaking until Tolan nodded his assent. "The stones I seek sit in a circle of eight stones and are carved with various symbols."

Tolan fought off his inclination to scream out in denial and concentrated on keeping his own knowledge inside. "These, my lord?" he asked, pointing at the stones nearby as they stood in silence under the waxing moon. "Mayhap a smaller circle existed within the larger ones?" He chose his words very carefully, not wanting to appear too knowledgeable or too lacking.

"We searched these the last time I was here," Geoffrey explained. "I can see no markings or carvings." Shaking his head, he glanced over at the stones once more. "There are some shapes and scratches, but not like those for which I search."

Tolan debated whether or not to ask the question burning in his own mouth. He should let this alone and not stir up more interest by discussing it further. Lord Geoffrey nodded at him.

"I trust you will keep my counsel and not speak of this to anyone else, Tolan. I look for certain symbols carved into the highest places on the stones. Flame, lightning, water, the sun, and more. I must find them. My very li . . ." Lord Geoffrey stopped and looked around as though he'd heard someone approach. "I must find them."

"I know of no such stones, my lord," Tolan offered. He said so even while knowing he lied as he spoke those words. Tolan knew that his duty, his ultimate loyalty, belonged not to this worldly lord but to the ancient ones who had sculpted this landscape and whose power yet lived in the earth beneath his feet. The ones whose blood pulsed through his body even now.

"Then we must continue searching," Geoffrey replied. Standing, he walked away with a brisk stride, not even waiting for Tolan to speak again.

Who would put Geoffrey of Amesbury to such a task? Who knew of stones carved with symbols of the old gods? The circles Tolan knew of or had seen always included more than eight stones. But the stories handed down to him spoke of other circles, hidden ones that always contained one pillar for each of the seven Old Ones and one for the priest who was needed for rituals. And an altar or recumbent stone for sacrifices. Eight stones standing around one. Tolan wondered who would be seeking out that circle now.

As the reddened area on his arm burned anew, Tolan suspected he might know.

They spent the next day searching or searching again the huge stones there. Tolan feigned it at the beginning, but by the end of the day, he did not doubt that there was some power here. The ground around some of the stones, the ones that carried small symbols of axes, felt the same to him as the edges of his own lands. But the vibrations never grew stronger or louder to him.

And that night, Tolan's dreams were filled with

images of ancient priests leading their people in procession into the circle. Carrying gifts and sacrifices, they worshipped their gods as they had for generations. When he woke, his hand was buried in the loose soil and he knew that the dreams had truly been visions of the past events on this land. Another gift from his own gods.

For the next sennight, they made their way across the area, wending along small roads and bigger ones, through the farmland and hills, turning north and then east until they reached a huge mound that could be seen for miles. These lands belonged to various local noblemen and some to the nearby abbeys and churches. But this mound had existed for longer than Tolan could even guess. The ruins on top spoke of long disuse, so Lord Geoffrey traveled past it without stopping.

When they reached the monoliths scattered in larger circles across the countryside at Avebury, Lord Geoffrey turned them south along the road that would lead past Tolan's own lands that bordered on Lord Geoffrey's. Tolan hoped they would simply ride on by it, but the nobleman called a halt and summoned Tolan to his side.

"This is your farm, is it not, Tolan?" Geoffrey pointed to the thick copse and the fields surrounding it.

"Aye, 'tis mine," he said, not able to keep the pride from his voice. Not many could claim that they owned land, but his family had acquired this and passed it down from father to son over uncounted generations.

"What lies in the woods there?"

A deep, piercing fear cut through him and simmered in his gut at the question. He turned away to try to control his reaction before answering, "Only thick growths of old trees, my lord."

"So you have walked the land there? You know it well?"

"I have, from the time I was a boy."

As Lord Geoffrey thought on his words, staring at the woods, Tolan could feel the rumbling coming from under the earth, traveling out in waves from the woods. He glanced at the rest of the group, wondering how no one else was aware of the life and the power flowing here. It called to him here more strongly than any other place he'd been.

"Why do you not cut those down and cultivate the lands?" the lord asked.

"I have enough work to fill my time, my lord," he replied. "I am hoping that my son will take over this."

"Who lives there now?" Lord Geoffrey turned his horse and nodded toward the small house built just outside the circle of trees. The small curls of smoke escaping the chimney gave proof of its use.

"A cousin. He lives here and oversees the fields that surround the woods."

The arrangement worked well for both of them—his cousin, Farold, got a place to live and meaningful work and Tolan got someone who oversaw his lands when he could not. Lord Geoffrey moved closer and leaned toward Tolan.

"Are you certain there are no stones like the ones I seek there?"

"I have seen no such stones, my lord."

Tolan held his breath as Geoffrey considered his words and made his choice. As he waited, his cousin, having seen their approach and having recognized him, walked toward them, waving in greeting to them.

"Go. See your cousin and catch up with us anon. I wish to sleep in my own bed this night."

With a barking command, the nobleman ordered the rest to ride south, leaving Tolan in their dust. Tolan took only a few minutes to greet his cousin and speak on matters between them before mounting and riding away at a fast pace. When he first heard the voice carried on the wind, he thought it was his cousin calling to him. Pulling up hard on the reins and bringing the horse to a halt, Tolan turned and searched for its source.

Tolan Earthblood, come to me.

His cousin even now returned to his tasks inside and there was no one else there in the fields or on the road. Loosening his grips on the leather strips, he had readied to touch the horse's sides to ride once more when he heard it again.

Tolan Earthblood, heed my call. I am here.

A woman's voice. A woman spoke to him, and yet he could not believe where the voice seemed to come from—the center of the woods. He found himself drawn to the edge of the earthwork that surrounded the woods. A huge ancient henge, like the others they'd visited these last weeks and yet not like any other in the world.

Blood of the Old Ones is in your veins and I call you to my side.

He cried out in pain as the area on his arm seemed

to melt and sear at the sound of the voice. Tugging his sleeve up, he saw that the area now carried a shape—that of a tree—and changed before his eyes. The rough form of a trunk, roots, and branches formed and melted, over and over, there on his forearm. And as it did, the voice whispered low in his head, the power in it growing stronger with each word.

Now. Come to me now. Serve me and I will make you lord of all you can see. Earthblood.

By the gods! Were the stories of Old Ones and their existence and ties to this land true? If they were, if the ring of stones existed beneath these woods, then the voice was . . .

Tolan stopped thinking on it and kicked his heels, making his horse rear and then charge into a gallop along the road. He only knew he must distance himself from this now. Only when he caught up with the others some miles along the road did the whispers cease completely.

"Tolan, are you well?" Bordan asked him as Tolan took a place behind the soldiers. "You look like you have seen something unholy."

"I am not used to such journeys," he said, not meeting the man's gaze. "All will be well when I get back to my cottage in the village."

And as they crossed the miles to Amesbury, Tolan tried to convince himself of that. But something deep in his soul told him he had never been so wrong.

CHAPTER 4

The sun rose and she did as well. No matter how she felt on any morning, Thea found it impossible to sleep past sunrise. Stretching out along the length of the pallet, she watched her breath float like a cloud across the chamber. Even knowing that the cold air of the morning would chill her, she tossed back the thick blankets and began her daily routine. There were tasks to carry out and people who needed her attention.

Those parts of her day ahead were not what caused the anticipation she felt growing within her, though. Bordan had told Langston, who'd been overheard by Kirwyn, who'd then told Githa, who told her that Tolan would return this day. She laughed at the convoluted way that she'd learned of it as she cleaned out her hearth and arranged a new pile of wood and kindling for the fire.

Tolan would return this day.

As much as she was content with her life as it was,

Thea could not lie to herself as easily as she could to others—she liked having Tolan in her life too much. She liked his attentions and his concern about her. She could imagine . . . nay, not that, but she could almost imagine being at ease with him at the end of each day.

Shocked by even that admission, she shook her head and laughed. How far she'd fallen from the vows she'd made to herself when Jasper died. Never would she allow another man to be close to her, close enough to hurt her as her husband had. Never again would she allow a man to determine the breadth of her life. Never again would a man limit her work. And here she was, just three years later, contemplating breaking every one of those hard-won promises.

Thea moved the pot on the hook over the flames and poured water into it from the bucket beside the hearth. Once it was heated, she washed with it, then ate and dressed. Gathering her satchel and basket, she prepared for the day ahead. Banking the fire, she wrapped her cloak around her and walked out onto the porch in front of her cottage. Without a thought, she faced the rising sun and closed her eyes, allowing its growing strength to seep into the coldness of her body.

She remembered not when she'd begun the custom, but it served well as a beginning to her path of healing and helping each day. Though it was still low in the sky, she could feel the increase of heat and light each day. Mayhap her family descended from those ancient priests who charted the sun's progress through the sky? She knew not, but the practice seemed to give her some comfort as she began her day.

Each year, during the darker days of winter, she found herself stopping anytime the sun's light broke through the clouds to take and savor that moment. Then, some months later, as summer approached, the sun stayed up longer and higher, its light and heat and strength would surround her for many hours each day.

The day passed slowly, for she found herself thinking more and more about Tolan than she usually did. Mayhap his absence had brought this need for him to a sharpness she'd not felt before? Oh, she did need him. Not just for the passion they shared, but also for the companionship and commonality of their duties to the people here.

For a widow, sharing a bed was not a scandalous thing and Thea liked the pattern that they'd fallen into over the last year. They each had their daily lives and their own responsibilities, but they spent their nights, many nights, together.

There were no demands, no duty owed, and no ownership of her life and soul. She shivered then, not from a lack of warmth but from the memories of the time when Jasper had owned her body and soul.

Never again. Never. Again.

Not that Tolan would ever . . .

She shook off this path of thinking and walked briskly along the lane to her next stop. The new babe was thriving and, even after a rough beginning, showed no signs of slowing. Linne was healing well and was taking care of her child with only a little help from Rolfe's mother.

A broken leg that needed tending. Cuts and burns.

Scrapes. A fever. Arranging for the planting of the new herbs in the shared garden. All these took her attention for several hours and it was only as the sun began its slide to setting in the west that she finally realized she'd not thought on Tolan since earlier in the day.

After eating a simple meal by herself, Thea found some garments that needed repairs and realized the repetitions eased her nervousness. Well, not nervousness but eagerness for him to arrive. It was long after dark when the sound of soft footsteps outside gained her attention.

Elethea looked up from the mending at the soft knock on her door. A more insistent one would mean one of the villagers needed her attentions. This kind signaled only one thing to her—the arrival of Tolan. She placed the torn tunic back in the basket sitting by the small hearth and went to see.

Lifting the latch, she eased the wooden door open a scant inch and glanced outside. In the dark of the night, he stood there, outlined by the full moon's light. He was taller than most men in the village; she recognized his form at once. Then he nodded and, in that deep tone of voice that never failed to send whispers of heat through her, greeted her.

"Elethea, how do you fare?"

She wanted to laugh. His words were so commonplace as though his arrival at her cottage in the hours when most of the village slept was how things were in Amesbury. Elethea did not doubt for a moment that many knew of their assignations. Still . . .

"I am well, Tolan." She stepped back and opened the door wider. "And how was your journey?" He'd been away, seeing to their lord's concerns, for almost a fortnight.

He accepted the invitation as he always did—in a calm, even manner. She doubted that anyone who'd met him, save for possibly his dead wife, had ever seen the passion that lived within this composed exterior. But Elethea glimpsed it—once in the fields observing him as he tended to his lands and every time he joined with her body.

Before closing the door, she took the small lantern from the rock that sat beside it and brought it inside. It was her signal to others that she was still awake and could help them. With Tolan's arrival, though, she wished for no interruptions.

He stood in the middle of the room and his head nearly touched the roof above. And he watched her with a dark intensity that her body understood. "I am well." He loosened his cloak and tossed it over a bench against the wall.

"But I have missed you, Thea." He crossed the distance between them in two strides and pulled her into his arms. "I have missed you greatly."

His mouth captured hers and she gave herself over to him, waiting for the passion within him to overwhelm the calm control he exuded. Two weeks without him left her restless and needing his touch. Needing the taste of him. Needing the strength and passion he would show her.

He took her breath away even as he kissed her that

first time. By the second and third and fourth kisses, she lost the ability to stand. Tolan slid his arms around her, holding her up and drawing her close.

"I think you have missed me, too," he whispered.

She laughed as he kissed down her throat and used his teeth on that sensitive spot just near her shoulder. Then she could only gasp as she arched against him, aroused by everything he did. His answer was to slide his hand down, caressing the fullness of her breast and then over her stomach until he reached . . .

The moan escaped as he grazed his hand over the junction of her thighs. Another as he rubbed harder there, the friction and pressure of his touch even through her garments causing her body to heat and weep its own moisture. She ached now, worse than the moment before, and she pressed against his hand, begging for more.

"End this, Tolan," she moaned out as his fingers slid between her legs, all the while continuing to caress and press the place where she wanted . . . him.

"Ah," he whispered after he claimed her mouth another time, "now I know you have missed me greatly, Thea." He moved his hand. "And this, mayhap?"

Elethea held her breath and his gaze as that hand slid down her gown and gathered up its length. His fingers on her skin made her shiver, her body arching in anticipation. Then he moved slowly up her thigh and she gasped with each inch closer, letting her legs fall open for him. When his fingers slipped into the sensitive, heated folds there, her head fell back and she moaned at the pleasure of it.

His mouth on her neck made her shiver again and she reached up to untie her own laces, wanting his tongue on her breasts. He chuckled; she knew he understood the madness he was causing, and when she'd managed somehow to loosen the edge of her gown and tug it down, his mouth was there, tasting and nipping along her skin.

He ceased neither his mouth nor his hand, pushing her body toward the edge of control. Somehow they'd moved a few paces and now she felt the wall behind her, giving her support, as he relentlessly pleasured her. He lifted his mouth from her and caught her gaze. She knew what he would do now. He liked to watch her face as she reached completion.

Her body wound tighter and tighter until she could not breathe or speak. He forced moan after moan from her until the tightness exploded within her and she arched against his hand over and over. Tolan's fingers teased that small bud within the folds until she could do nothing but feel wave after wave and pleasure coursing through her body as her release happened.

Tolan watched the way her eyes glazed over in passion as he stroked her deep and fast. Her body reacted in ways she probably did not even know, but he could see them and feel them. His hand between her legs grew wet with her arousal and the bud beneath his finger stiffened much like his own cock did.

Her mouth grew rounder and she licked her lips as her body kept pace with his hand, rocking against him, demanding more and more. Then he brought her to release and those breathy gasps turned into a low, long moan as she surrendered to her release, screaming out in the quietness of her cottage.

His body throbbed and ached for its own release, but this time was for her. It had been too long. Too many nights without being inside her body and finding that moment of joining and complete pleasure. He held her there, pressed against the wall, his hand sliding in gentle caresses as her body eased down from the height of passion. When she sighed, he smiled and kissed her one more time.

"I have a perfectly comfortable bed right over there," she said, nodding behind him.

"Aye, you do." He nodded as he spoke. "But I could not wait. It has been too many nights since I watched your face as I pleasured you." A blush filled her cheeks that had just cooled down from her passion.

Tolan removed his hand and let her gown fall. She did not cover her lovely breasts and he wanted to lean over and suckle the rose-colored nipples. He would. And she would scream again for him many more times before dawn's light brightened the sky and woke the village. Thea trembled when he stepped back and reached out to grab hold of his arms. She let out a soft laugh as he held her, waiting for her legs to gain their strength.

Something deep within him felt satisfied that he could cause such a reaction in her with only his touch. His cock, still hard and erect, reminded him that there were other ways to seek release.

"Can you stay or must you return to your house?" she asked, reaching up for her laces.

He stayed her hands with his, sliding his finger along the edge of the opened gown and shift. She arched as he flicked his finger over her swollen nipples. He took one between his finger and thumb and rolled it, eliciting another gasp from her. Done but not, she responded without shame or delay to his every provocation. And he wanted her more for it.

Even now his flesh throbbed with need and his soul desired her in a way he could not describe. Crouching before her, Tolan loosened the laces more and pulled her shift and bodice out of his way, allowing her breasts to spill out before his gaze. Now he could touch them and caress them and send her careening into passion once more.

Cupping them and stroking the taut tips with his thumbs, he once more watched as a lovely blush rose into the skin of the breasts and then into her neck and cheeks. But this was not embarrassment, it was arousal. Tolan leaned in and tasted first one and then the other, licking around the edge of each nipple before pulling it into his mouth and sucking it. Her reaction was immediate; she arched against him and grabbed his hair. When he lifted his mouth from her skin, she pulled him back. Laughing, he looked up into her dark brown eyes and smiled.

"I am staying the night, Thea."

Even while he was suckling her, his hands made quick work of removing her skirt and sliding the shift down over her hips to the floor. Then Tolan wrapped his arms around her and lifted her to his chest, enjoying the feel of her nakedness as he walked those few paces across the chamber.

"Let us put that perfectly comfortable bed to use," he urged.

It took little effort or time to reach the bed and soon he had her pressed down, on her back, and was exploring every inch of her flesh with his mouth. She liked him between her legs and he liked being there, stroking and tasting that intimate place. His tongue made her cry out, but his teeth made her scream. When he used his fingers to plunge deep within her, her body arched off the bed.

He wanted to wring every possible sound and motion from her body.

He wanted her surrender.

He wanted to give her an overflowing measure of passion before seeking his own release.

He wanted . . . her in every way a man could want a woman.

That desire, that need, surprised him only in the strength of it, not the fact of it. The realization simply pushed his need for her higher and he relentlessly teased her to the edge of release. Then, just before he knew her body would tighten within, he would ease his touches and caresses and let her slip back just a little from that precipice.

He knew he needed to be inside her most, so he kissed a path up her body, even while his hand stroked her flesh. She opened her mouth to his and suckled on his tongue as he had on her breasts, the salty taste of her own essence shared now with her. Leaning to one side, he gave her room to reach the ties at his waist, never slowing his hand or breaking their kiss. When his cock was freed, it took no more than a second to move to lie between her legs and thrust deep within her.

His flesh fit in her tight sheath and she let out a gasp and then a moan as he filled her completely. He wanted to pause and savor this moment of joining, but now she urged him on with words and by meeting his every thrust. He let go of his control and did as she asked—he took her. Deep. Fast.

Their cries mingled and echoed in the small cottage. He marveled at her uncontrolled reactions to him, to this, for it was the opposite of the way she behaved in front of others. Here, together, there was nothing to hold back her response to their pleasure.

Tolan had missed everything about her while away from Amesbury on the lord's business. Not just these physical acts, but also the way she smiled when she greeted him. Especially when she came upon him unexpectedly and her brown eyes lit at the sight of him. He loved the way she saw to the needs of the injured and sick of their village, her touch gentle and her care thorough and competent. More than competent, she was as successful a healer as he was a farmer.

Though the fires of passion exploded into being several more times that night, it was as the light of the morning sun began to creep into the lower edge of the sky that Tolan knew the truth. Elethea was the woman he wanted in his life. The woman he wanted as his wife, to be at his side and in his house and bed . . . but most importantly, in his heart.

The miles that he'd crossed and the days away from her had made that clear to him. He'd remained unmarried since Corliss's death those years ago and he'd raised their son on his own, believing that the call to his other duties might come at any time. Now, though, as the signs grew and the whispering voice had forced him to accept the reality of it, he knew he must have her at his side through whatever was coming.

At her side, he could protect her from the danger that grew and would surround them. And at his side, her presence would give him the strength he needed to face these unknown challenges. He had faced the fact that he wanted to marry her and marry her before Lord Geoffrey could, in any way, interfere. He only prayed Thea would say aye.

As the sun's light crept in through one window, she roused in his embrace, sliding her leg over his and smiling a soft, satisfied grin. He held her close and tried to think of the perfect words to say to her. Her gaze narrowed on his and she spoke first.

"What is it, Tolan?" She reached up and caressed his brow and cheeks with her fingers. "Is something wrong?"

"Nay, Thea. All is well." Tolan eased back just a bit, still keeping her near, but with enough room to speak. "I have a matter to discuss with you. That is all."

"This sounds serious." Thea pushed up to sit, her

long brown hair flowing over her shoulders and pooling on her lap. It hid nothing of her charms from his sight.

"It is serious. It is a matter of marriage."

From the hint of a frown, quickly hidden, Tolan suspected that the topic did not please her and her answer would not please him.

CHAPTER 5

Thea tried to pull away from him and from this topic, but he would not allow her to do so. He did not force her and yet he slid his arms around her, holding her close and not releasing her. She tried to tamp down the panic that always rose within her at the mention of marriage.

"Thea," Tolan said quietly as he did let go of his hold on her. "Stay," he urged in that voice that she wanted to obey.

"We both have duties that call us, Tolan," she said. Sliding from the bed and gathering up the clothes that lay strewn around the chamber, Thea began her morning tasks as she always did.

The silent reply made her more nervous than if he'd yelled or berated her as Jasper had when he was angry. Glancing over her shoulder after she'd pulled on a clean shift, she saw him lying there naked, with his hands tucked behind his head, just watching her.

"What misgivings you have—are they about me or being married once more?" he asked. She wasn't sure if it was his insight or memory that made her more nervous.

"I do not wish to discuss it," she said, quietly but with determination in her voice. She must bring this to an end. It would stir old memories and old hurts better left buried deep and untouched. "I have no complaints about how things stand between us."

Those words caused him to climb from the bed and stand before her—closely before her—in a matter of seconds. Part of her wanted to back away. Another part wanted to issue words of apology and beg for . . . Thea took a deep breath and shook her head. She must not let the past live once more in her life.

"You never speak of how things are between us, Thea." He glared at her, angry for the first time she could remember. "You never ask for anything of me, but that," he said with a glance at the bed. "Do you never wish for more? To stop sneaking from my bed to yours and to stand together before the others in the light of day?"

Did she want for more? Since their first time until now, she'd not thought on anything past the pleasure they shared. She could not think on anything more. The bed play was the only thing that broke through the numbness she'd wrapped herself in for so long. She'd offered him only the use of her body because she had nothing else to give him.

"Is that what you want, Tolan?" she asked softly, unable to give him even a reply to his question.

Tolan opened his mouth to speak, but a loud knock on the door interrupted whatever he'd planned to say. He tugged on his trews and shirt and waited for her to open it. Thea pulled a gown over her shift and walked to it.

"Someone might be hurt," she murmured as she lifted the latch. "Oh, good morrow, Kirwyn." Tolan's son stood there.

"Is my father within?"

"Aye. Come in," she said. Tolan's son knew how it was between them. Though they never spent the night in Tolan's house if Kirwyn was there, the boy was old enough to understand about his father and her.

"I heard that you'd returned last evening," Kirwyn said. "But you did not send word to Githa."

"Good morrow, Kirwyn. Aye, I returned late last evening and thought you would already be abed." Tolan walked to his son and hugged him. This showing of affection was one of the things she liked about him. "Is something wrong?" He stepped back and searched his son's face as though the answer would be found there.

"Lord Geoffrey's man came for you."

"Did he say what it was about?" Tolan asked as he pulled on his boots and found his belt and cloak.

"Nay. Nothing more than you are summoned this morn to wait on Lord Geoffrey." Kirwyn missed nothing as he watched his father dress and ready himself.

"You must eat first," she said. "Have you broken your fast yet, Kirwyn?" Boys of his age were always hungry, Thea knew. "Sit, I will get you both something to eat before you are on your way."

She poured water into cups for them and gathered together some cheese and bread and some dried fruits. It took little time to make porridge and soon they were all eating. Though she tried to catch Tolan's eye, he was avoiding her gaze. She did not forget his interrupted anger and knew it had not gone away. This meal was consumed in an awkward silence, broken up by only Kirwyn's questions about his father's trip with the lord. Curious also, she listened to their conversation.

Soon, they finished eating and it was time to take their leave of each other. Others in the village and at the keep waited now on both of them, so Thea began gathering her supplies for the day. Tolan stood and carried their bowls to the washing bucket before nodding at the door. Kirwyn thanked her before lifting the latch to leave.

Just as he stepped to the doorway, Tolan turned back and strode back to her. Grabbing her by the shoulders, he pulled her into his embrace and kissed her until she was breathless again. While still holding on to her, he leaned back and stared into her eyes.

"Aye. I want more with you. I want you day and night. I want you to be at my side before all the others, not hiding away. I want you to marry me, Elethea."

His words sounded like pledges, promises made to consecrate a future together. Just like marriage vows. Before she could say anything, he kissed her again, possessing her mouth and taking her breath and almost her will.

Then he was gone, the door slamming behind him as he walked off with Kirwyn toward their cottage.

She slid to her knees, weakened by the strength of his passion and by what he asked of her. Thea leaned forward and touched her forehead to the floor, curling over her legs, trying to sort through the conflicting feelings and thoughts that raced through her heart and her mind.

She lay there for some time before the sunlight pierced through the dark chamber's window and fell on her. It illuminated the floor around her and she watched as dust sparkled in the air before her. Though the light was not hot, her body began to pulse with heat. Her skin glowed and she leaned back on her heels to examine it.

It had to be some kind of illusion. Truly, her skin could not glow like the light of the sun. Holding her hand up before her face, she blinked and blinked again, trying to make sense of what she was seeing and feeling. Her sleeve slid down from her wrist and exposed her forearm where the bandage had fallen away.

The red area had not responded to the salve she put on it. Indeed, it had grown larger and darker. When the sunlight touched it, it began to shift before her eyes. The redness swirled around and around until it was a circle, a disk-shaped mark there. It burned much like skin that had touched fire, but this did not blister. The area reached a certain size and shape and then continued to pulse as though alive.

Thea pushed to her feet and stepped out of the light, into the shadows of the corner of the chamber, suspecting that the stronger light was causing her eyes to be false to her.

Her skin yet glowed and the mark continued to shift and glimmer and burn as though the sun lived there on her arm. She touched it with her finger and she could feel no difference there. Thea wanted to observe it more, but a call came from outside, forcing her to forget the mark.

"Elethea!" a man called out loudly. "Elethea!" She pulled the door open to find Rolfe there, agitated and sweating. "I pray you, please come now. Linne is bleeding."

She paused only long enough to grab her basket and then followed the large man along the path to his cottage. His mother stood at the door, holding it open so she could enter.

"What happened?" Thea asked as she ran to Linne's side. The young woman's body was shaking as tremors moved through her. "Linne!"

She reached out and turned Linne's face to her, but the woman was not conscious. Without delaying, Thea tugged Linne's gown up and carefully felt between her legs. Blood, too much blood, poured out there.

A sinking feeling took hold of Thea, making her throat burn as she realized the young mother would not survive such bleeding.

"Please, Elethea. Please save her," Rolfe pleaded. He paced behind her, carrying the babe in his arms now. His mother stood ready to help.

Trying to gain control over herself, she took in a deep breath and let it out. What could she do? Packing would not help stop such bleeding.

"Elethea! Do something!" Rolfe bellowed. His deep voice and distress woke up the babe, who cried loudly. At least the baby was strong. If she could not help Linne, at least the babe would live.

Then, although Rolfe continued to beg her, the sounds all faded away. She waved him and his mother away and peered at Linne. Thea's hand remained on the woman's thighs, which, like the rest of her, were growing colder and colder as she bled her life away. She needed to keep her warm. Placing her other arm—the one with the new mark on it—on Linne's belly, Thea thought about the sun's heat.

How her skin had heated as the sun touched it.

How her skin had glowed with the sun's light.

Spreading her fingers over the still-extended womb, she thought about sharing that warmth. She thought about sending it deep within the woman to end the bleeding that would kill her soon. Thea thought about sending the life force of the sun into the dying woman to keep her alive.

She did not remember closing her eyes, but when she opened them, Thea saw that Linne's whole body glowed as Thea's own skin had earlier. And the bleeding stopped flowing onto her hands under Linne's gown. Thea remained still for several minutes, praying that the bleeding had truly ceased. Then she slid her hand out and wiped the blood off it.

"Elethea?" The whisper caught her by surprise, for Thea thought herself still caught up in the strange silence.

"Linne, you are awake. How do you feel?" Thea slid closer and knelt by the woman's side, taking her hand.

"I feel warm," she said softly. "I was cold, so cold that I could not stop shivering. But the sun came out and now I am warm again." Glancing past Thea, Linne frowned at her husband. "What is wrong, Rolfe?"

"I thought . . . I thought . . ." The man could not get out the words to explain what had happened. "I know not what happened."

Rolfe stared at her and Thea wondered what he'd seen. She could not explain it, either, but it seemed as though something moved through her into Linne and stopped her from dying. But that was not possible. That would be . . .

Dangerous.

Women were thought to be in league with evil if things such as what had just happened were spoken about. Women were killed over such matters.

"I placed some herbs and bandages in as a packing, Linne," she said quickly. A complete lie. "You must rest until I return on the morrow to remove it. I would not want the bleeding to begin anew."

"You will rest, Linne," Rolfe repeated. "I will not lose you." It was an order given with such love that tears came to Thea's eyes as she heard it.

Thea stood and shook out her gown, blood staining the front of it now.

"Can she feed the baby?" Rolfe's mother, Hilde, asked from where she stood.

"Aye," Thea said, nodding at Hilde. "But she must

remain abed until I return on the morrow." Hilde crossed her arms over her chest and nodded. Thea knew that no one would disobey Hilde when she was in charge.

Thea tossed one of the lengths of cloth she'd brought with her over her basket and walked to the door. It hid the fact that none of her rolls of bandages had been used. And that her herbs remained untouched.

She left and walked aimlessly up the path of the village. Her mind could not figure out what had happened. Well, she knew what had happened—Linne had not died when she should have. But the how and why of it were the true mystery.

Thea thought on what had happened and realized that, for the first time after a birth or healing, she had not grown overheated. Usually by now, she was seeking out a cool place or the cold water to temper the increasing heat within her. Yet, just now, it was Linne who spoke of the heat.

What had happened to change this pattern?

Her talent for healing had always been strong. Though her mother taught her the way of it, Thea had gone on and learned how to do much, much more. Some treatments and concoctions just seemed the right thing to do or make, while others were learned through observation and trial. Her skills at delivering even the most difficult births and keeping both mother and child alive had put her much in demand.

And Jasper had hated her for it.

He'd hated that she gained attention for being something other than his wife. He'd hated that she'd answered every call, no matter the hour of day or night, refusing no one in need. He'd grown to hate her. She shivered then as memories of his hatred rose from the place within where she tried to keep them.

The only good thing was that their marriage had only lasted for three years. Longer than that and Thea doubted not that she would be the one buried in the graveyard next to the church instead of Jasper.

Shaking off the past, she walked back toward her cottage, needing to change her gown and wash before the day was full upon her. When someone called out her name in greeting and she glanced up to reply, she saw Tolan on his way up to the keep. He walked with purpose, for he was an important man to Lord Geoffrey.

Important enough to accompany the nobleman on this recent journey. Indispensable to the success of the lord's lands. Too important for a woman like her to marry. If she had not had her own reasons to avoid marriage already, then Tolan's status and importance gave her additional ones.

Thea made quick work of changing out of the bloodied gown, washing the worst out of it and dressing in a clean one. With her basket and satchel filled, she felt ready to follow through on her plan, the one she'd set for herself when Jasper died.

She would use her skills and talents for the benefit of those living here and never expect more than the joy that it gave her. When she had first married, she expected to have children, many of them, but Jasper's beatings had taken away her ability to have them. So she would find joy in bringing new life into the world for others.

And Thea would never marry again. She would never give a man that kind of control and power over her very life and breath. If that meant giving Tolan up when he sought a wife, then she would have to find the strength to do that. For no man who needed sons as he did would marry a woman who could not bear them.

She did as was her custom when bothered or worried—she threw herself into her tasks for the rest of the day. Thea visited the ill and injured in the village most of the morn and then spent several hours preparing the small patch of ground she used to grow herbs. Tired and sore from her efforts, she returned to her cottage to end the day with a simple meal.

Though Tolan's absence that night did not surprise her, it did bother her more than she had expected. After all, they were nothing more than friends who shared a bed when it was convenient. She should have no more expectations than that. Thea suspected that something had changed between them and wondered if they would ever go back to the relationship they'd had when this day began.

When he did not knock on her door the next night or the one after, Thea had to face the truth. And if she cried herself to sleep, at least no one heard her.

CHAPTER 6

Southern coast of England

William de Brus had waited as their ships were unloaded and watched as their supplies and people reached the shore. It had taken most of that day to accomplish, but now, before nightfall, they were miles inland and camped in a heavily wooded area next to a river. It would shield them from prying eyes and give them a chance to organize themselves.

A large force of fighting men would gain notice much too quickly and be confronted by the local lord and possibly the king's men. So they'd decided to break up into two smaller groups and hide themselves in the guise of pilgrims.

"Do you think we will go unnoticed?" Roger de Bardem, William's closest friend and commander of the men who fought with them, asked. They stood at the edge of the encampment waiting for the sentries to report. Anxious to return to his wife Brienne's side, William wished things settled for the night.

"We have all been raised as faithful Catholics, Roger," William offered. "'Tis less a falsehood than many others we have told."

"Except for them," Roger said, nodding at the group of priests, men and women, who even now chanted some prayer to their gods for delivering the group safely to the southern shores of England.

"Father Ander assures me he can accomplish this. Corann agrees. So we will travel north as pilgrims of the Holy Church, giving thanks for blessings received."

"And the king will not hear of us?" Roger asked, crossing his arms over his chest and meeting William's gaze now.

"If he does and sends someone to investigate, I will use the good name of my *father's* family to ease our way. The de Bruses own properties, hold titles, and owe homage here in England as well as France and Scotland." William smiled.

Though his true father was King Alexander III of Scotland, William's bastardy was an open secret. But respect for the man who'd married his mother in deference to the king's wishes would help them more here.

"But I suspect that Edward is too busy seeing to important matters of kingdom and country to worry over some pilgrims journeying into his lands."

Chaos swirled around them in the world and loomed even larger a threat because of the ancient goddess's attempts to escape her otherworldly prison. A king, his own father, had fallen and more, William suspected, would follow. Caught at a disadvantage because of their lack of knowledge, the Warriors of Destiny, descendants of the ancient Celtic gods, were trying to find their way in this newly risen war between good and evil.

Only the priests had continued strong in their faith and their ways and had searched for those of the bloodlines to guide them in this conflict that had the potential to see evil triumph and humanity be destroyed.

The first two battles had been won but at a terrible cost. Now the third one was ahead of them. They must reach the area where the prophecy foretold the next circle of stones and the two bloodlines who guarded it. William prayed to whoever would listen that those guardians would have more knowledge than he and Brienne and Soren and Ran had had coming into this.

"Here they come, Will," Roger warned.

Father Ander and Corann were inseparable now, always with their heads together discussing matters of faith and the challenges they faced. For one raised in the orthodoxy of the Catholic priesthood, Ander had taken his newfound role in this endeavor with more acceptance and enthusiasm than anyone would have guessed. And Corann, though raised in the faith of the Old Ones, faced his own challenges since being designated as the leader of those priests on the death of their mentor, Marcus, just over a fortnight ago.

"Father. Corann. How goes it?" William asked.

Ander held out a parchment to Will and he examined it. A list of abbeys and churches and a rudimentary map of the journey ahead of them. It ended in Amesbury.

"You think the circle we seek is in Amesbury, then?" he asked, showing the map to Roger.

"Nay, not Amesbury itself, but the whole area is strewn with ancient stones and curious mounds. There is an abbey in Amesbury and I will seek out more there," Ander advised and he swept his hand across a large blank area of the map.

"So much we do not know," Roger whispered.

"Ah, but we know more than we did before," Corann said. "Yet we are not as arrogant as the others. And so far the gods have favored our efforts."

"We will seek information on the morrow at the priory, William. The church here is now being called Christ's Church, for it is said that He disguised Himself as a simple carpenter to fix a problem with a wooden beam in the roof. Surely, it is an auspicious place to begin our quest on behalf of good?"

Before William could remark on the priest's comments, his name was called.

"William?"

He turned to the soft voice he knew and loved. Brienne walked to them, shimmering with the aura of her power, and gifted him with the smile he craved as much as he craved her. "Supper is ready. Come, friends. We must all seek our rest this night in preparation for our journey."

"Rest, my arse," Roger said under his breath but loud enough for the other men to hear.

William laughed, but since Brienne's voice called to the warblood within him, it sounded like a roar. His vision changed, too, and everything he saw now was tinged in red. Knowing it was not needed, the war-blood sank back into William's blood and waited . . . always waited.

"On the morrow, I will visit the priory here to establish our groups as pilgrims and to see what I can learn of the lands to the north," Ander said, looking to Corann and William for their agreement.

"Ran is taking the river north to explore the lands to which we journey," Corann said. "No doubt Soren will follow in the skies."

No doubt. Soren carried the bloodline of the god of sky and storms, so he could move as wind or clouds. His wife, Ran, was blessed by the goddess of water and sea and would become one with the river to travel along it. Though traveling by boat would be faster than riding and walking, the river narrowed and changed course too many times for their large ships to fit. And too many small boats would be needed for the whole of the group.

"We will talk when you and they return," William said, nodding at the two priests.

Once they'd left, he and Roger discussed the guards and timing of their patrols before he took his leave of his friend. The warblood would not be held back much longer from seeking its mate, and William could feel his control growing thin.

"Will?" Roger said quietly. When he faced his friend, Will nodded. "Is there ever a moment when it isn't there, pushing you and changing you?"

The profound changes in everything they had believed and learned over these last weeks were shocking, even now to him. Will was part of this plan set in place eons ago by ancient gods to protect mankind. Even knowing his part in it did not make it feel any less surprising.

"Nay. He is always there, always ready. But there are moments when I wonder how I did not know it all my life. I suspect that all the accolades for my fighting abilities and the tourney wins were due to him."

"He? You speak as though it is not you."

Will stepped closer to his friend and tried to explain. "There are times, before he takes over, when I can still hear and think only as William. But then the warblood makes me able to see and hear and fight better. He is a better version of myself."

"Better?" Roger asked. "But how can that be?"

"Stronger certainly. Clear-minded and focused." Will shrugged. "I know not how else to explain it. I just know it to be true."

He had thought on it more and more and could not explain it otherwise. Brienne had said the same thing about how it felt to her when the fireblood took over. He did not know Ran and Soren well enough yet to delve into such matters, but he expected he would hear the same thing from them.

So all he, they, could do was to accept the changes in his life, accept the call to protect humanity, and accept that his life and his future would never be in his control again.

He nodded to his friend and stalked off to find his wife. It had been too many days since they had a moment or an hour's privacy, and the warblood ached for her, even as he, the man, did.

"All is well?" she asked at this approach.

"For now, 'tis," he said in that voice that contained both the man he was and the warblood who rose now. "On the morrow? Who knows?"

He was their leader and needed to be strong for all those who followed his orders and plans. But here, in her presence and in her arms and within her body, he could be himself. She walked into his embrace and offered her mouth to him. Will kissed her gently, touching their tongues, and accepted the warmth that lived within her.

"We will face the morrow as we do each day—together, my love."

The warblood liked the taste of her and the way her words sounded. He pushed his way into control of the human and showed himself to his mate. Growing and pushing to his true height, he touched the canvas of the tent over his head before stopping. The color of her changed, too, and the orange that surrounded her being sparkled and glimmered like the flames that lived inside her. He liked the fire. Even the pain of being burned did not stop him from seeking it, seeking her.

Now the constant hum of words in his thoughts and in his blood changed when she was there. At every other moment, he thought of killing and conquering and death and destroying his enemies. But when she was there, it was only her.

She was the fire who heated his blood and his soul and burned his body. She was the fire who could withstand his strength. She was only his.

His to take. His to possess. His to keep and protect. His to love.

He laughed then, and the sound of it echoed around them and escaped the confines of the tent. Love was human. It was the part of the human that remained in place when the warblood took his place in this world.

"Come, my love," she whispered. "Let us seek a place away from the others."

His blood surged then, desire for her almost overwhelming his control. But he would never harm her or allow her to come to it. The warblood took her hand and followed her deeper into the woods, to a place where none could hear them or his roar when he claimed her. She worried over that.

But she did not worry long, for he pleasured her relentlessly through that night until she forgot about everything else. A strange feeling haunted him through their hours together and did not leave no matter how many times he sank into her soft, human body and heard her cries of passion and release.

Unable to define it, the warblood pushed it aside and did not allow it to control him. He took her body, heart, and soul that night and offered her all he had in return.

Only when he returned back into the human's blood, only as William regained his place, did the warblood recognize the feeling he'd noticed.

Loss.

Loss of her.

He would lose her.

Unacceptable! he thought as he pushed through the

barrier separating his mind from the human's. He would not leave and allow her to be unprotected. He could not lose her. He would not. If he could not be present at all times, he would be watching. He would . . . watch.

"Will?" Brienne tugged on his hand as they walked back to the camp. He stopped and turned to meet her questioning gaze. She frowned.

"What is it? Have I forgotten something?"

"Your eyes. They are . . . they are the warblood's eyes, Will."

At first he'd thought the red tinge was caused by her nearness and the power that surged from within her. But now he realized it was his own eyes that had changed.

And not only had the color changed, but so also had his ability to see farther away and clearer. Will glanced back at her and nodded.

"So it is," he said as he took her hand once more and led her back to the others. "The warblood is still here, Brienne. He's still here."

Will could not explain it more, but he knew that the warblood would never be completely absent from his conscious mind ever again. As he sought a reason, it came to him.

The warblood was watching. Like a sentry on duty, the creature within now stood guard. And the only reason he could think of disturbed him greatly, for the warblood must think his mate was in danger.

Over the next days, as they began to travel north, into the heart of England and farther along their destined path, the warblood never left Will completely. His gaze stared out over the lands as they crossed the miles to the place where they would once more battle the evil one and her followers.

Ran discovered no open dangers along the path of this river, called Avon. Soren reported that nothing seemed out of place from his view above. And Father Ander mentioned that being on the hallowed ground of the church seemed to mute his and Corann's ability to sense the others and might be a way to hide from de Gifford, who must arrive here soon.

All important things to consider as the huge group broke into two and headed to Amesbury a day apart. But the most important thing was never far from Will's or the warblood's thoughts—Brienne must be kept safe.

CHAPTER 7

Tolan's world was spinning out of control. Each day something else happened that he could not stop or change or divert from its course.

The orderly progression of his life and purpose through the seasons was gone. He'd liked the predictability of how he lived, especially since he understood how the spring would wake the earth, the summer would bring it fertility, the fall would see its bounty collected, and the winter would see it seek its rest. Until it all began again.

Now the woman he wanted to marry was opposed to such a thing. And his son was gazing with calf eyes at a young woman with alarming regularity. Worse, the man whom he served was looking for the one thing he'd sworn to keep hidden.

As he strode along the perimeter of the field that Lord Geoffrey wanted cultivated, Tolan knew that this part of his life was the only one he knew for a certainty. He crouched down and examined the soil closely, running his fingers through it to loosen the clumps. He'd been right to promise this land would take seed in just a few weeks. As he wiggled his fingers, he could feel the first traces of life returning to the once-deadened soil.

Standing and brushing the dirt from his hands, he was content that at least this would go as he knew it should. He nodded to Langston and pointed at the men who stood off in the distance.

"Tell them to leave this be for another sennight," he said. "Then we will plant."

"It looks barren to me," the man muttered as he shrugged.

Tolan smiled and shook his head. "Well, 'tis not. The harvest will tell you so."

Langston walked off to speak to the men, the eighth task of just this morn, and Tolan wondered what else he could find to keep the man busy.

No, what he needed to do was to discover the reason why Lord Geoffrey sought the circle Tolan knew lay buried deep in the impassible thicket on his lands. Though his father had passed on the knowledge that it was there and even though Tolan remembered catching a glimpse of it decades ago when just a small boy, the trees had grown into an impenetrable barrier around it. No one had seen it for years.

Yet the nobleman knew about it and, clearly, he was terrified of the consequences if he did not find it. He might not know what it truly was, but someone did. The person who gave Lord Geoffrey the orders to find it. A person who was powerful enough and knowledgeable enough to know the importance of the stones and what their purpose was.

Tolan turned and walked toward the outbuildings, searching his memory for what his duty was now. If he thought the circle under threat, what was he supposed to do? Who else knew the truth and how could he guard it against those who would threaten it? More than that, if he heard *that* voice calling, could or did others? Would more answer the summons?

The mark on his arm pulsed then, reminding him that he might have little time to ignore this matter. If letting others get to the circle would truly bring about the end of the world, as his father had told him, what choice did he have other than to make certain that did not happen? Even if he did it alone. Even if no one else stood with him.

He'd thought on this for hours as he'd lain awake and alone these last two nights. If he was truthful, he considered all this while trying not to think about Thea. And the nights were long enough for him to spend time doing both.

Tolan planned to travel back to his farm alone and seek out the circle. He would see for himself what was at stake and from where that voice had spoken. Once the rest of the main fields were prepared and sown, he would be able to go there—in three or four days at the most. So he began collecting the seeds that would be the first crop to be ready. A knock on the door interrupted his work about an hour later. Expecting it to be Langston, who could never sort out his own tasks without guidance, Tolan lifted the latch, tugged the door open, only to find Thea standing there.

"Thea, I did not expect you," he said, not knowing what else to say. "Are you well?"

"I am," she said with a nervousness that had never existed between them before. "I know you are a busy man with many duties, but I wanted to ask you to come to my cottage for supper this night."

On any other day such an invitation would have made him smile, but this was different. Her unease sat around her like a swirling cloak, almost as protection against . . . him? And he did not like it. It reminded him too much of the first times he'd met her when she shrank away from even an inadvertent touch of his hand.

"Thea, come in," he said, taking her hand and tugging her inside the building and out of sight of anyone passing by. At least she did not resist his touch now.

"I did not mean to interrupt you at your duties now, Tolan," she said softly as he pulled the door closed behind her. "It can wait until later."

"Nay, it cannot," he whispered, pulling her kerchief off and wrapping his arms around her. "I cannot."

He kissed her then, letting her feel his desire for her. He knew there was more between them than simple lust and he would make certain she knew that. If she thought that he would reject her for speaking her mind, she needed to know he would not. More than all that, she had to know that he was not the brute she'd married and nearly had not survived.

Thea softened beneath his mouth as he gentled his kiss and he felt her hands glide along his back. Sliding his hands up into her hair, he held her to him with only enough strength to keep her close. If she'd stepped away, his hold would not prevent it.

"Nothing has changed between us," he whispered against her mouth.

"I heard what Lord Geoffrey expects from you, Tolan. I will not be in the way."

Ah, so the conversation was not as private as Tolan had requested it be. Word spread from those living in the keep to the villagers with a quickness that always surprised him. Content to keep his own counsel, Tolan did understand that others found joy in sharing bits of news and gossip.

"We can speak of that later," he said, releasing her. "And other matters." He kissed her once more and stepped back. The frown was still set firmly on her brow, so he reached out and smoothed it with his thumbs, cupping her face. "I will be there."

Thea nodded and picked up her kerchief from where he'd flung it and he watched as she covered her hair. He would have mourned for the loss of seeing it except he knew he was the only man to glimpse it uncovered, loose, and swaying around her naked body as he drove her toward carnal satisfaction. Even now he caught himself watching the way her hips moved with each step away from him.

Shaking himself free of her spell, he turned back to his task as she headed toward the village with her basket on her arm.

The day moved along and he tried to concentrate on what he needed to accomplish and not on her, but he could not. With all the strange possibilities surrounding him and trying to take control of his life, she was the only constant.

The only one on whom he could depend. She worked in service to those living here much as he did. They shared a common purpose here.

As a shiver slid along his spine, Tolan knew he would do what was necessary to keep her safe. A glance toward the shadows of the woods there told him that the men who had followed him since he left the keep two days ago still did so. Every step he took was being observed.

And Tolan did not know why.

The orders would have come directly from Lord Geoffrey, so it meant that he suspected Tolan of something. Was it over the matter of marriage that Geoffrey had discussed? Were they watching to see with whom he spent time? Had Tolan's refusal of the nobleman's help in finding an appropriate wife angered him?

Or worse, had his ritual in the field been witnessed?

He remembered being as careful as always when he carried out the prayers. He'd always waited until the village and farms were long settled for the night. He would have felt their weight on the earth if they stood nearby.

Startled at that realization, he turned back to his preparations within the shelter of the building and waited for night to fall.

It had happened again.

As Thea laid her hands on old Rigby's leg, mangled

months ago when the millstone broke, she felt the heat passing from her blood into the still-healing bones there. Under the guise of examining the fractures that were taking too long to heal, she slid her hands along the length of his lower leg first.

Fortunately, he was lying back and not watching, for her hands began to shimmer. Leaning forward to cover the strange sight, Thea let nothing disturb her thoughts as she rubbed the tight skin over the broken places.

"Ah, where was that during the cold winter nights?" Rigby said, laughing. "That eases the ache well."

Thea nodded and reached out to her basket, pretending to dip her hand in some unguent now that Rigby's attention had turned. "I am gladdened that it helps. A new recipe."

She continued for some time, until all the places she touched felt warm and supple beneath her hands. Though she'd set his bones, she'd been able to do nothing about his knee or his foot. Those two areas had taken the most time to warm, so she did not rush it or think too much about the reasons she was doing this. Thea finished by spreading some unguent that she had made to keep his skin soft and wrapped some bandages around it.

"You may sit up, Rigby, but only with help." She felt his wife hovering behind them, waiting for word of his condition. "I think the healing is going well." He let out a sigh that was matched by that of his wife. "I know it has been slow and you want to be back on your feet."

Thea pushed to her own feet and placed the jar in her basket. Rigby's wife, Eldreda, walked to her side.

"My thanks for your help, Thea," the older woman said. "He could have died from such injuries, but your care saw him through." The woman patted her shoulder and nodded to her husband. "He will do as you say."

Thea almost laughed aloud at the words and tone spoken by Eldreda. Very few people would disregard Thea's instructions if she could use a voice like what Eldreda used on her husband. From his expression, he'd been thinking of doing something Thea had warned him not to do.

It was hard for a man who knew only work and physical labor every day of his life to lie back and be at ease. And every day that someone else ran his mill meant a day closer to be unneeded. A dangerous state to find oneself in when a person's value was measured by how much the lord needed your work or service. Though she was not tied to the land as others were, Thea knew that her place here, especially as a widow, was based on Lord Geoffrey's preference.

"I pray you will walk soon, Rigby," she said. "But that depends on you continuing to follow my instructions and not doing too much too quickly."

"Oh, aye, Elethea," Rigby said as she and Eldreda helped him to sit on the pallet. "I am a man who knows when to listen to a woman's words."

Eldreda burst out laughing at his declaration and Thea could not help but stare at these two. Another example to her that all marriages were not the same and that some men could abide by their wives having a say.

"I must go to check on Linne," she said as she gathered her cloak and her basket on her arm.

"A miracle, eh?" Eldreda whispered as she walked with Thea to the door. "Hilde said she'd not seen a woman survive the bleeding that Linne suffered."

"A miracle to be sure," Thea added, unwilling to say more.

"Here now, for your help, Thea," Eldreda said, handing her a loaf of bread and a sack of flour.

"My thanks." She turned back to the older woman. "Try to keep him from standing until I come back," she explained. "Or send for me if there is a problem."

"I will."

Thea walked off then, to Linne's cottage, even while feeling that what had just happened with Rigby overwhelmed her. She needed time to think on it. To try to understand how she could be healing with her touch. That suspicion shocked her to her core.

Herbs cured illness and eased symptoms. Concoctions, teas, and ointments made people feel better. The touch of hands could make tightness go away, but heal? It was like something out of a legend or, worse, deviltry. She made the sign of the cross in reaction to such a thought. God-fearing people did not believe in such things.

The stinging on her arm made her hiss. Tugging back the sleeve, she found the area there was now larger and more defined. More frightening was that, as she watched, it moved and changed shape, until it was perfectly round like the sun. But this time it did not fade away as it had done before. It remained there, undulating as though something swirled under her skin.

"You are deep in thought, Thea," Linne said.

Blinking and shaking herself from her reverie, Thea found that her feet had taken her to Linne's home. The young woman sat on a bench, outside the door, in a place where the warmth of the sun would reach her. Young Medwyn at her breast, Linne was the image of health.

"Aye," Thea said, smiling at the young woman who should be dead and buried. "I am almost out of herbs for one of the ointments I make. Just thinking of how to manage it."

"You are always thinking of others, Thea."

Linne rubbed the babe's head and Medwyn answered with a burp and a sigh, sliding off her breast, asleep. Thea never felt so empty as she did just now.

"Will you come for supper?" Linne asked. "We will not keep you late." A wink spoke of Linne's knowledge of the pattern of Tolan's visits.

"I would like that," Thea said. It would keep her from sitting in her cottage, listening for every sound that could mean Tolan approached. "But I have made other plans this evening."

But later, after spending the remaining hours of the day before the evening meal in her garden, pulling at weeds and the preparing the soil, she did exactly that.

And when she sat in her chair listening for his

footsteps outside her door, Thea was no more at peace with the changes happening in her life than she was clear in her understanding of what caused them. She only hoped that Tolan would be the one person she could trust, even if she did not want him to know all the secrets she bore.

Southampton, England

Hugh smiled smugly as his ships approached the port of Southampton on England's southern coast. The only reason his ships made it across the channel from his lands in Brittany and Normandy was that the attentions of the Warriors were turned away.

They thought and acted like the humans they used to be, not the beings of power that they were now. The first four had not yet accepted or understood the extent of their powers or their range. And Hugh was glad he had not told them all of it. Or he would have yet been stranded on the sea.

As they grew closer to the shoreline, Eudes, his commander, walked to his side and waited to be acknowledged. Hugh nodded.

"My lord, everything is readied."

"Our man?" The spy he'd left within those who fought with the Warriors had sent word of the discovery of the prophecy.

"He should be waiting when we dock," Eudes said confidently. Not comfortably, though.

"Send him on to my cousin as soon as he gives his

report," Hugh said, turning to face the man who was his half brother. "Is there a problem?"

"Only that we are behind them."

"Worry not. They are wandering and we will march with purpose and arrive from a different direction," Hugh said, closing his eyes and searching for signs of the others. Another ability they had yet to master. "And they have no idea of where we are."

Ripples in the air told him of their position. The four others were north and west of him now. Stretching out his mind, he could only detect the presence of the other two, the ones whose powers had not yet erupted.

There was still time. Time to find them and bring them into the goddess's following. Time to teach them about the price of resistance and the reward of loyalty.

He shivered then and the skin on his back pulled against his shirt and tunic. Burned too much and too many times, it was now beyond repair and the price he'd paid for failing Chaela.

When he'd arrived on his lands, he sought out the place where he could reach her, and their merging, well, it had gone as badly as he suspected it would. No matter that he had groveled and begged her forgiveness in any and every way he knew how, she had never slowed in her punishment of him. Even now the pain of it tore through him, making it difficult to breathe.

It would never heal and the torment he would feel when he turned into fire would remind him of his weakness. She had burned him to cinders and allowed him to reform, only to repeat it over and over until he could no longer heal every part of himself. The area on his back, from his hips up to his ribs, would forever remind him of her terrible wrath.

But . . .

He knew that the ultimate reward he would reap when he opened the gateway and released her from her prison would more than compensate him for this physical torment now. And Hugh would gladly suffer now knowing what was to come.

Glorious, complete, and utter power over mankind. Kings would no longer matter. Armies would not, either. When Chaela gained control, he would oversee the breeding of more bloodline descendants and would rule over them as they worshipped the goddess. And he would take his place at Chaela's side as her consort and they would destroy anyone who stood against them.

The first to feel his wrath would be his ingrate of a daughter—he would destroy her before the eyes of those she led astray.

Then he would take the Norse woman—Ran. He craved merging with her . . . and taking that magnificent body of hers even while she fought him. And she would fight him. But her strength would not be enough against him and Hugh would relish every moment of her struggles until he broke her mind, body, and soul. Then he would keep her as his concubine, breeding sons on her filled with their bloodlines. Strong sons. Many sons.

Hugh shivered again. This time it was his cock that reacted at both the thought of joining with Chaela in human form and the satisfaction and pleasure that would also follow when he broke Ran. His body began to turn then, the flames igniting within and spreading out.

Until the anguish stopped him; his human flesh was unable to bear the fire's touch. He needed more time before he could face that agony again. Letting out his breath, he concentrated on the land as it grew closer.

"My lord?" Eudes asked.

In no mood to deal with his curiosity or his questions, Hugh sent him away with but a glance. He must ready himself to do what he had to in order to find the gateway and open it. Now, though, Hugh stood silently and tried to force his mind off the searing pain that threatened to slow him.

Pain was nothing but a guide to what he truly wanted. Pain would never break his resolve to see the Warriors defeated. Pain would simply be a precursor to the great pleasures that awaited him when he pleased his goddess and freed her.

CHAPTER 8

Tolan stood before her door for some time listening to the sounds of the night. Lifting his head and closing his eyes, he took in more—not only the sounds but also the smells. The earth beneath his feet was coming alive and he detected the odor of the living things waking from their winter sleep.

As he turned his head, whispers caught his attention. Unable to hear them clearly, Tolan walked around Thea's croft, drawn to the area where she grew her herbs. The sounds grew louder still, but there were no words being spoken. Thinking he might be interrupting two trysting lovers, he stopped and waited.

The smell was familiar, for it was that of the soil as it was turned over in the spring, refreshing it with the touch of the sun and air after its months of rest. And it grew stronger and stronger. He walked to the stone wall that enclosed the garden and looked within.

Indeed, some of the soil had been turned over and

loosened from the winter's grip. A small section of Thea's garden was ready to be seeded for the summer's growth. If the strength of the smell of it had not surprised him, the way that the area glowed did. He walked with a care over to that corner and crouched next to it.

The warmth was unmistakable, for it was like that of the sun's kiss on the soil after a long, cloudless day, and here the heat lingered. . . . He'd felt the same warmth when he worked the fields in the bright sunshine. Even now his hands itched to touch the soil and turn it. Yet here it was something different, something . . . more. Almost as the earth felt to him after he'd touched it or called life to it.

Glancing about, Tolan realized it was the corner of the garden that was shaded by the large oak tree that grew there just outside the wall. Standing, he wondered how this had happened.

The only person who worked this garden was Thea. She allowed no one else to tend to her herbs—they were too important in the concoctions and teas and unguents she made to treat the sick and injured to let someone else oversee their care.

Only Thea. Only Thea touched this garden.

Thea.

For a moment, the truth he'd never seen before shocked himself so much that he could not consider all the possibilities or consequences of it. Could it be that she was like him? That she had the blood of the ancients within her? If so, she'd never given any clue to it. Brushing the soil off his hands, he began to walk to her door, thinking on the woman herself.

She'd learned his healing skills from her mother, much the same as everyone did. But Tolan knew that Thea had long ago surpassed anything she'd learned from old Welsa. Her talent went beyond knowing the recipes for making the things she used. Her talents went beyond what he knew of most healers. And those talents had been noticed and coveted even by Lord Geoffrey.

It had been the nobleman's idea that she wed Jasper, a Norman in his service. That kept her here, working for him, when she might possibly have moved to live with distant relatives and taken her skills with her. And now Tolan wondered if Jasper's death might have been more than accidental.

Thinking on it in this way, Tolan suspected that Jasper's beatings had gotten too violent and that threatened Geoffrey's use of her skills. That fall from a horse that broke Jasper's neck could have been caused by many, many things. But it would mean that Lord Geoffrey knew much more about the bloodlines and the ancients . . . and about Tolan.

'Twas too much of a coincidence for these things not to be connected. If Tolan had grown up with the stories being passed to him, then it seemed logical that others had as well. And it made sense that some others, even while connected by the blood of the ancients, might never had learned of them.

Like Thea?

The thought sent him staggering, along the path that led to her door. He waited there, listening once more, before he lifted the latch and entered quietly, not bothering to knock. Her soft snoring made him smile and he decided not to wake her . . . yet. Tolan leaned against the now-closed door and thought on his new suspicions, gathering his thoughts and trying to come up with a way to ask her about them.

If she was of the bloodlines, she would have been warned against revealing it to others, as he had. It would have been part of her training. If she herself had no knowledge of it, then . . .

Tolan glanced over to find her sitting before the fire, her head tipped to one side, in the high-back chair. Her work chair, she called it, and sure enough, her sewing basket sat on the floor at her side. She was dreaming now, whispering words and a name. He crouched next to her and waited, not wanting to frighten her.

"Linne!" she called out then. "Linne. No!"

As he watched in silence, she held out her hands as though touching the young woman who'd just given birth a sennight ago. Tolan knew that Linne had also nearly died when she began bleeding again a few days ago. Whatever treatment Thea had rendered had saved the new mother.

How she'd saved her became clear to him in the next moments as the hands she held out began to glow, giving off both light and heat. Tolan staggered back as it surrounded her completely. She sat in the center of an aura of gold, unaffected by the power that she exuded. Though hot, this power did not burn. Enthralled by this, he watched and waited for her to wake.

A few moments later, her eyes fluttered and opened slowly, the glowing still strong and bright around her.

She met his gaze, and that frown formed on her brow once again.

"Tolan? What . . ." She looked at her outstretched hands and then back at him. "I . . ."

"How does it feel, Thea?" he asked, nodding at her hands. She stared at them, her eyes wide and her gaze confused.

"They are warm," she answered as she let them fall onto her lap.

"Is that how you heal people?" he asked.

Certain that his question would stir up many, many more between them, he asked anyway. Tolan understood how their common purpose could run much deeper than either of them had ever imagined. He had kept his secret for his whole life, even through his marriage to Corliss. To speak of it to someone else who might be the same as he was extraordinary and unexpected.

Watching her filled with this unexplained power made him also realize that he trusted her in a way he did not trust others. Another word pushed into his thoughts and his heart, but it was too soon and too uncertain to name it such.

"I know not, Tolan," she said, sitting up straight and watching as the brightness in her hands faded. "I was dreaming."

"About Linne."

"Aye. About Linne. How did you know?" she asked, standing now to face him.

"You called out her name. Several times. And you reached out as though you were touching her."

Though her hands had changed, the golden color yet outlined her. Tolan reached out to touch her cheek. The aura shimmered and did not change. She shone like the midday sun before him while everything else faded into colors and shades of shadows.

"Did you lay your hands on her, Thea? When she was bleeding?"

She nodded as though afraid to utter the words.

"And you have done this with others?" Another nod. "For how long?"

She let out a breath, unsure of how to answer him. Though fearful of exposing this to others, for she could be labeled a witch or devil worshipper, Thea did not fear Tolan knowing it. He was a fair man and mayhap he could help her find some explanation for the ability she could not define.

"I have always been a healer, from the first days my ma showed me the way of herbs and medicaments. But this"—she held up her hands between them—"this is new."

The heat seeped away, but her skin shimmered brightly enough to cast a light across the chamber. Thea waited to see his reaction, to this ability that she could not explain. Instead, she realized that Tolan was different. Or was it her own vision now that this power inhabited her? She looked away from him and noticed that the rest of the room seemed pale when compared to him.

Was it the glow of her skin that made it seem that way? She thought about the feeling leaving her hands and it dimmed slowly until it was gone. But it was replaced by something completely different . . . and not from her.

She could not breathe in that moment as she stared at him standing a few paces away from her. His physical appearance was no different; his shape was as tall and muscular as always. No, the thing that had changed was that he now stood outlined surrounded by a green light.

No, that wasn't it. His body gleamed as though encased in green. Green like the grass that covered the lands. Green like the plants that would begin to shoot from the soil. Green like the color of the leaves on the mighty oak trees that grew all over the area.

He must have noticed her surprise, for he stepped closer and reached out to touch her. The hand and arm shimmered, casting off flashes of green as he moved. As her skin had given off the golden light like the sun.

"Tolan." She touched his hand, not knowing what to expect. "You are . . . shining."

Now he was the one looking surprised. He shrugged and shook his head. "I do not see it." Holding out his hand, he shook his head again. "Nay."

His expression changed then, and she had the feeling that he knew her next words and would not like them.

"So, is yours related to your abilities with growing things?"

Although he paled, the green shimmer remained around him. "Aye."

One word, but it explained so much about his continued success in times when famine or drought or pestilence struck other lands or farms or fields. Had he inherited this power from his father? There were stories about how many generations of his family had served Lord Geoffrey and his ancestors, so there must be a connection there.

For that moment, she no longer felt alone and frightened. She let out the breath she did not realize she'd been holding inside her and asked the first question that came to her mind. "How long have you known?"

The crackling sound of brush underfoot pierced the silence before he could answer and he raised a finger to his mouth.

"Put out the fire, Thea. 'Tis time to sleep," he said in a loud voice. He nodded at her and she did just that. "I will return anon," he then whispered. "I will see if I can chase him off."

Tolan walked over and opened the door quickly, peering into the darkness outside. Then he strode over to the side of her cottage and relieved himself. 'Twas then that she heard the scurrying footsteps down the path away from her home, using the sounds of Tolan's actions to cover the noise of his retreat.

Tolan had known someone was there. She banked the fire for night and when she turned, she found him in the doorway staring at her.

"Who was it?" she whispered once he'd closed the door.

"A guard from the castle. My steps have been shadowed since I spoke to Lord Geoffrey days ago."

"Why? What does he suspect? This?" she asked,

motioning to the aura she could still see outlining his shape.

"Come with me," he said softly, holding out his hand to her.

She took it without hesitation and followed him out. Slowing only to grab the small lantern by the door, they walked quickly around her cottage. He did not stop until they stood beside the low wall that surrounded her garden.

"This is when I first suspected you were more than you seemed, Thea." He pointed to the only part of the small plot that she'd been able to work so far.

She'd spent hours here today, thinking and turning the soil, and thinking and then just drifting off lost in her thoughts. Now, looking into that corner, she noticed how the soil glimmered the same way her hands had. Opening the gate and walking over there, she stared at it.

"I think that you have been putting whatever power you have within you into the herbs you grow and the medicaments you make and use. You left your mark there on the soil."

"What?" she asked, shaking her head. "Do you not hear how ludicrous that sounds? Power? Are you saying I have some kind of magic within me and use it? That is against God's laws and the Church, Tolan." Thinking it was one thing, but hearing it said aloud brought the possible danger much closer.

"Do you pray while you work? Do you offer thanks when something works to cure or aid someone who seeks your help?"

"Certainly," she said. "Do you not pray during your work? While you till the soil and prepare the fields?"

"Aye."

A strange expression crossed his face then, one of surprise mixed with guilt and satisfaction. From that look in his eyes, she wanted nothing more in that moment than to watch him as he tended to his fields.

"I think it is those prayers that are imbuing your herbs and your other concoctions with healing power." He paused and then met her gaze, his now serious. "And that is why my fields are fertile and my lands and the ones I care for do not suffer as others do."

"Show me."

She had not planned on calling his abilities into action, but he nodded and came to the corner where she yet knelt. He tugged up his sleeves and would have thrust his hands into the soil when she stopped. There was a bandage on his forearm.

"Your arm." He stopped and looked at her. Sliding her sleeve up, she revealed a matching bandage, one she still wore to cover the mark there. "I have one as well." They peeled them off at the same time, unwinding the linen to reveal the skin underneath it.

Where hers was shaped like the sun, his had the appearance of a tree. And like hers, his moved as though alive, its branches waving as though blown by a gentle breeze.

"Does it hurt?" he asked, sliding his thumb across the skin marked by it.

"At times, but not now. Yours?"

"The same. It appeared a few weeks ago and grew to this size. It seems to react to you, though. Look."

Both of the marks grew brighter as they held their arms closer. As did the green color surrounding him.

"You are brighter now, too," he said. "Can you see it?"

"I feel something, aye, but do not see it."

"But you could when you healed Linne?" he asked.

"Aye. And when I healed old Rigby."

"He has suffered so much, Thea. Does he know?" He sat back on his heels, and the look of admiration in his eyes nearly made her cry.

"Nay, not yet." Shaking her head, she rubbed her eyes. "I only knew when it happened. He felt the warmth of it when I laid my hands on his leg. Tolan, he has been in such pain, it will take some days for him to realize it is gone." The feelings threatened to overwhelm her then, so she nodded at the ground. "Show me what you do."

There were so many more questions, but they would hold for now. This was what she wanted most to see.

He nodded and then leaned over, plunging his hands deep into the soil. The green glow spread into the ground, and the earth began to churn under his touch. Soundlessly, it moved as though someone stirred it. Tolan's eyes were closed and his lips moved in silence. This went on for several minutes until he opened his eyes and gazed down at the place where his hands connected to the earth.

"I see it now, Thea," he whispered, staring at the same thing she saw. "I did not know."

His eyes closed then and he finished this ritual of his, sliding his hands free and rubbing the loosened soil from them. Reaching across the small gap between them, he entwined their fingers and just stared at her.

"I cannot wrap my thoughts around such an idea or such a thing," she finally said, nodding at the corner of the garden that was perfectly prepared for the seeds she would plant and nurture.

"I have known about this since reaching manhood, but never dreamed there would be another. Not here. Not now," he admitted.

"There is so much I need to know," Thea said, releasing his hand and standing. "Will you tell me what you have learned?"

She watched as Tolan stood, still vibrating with the power of the earth and shining with its color. He grew serious now.

"I do not think 'tis safe to discuss these things here. Not with a guard shadowing me." He closed his eyes and let out a breath before speaking again. "But he is gone for now."

"How do you know that he has not returned?" Thea glanced toward the front of her cottage and could hear and see nothing.

"I have only just discovered that I can feel the footsteps of others who approach. I can feel their weight on the soil as they move."

Stunned by such a thing, she waited on him.

"I planned to go back to my farm in a few days. To sort things out there. Come with me, Thea. We will have privacy there to discuss these matters and others."

"Durrington, Tolan? You return to Durrington?" His farm was several miles away and was rumored to be large and prosperous, though she'd never seen it and he spoke of it only in passing during their times together.

"Aye." He nodded. "I passed it while on that journey with Lord Geoffrey and wish to go back."

"I will go with you."

"Until we go, speak not of this to anyone else and use your gift only if necessary. We must gain a better understanding of why the lord has sent a guard to watch me."

"Do you think there are others, Tolan? Others like us?" she asked. If there were two, mayhap there were others?

His only reply was to nod, grimly and once. She accepted his hand and they walked back to the door of her cottage. He bade her farewell and promised to speak to her about the arrangements in a few days, but he did not follow her in or stay the night. 'Twas clear to her that he was concerned about the lord's reasons for following him, and rightly so.

When she finally sought her bed, sleep did not come for several hours. The excitement of discovering the truth about him, about them, and witnessing his use of his gift as he called it, kept her awake. As she tossed and turned, the one question that plagued her relentlessly through the dark of the night was the same one she'd asked Tolan.

Were there others like them?

But the question she had not had the opportunity

to ask him was mayhap the more disturbing one to her—if she had the power of the healing sun within her and he had the power of the earth within him, what powers did others have and to what purpose did they use them?

CHAPTER 9

His plans to visit Durrington did not happen as he'd hoped when he invited Thea along with him. Since Tolan also intended to speak on more personal matters, the delays and changes in his plan frustrated him even more. And the guard's continuing presence, though now more discreet, angered him.

Two days after the revelations in Thea's cottage, Tolan tried to speak to Lord Geoffrey about it but was sent away without seeing the nobleman. Tolan did not, however, miss the strange stare from the man he served as Tolan walked out of the keep and toward the gates.

Lord Geoffrey, with that strange, rambling journey, his eerie questions, and his piercing stare, knew more than Tolan hoped any man ever would. For now, he must have a care not to be seen doing anything that seemed to be more than any other experienced farmer would do.

An experienced farmer whose tasks seem to grow more numerous with each passing day as the growing season approached. This year, it seemed that Bordan and the lord assigned more and more things to his list of responsibilities. In a way, it felt as though it was an attempt, like Thea's marriage to Jasper, to keep him near and busy.

The one thing Tolan did not wish to do was to ignore Thea. So when he saw her going about her visits, he followed her until he could pull her unseen into the shadows behind the miller's house. They'd not spoken since the revelations two nights ago. Worried over what her reaction would be, he was reassured by the laugh she uttered.

He would hate to lose the closeness they had. He would hate to lose the ease between them. He would hate to lose her. And they'd still not spoken of many things that would not wait for their journey to Durrington.

"How do you fare, Thea?" he asked as he pulled her to him and wrapped his arms around her. The glow surrounded her, and heat filled her. "Are you well?"

"I am, Tolan," she said, just before he claimed her mouth with his and made speaking impossible.

How had he never noticed the way she carried the health and the heat of the sun within her? Never had his father spoken of any others like themselves, so Tolan had never been looking for others. He thought his duty was simply to tend the lands and keep the circle safe.

"Can you walk with me now?" he asked, holding out his hand to her. "I would speak to you."

"Tolan—"

"Thea," he answered back. "A simple walk and I promise not to ravish you before the others." He shook his hand and waited for her to accept. "Tell me where you must go and I will walk with you there."

Finally, she grasped his hand.

"To the last croft before the west field. Bringing some ointment for Riletta's joints," she said. He walked in that direction, entwining his fingers with hers as they did.

"I am headed in that direction as well. Come."

And he made certain to walk right down the main path of the village. She tugged her hand from his and stopped at the last moment before they stepped from the shadows that hid them from the view of others.

"I am not ashamed, Thea. Not ashamed to be seen with you, or visit you night or day. We are not a secret. Not to them," he said, nodding to the villagers in sight. As he watched, she glanced at him and then to their neighbors and friends. She looked back at his out-stretched hand.

Tolan tried not to laugh aloud when she accepted it. Some barrier had been crossed then, but he did not press her for more now. They walked several paces out of the shadows and onto the path. Granted, the first few people to see them did stop and gape a bit. Then smiles and winks greeted them, warming his heart and relieving a great deal of concern.

"I am not ashamed of being with you, Tolan," she said softly as they walked along. "I just did not wish to the center of gossip and whispering."

Again.

She did not have to say that final word for him to hear it, for he understood her meaning quite well.

"I know why you do not wish to discuss marriage between us." He kept his voice soft and held her hand as he spoke words he knew would be disturbing to her. "And I will respect your wishes on that." *For now.* "But there is too much that is good between us to allow you to walk away or to step aside, Thea."

He was pleased when she did not pull them to a stop or resist his words. His blood began to race when she squeezed his hand. From where he walked, he could see the tears in her eyes and the way she swallowed several times against them. Tolan gave her time to gain control. Once again, she surprised him.

"There is much good between us, Tolan. And I do not wish to walk away from it. From you."

They walked in now-companionable silence toward Riletta's cottage and Tolan tried not to smile. So, no matter what she would do or say from this moment on, he would hold that declaration in his heart. When they reached the edge of the village, where the cottages ended and the large furrowed fields began, he stopped once more.

"Come and eat with us this night."

"But Kirwyn—"

"Kirwyn is old enough and he knows how it stands

between us. Blythe will be there as well." At her up-raised brow, he nodded. "My son tells me his heart is set on her."

"Truly? Now?" she asked.

"Aye. Against my counsel and my wishes," he said, crossing his arms over his chest. "The only thing I can do is to keep a watch on them and make certain things proceed as they should."

"As though you could stop them?" she asked. She gave a laugh then and the sound of it echoed around them. "I will come this night, even if only to watch you try to hold back the rain."

He wanted to be angry, but seeing her laugh forced him to shake his head. "I just want the best for him. I want him not to make the mistakes of youth. I want . . ." He shrugged. "I want what any father wants for his son."

Pain flashed in her eyes then and was gone an instant later. Though it was fleeting, the depth of it filled him with a sense of loss.

"I must see to Riletta now, Tolan," she said. "I will see you at supper, then?"

He did not give her time to object then. Tolan reached out and drew her to him, kissing her gently on her mouth. Nothing that others should not see. Nothing that a couple in love would not do. Just a kiss.

Watching her walk away then, Tolan knew some-thing had changed between them. Something was there, something was different . . . and somehow bet-ter. Now, as he strode out to the fields there, the sense of anticipation grew within him.

And not even the knowledge given him by the surrounding earth that two large groups of travelers were nearing Amesbury lessened it.

As Thea watched Tolan speak to his son through their meal, she realized that just about nothing was the same in her life as it had been just days before.

She carried some power within her—that knowledge helped her accept that there was more to her healing than simple skills passed from mother to daughter.

She was not alone—at least one other existed who carried some unexplained power within himself.

She was in love with this man.

Though the first two realizations were so extraordinary that they challenged even her ability to accept it, it was that last one that made her the most gladdened. Even understanding that she could not be his wife did not diminish her joy just then.

He loved his son, that much was clear to her as she watched them during their meal. And he was trying to raise him well, especially without the guiding hand of a mother for the boy. Though Kirwyn was as any young man his age was—rebellious and opinionated— he loved and respected his father. Her heart hurt in her knowing that she could never give Tolan a child like this one.

It was not just her fear of putting herself under the personal control of a man that kept her from even considering marriage again. Nay, that darker secret she carried—kept her from marrying this man. Tolan needed more children, especially sons, to carry on his family's legacy of tending the lands. Between duties here to Lord Geoffrey and Tolan's own farm in Durrington, he could not do it alone.

Worse for her, now knowing that the power he had was passed down in his blood, he needed a son of his own flesh and blood to continue the power that kept these lands fertile. Then the truth struck her, for if he needed to pass his power down through his sons, so she needed to pass it on to her own children.

Children who would never be.

"Thea? Are you well?" Tolan asked, drawing her from her thoughts.

"I am," she said, nodding. "Just tired."

"Kirwyn, see Blythe home," Tolan said, standing. "Come, I will take you to your cottage."

Thea gathered the bowls and spoons and began carrying them to the bucket to wash them. Kirwyn and Tolan were used to being on their own, with few seeing to their care, but at least she could see to this, since Blythe had prepared the satisfying stew, vegetables, and bread for the meal. After but a few minutes, she took her leave of the young man and woman, with thanks for the hospitality offered and shared.

Soon, it was only Thea and Tolan walking through the shadows of night back to her cottage. After his words earlier and his presence now, she felt at ease. He said he understood why she would not consider marriage . . . she hoped he did. But knowing that he had witnessed her humiliation at Jasper's hands horrified her. They reached her cottage and he followed her to the door, his intention clear.

However, now there was one thing she wanted from him. After all the changes in her life and the challenges she feared they would face, she wanted to feel his strength around her. Thea wanted to hold the rest of the world away for a few hours and reclaim her equilibrium for at least that time.

Before he could speak, she turned to face him and slid into his embrace. He'd exposed part of what she feared most, but now she must tell him the rest.

Tolan leaned down and opened his mouth to her, accepting her kiss and returning it. 'Twas her turn to lead in their passion, and her desire for him grew with each kiss, each caress.

Thea stepped back and undressed him. He neither resisted her efforts nor helped her, but he never took his gaze from hers. He'd also never questioned or limited her in her demands or requests. He seemed to accept that, at times, she needed to control the ebb and flow of their passion.

Now was one of those times. This night was one of those nights. The feeling that control of her life, of their lives, was slipping away intensified what she wanted from him.

She tugged his belt loose and dropped it to the floor and then pulled his shirt up and over his head. His chest was massive and smooth, the muscles well defined because of his work. She traced the lines between them and leaned in to kiss each of the brown nipples. She swirled her tongue around each one, leaving the tiny curls of hair damp. The sounds of his indrawn breath spurred her on, so she kissed and licked her way down his stomach, loving the way his muscles tightened beneath her mouth along the path.

Pausing to untie the laces at his waist, Thea eased his trews down to his hips. Once more she kissed the exposed flesh there, enjoying each time he hissed or he canted his hips. She could feel the ridge of hard flesh next to her cheek, so she rubbed against it, as a cat would against his leg. Her reward was a groan.

She knelt before him and opened his trews now, pushing them down over his hips and sliding her hands around to feel the power in his buttocks. He would thrust into her soon with these and she could almost feel the strength he would use. But they were not her target. Nay, she wanted to taste his cock. One glance at him told her he was waiting for exactly that—his openmouthed breathing was shallow and uneven.

Thea cupped his bollocks and then licked the length of his male flesh. Along its length and then around the thick head, she tasted and teased with her tongue and teeth, listening to his gasps. Her own flesh grew damp between her thighs as she took his manhood in her mouth and suckled on it.

Tolan slid his hands into her hair then, pulling it loose from its bonds and sending it floating around her. She grasped his flesh in her hands and held it tightly as she sucked harder and harder. His hands held her there, guiding her head as she pleasured him. Then, suddenly, he grabbed her by the arms and dragged her up his body until their faces were even and she could see the desire in his gaze.

"Fair is fair, Elethea," he said in a voice hoarse from passion.

Her body trembled then in excitement and anticipation. He gave as good as he got and her body understood the promise and the threat in his words and tone. He carried her over to the pallet, stripped off her garments and then lay down and waited for her to decide the next part.

The core of her flesh wanted him there. Her breasts ached for his touch and his bite. Her mouth, though, her mouth hungered for more of him, so she crawled over to his side and took his erect cock deep into her mouth. But Tolan was not a man to lie back quietly during bed play, and when he took her legs and lifted her body to straddle his, she laughed against the heated flesh in her mouth.

"Now—"

That was the only warning she got before feeling his mouth on her heated flesh. Torn between sucking on him and the incredible pleasure he was giving her with his tongue and teeth, she let go of any control and met him measure for measure. Until he spread her open and thrust his tongue deep into her channel. In this position, the growth on his unshaved chin provided a wonderful friction as he plumbed her depths, and she could not stop from thrusting against him.

And when everything within her coiled tightly, she stopped trying to think and just felt it . . . felt him. Heat spread through her and she felt the first tremors of her release. Tolan did not stop his attentions. Instead, he moved against her sensitive folds harder and faster until she found that moment when everything simply paused and then she fell over it.

On her hands and knees, crouched over him, she moaned out her satisfaction. But he did not wait, turning her to face him and guiding her swollen folds down the length of his still-rigid cock. It was delicious, stretching her and making her gasp as she took every inch of him into her body.

"Ride me, Elethea," he urged, his hands on her hips as he thrust impossibly deeper inside her. "Ride me, I beg you."

And she did. Lifting herself up, she leaned over closer to him, skimming her breasts on his chest. Her nipples grew taut points and she watched as he took one and then the other in his mouth. She arched now against his mouth, urging him on.

Her body grew hotter and hotter and she saw the golden glow of her skin brighten with each moment. Tolan noticed it, too, and smiled, never letting go or slowing. He pushed himself up to sit and slid his arms around her then, their thrusts growing deeper and slower because of the position now. She wrapped her legs around his waist and kissed him, sharing the heat with him.

Thea could look into his eyes now and she held his gaze as they remained joined as one flesh. The color that now surrounded him shimmered in his skin, and his eyes began to shine with it.

Green.

Like the color of the earth at the height of its power.

Life-giving. Fertile.

A momentary regret that it could not help her flashed in her thoughts and was gone in the onslaught of pleasure. His eyes grew brighter and brighter until she could see nothing else. Tolan rolled them and brought her beneath his body, covering her. Filling her. Completing her.

His body thrust into hers, and she felt his flesh grow harder then. He called out her name and released his seed within her. Her body answered, shuddering and trembling and once more reaching its own release.

It took some time for their racing hearts to calm. They lay entwined, his face tucked into the curve of her neck and his breath against her skin. And then the words that had threatened for some time escaped and could never be called back.

"I love you, Tolan."

As though the world paused then, the silence surrounded them so completely that she could hear nothing. He lifted his head and gazed into her eyes.

"And I—" He began to say the words, but she pressed her hand over his lips.

"Say it not," she whispered. "I have never loved a man before, Tolan. I wanted the chance to say the words even knowing there can be nothing more between us than . . . this." He rolled off to her side and she hated the distance, even while knowing it must happen.

"All you have to do is say aye."

The words that would have been uttered to lure Eve into sin could not have sounded more tempting than his did to her. But Thea knew all her truths and just could not find the strength to expose herself to Tolan, no matter what they seemed to share. She shook her head and smiled sadly.

"I will not marry again, Tolan. Not now. Not you. Not ever."

The declaration hung out in the space between them and she watched for his reaction. Men did not like to be naysaid. Men who controlled others did not react well to being told that their will would not be done. But one of the things she loved about him was his ability to be slow to anger. He reached over to her and she controlled the urge to flinch that yet lived within her.

"Marry or not, Thea," he whispered, rolling closer and bringing their bodies skin to skin. "'Tis your decision. But it matters not to me what we call . . . what is between us." He kissed her gently on her mouth and then smiled back at her. The green glow around him seemed to simmer, gently rolling shimmers moving, outlining his body. "I will not forsake you."

"You do not understand, Tolan," she began, before he silenced her with another kiss, this one more possessive than his last one.

"Nay, I do not understand, what with so many changes in our lives. And with so many portents that are rising. And so many concerns that must be seen to."

He gathered her close, laying his leg over hers and sliding his hand behind her head to hold her near him. It would have been an uncomfortably close embrace with any other man, but not with him. With Tolan, it felt safe and reassuring. It felt like . . .

"The only thing I know," he said, meeting her gaze, "is that I love you as well, Thea, and I will not let you go."

She could not stop the tears then. His words were a soothing balm on her long-abused heart and soul, much as his kisses and caresses appeased her body. All the dreams of her girlhood had been torn asunder during her marriage and she'd not dared to hope that there could be a man like this for her.

"Hush now," he whispered as he reached up to wipe away her tears. "I would hope you are gladdened by such words."

"I am, Tolan, but—"

He kissed her into silence then. He kissed her breathless. And then he kissed her in love.

It was a long time before either of them could speak again.

"You are glowing," she said, realizing that his body gave off the color all the time now.

"And you are shining like the sun," he replied, tracing one finger down her spine.

"Are we alone in seeing this, Tolan? Do the others not see these changes?"

"I think there are others who can, but not many," he said. From his tone, he'd revealed something just now to her that he would not freely admit to many, if any, others.

She lifted her head and looked at him. "Here? In Amesbury?"

"Nay, I think not in Amesbury." He closed his eyes

then and she could see them moving behind his eyelids as though watching or searching for something. "But those who can are close. Very close."

"Who are they?" she asked, sitting at his side.

"Some are for good and others are for evil. Our task will be harder now." His eyes yet glowed when he opened them and his voice sounded very strange to her ears when he spoke them—almost as though it was no longer him. "We must get to Durrington soon."

Then it was just him—his eyes and voice returned to what she was used to—and he took her in his arms and held her there for the rest of the night.

When he slipped out, she knew not, but she woke to an empty pallet. Touching the place where he'd been, she found it still warm and knew he'd left not long ago.

It mattered not this morn, for he had spoken the words she'd never thought to hear and had spoken her own to him. No matter what came next, she would hold that in her heart.

No matter what.

Tolan made his way around her cottage before walking back to his own. Something had changed within him this night. Oh, not just that he'd declared his heart to her, but also something in this new power shifted and released.

He could feel the weight of two approaching groups on the earth around him. One, or two, came from the south, from Christchurch, and would arrive within a day. The other came from the southeast, from the coastal city of Southampton.

And power exuded from both groups. One being of great power from the southeast traveling at a brutal pace. A number of them coming from the south but separated by distance and time.

Time had run out for him. For them. They must learn as much as they could about their newly risen powers, and the one place he knew he must search was the hidden place on his land. With Thea at his side, they would uncover it and seek out the truth.

A crackle of brush behind him reminded Tolan of his follower. He walked to the enclosed garden and stood in the silent darkness. His presence here was no surprise to anyone now. The few people in the village who might not have known about him and Thea did now after his public display and after he'd welcomed her to his home with Kirwyn present. It had claimed her more effectively than even the words he'd spoken to her a few hours ago had.

He stared at the ground, and his blood began to heat and his hands itched. The soil needed to be turned and readied. It called to whatever lived within him now. Usually, to use the ritual, he needed to thrust his hands into the ground, but something told him that was not necessary.

Tolan focused his thoughts on the cold, hard earth and urged it to move. Urged it to turn. Urged it to accept the seed and the water and the sunlight that was coming to it soon.

As he watched, the soil began to churn by itself, each section of her garden readied itself. But no hoe or plow or other tool was used this time. Tolan only had to think of it and the earth there did his bidding. In a short time, the smell of freshly tilled soil filled the air around him.

He wanted to laugh aloud, but it would draw the close attention of his watcher to this patch of land. And it would raise questions in that man's mind and he would take them back to his lord. Tolan could not risk such attention, so he offered up thanks silently before walking off to his own cottage. And wondering with each stride what other abilities lay within him since this gift awakened.

If he could move the earth with his thoughts, what could Thea do if the power of the sun's healing light dwelled within her? Could she heal the most grievous of injuries or illnesses? That kind of thing would be dangerous if witnessed. Cries of witchery would be made and every sort of authority would be called in to investigate.

Tolan stopped and stood still for a moment. As though the very earth beneath his feet shifted, he understood that nothing in his life or in the lives of those around him would ever be the same again. Those who traveled here brought with them some kind of reckoning that the whole of mankind would face. Good and evil would stand at odds unlike any other time in memory, and whatever fueled his power would be called to choose.

He smiled grimly then. That was an easy choice. For never would he stand on evil's side against good.

A chill wind cut through the trees and sliced into him. He shivered against its touch and wondered if he would come to regret his words . . . or his choice when it was all over.

In this moment, the only thing he knew was that they would leave at night. This night. He would leave horses saddled and ready over on the other road and leave from Thea's cottage. They could be on his lands by dawn on the morrow.

They would need all the time they could find to prepare themselves and their loved ones for the coming darkness.

CHAPTER 10

Amesbury Abbey

Corann stood at the back of the church and stared in wonderment at the accomplishments of those who designed and built it. Decades of living on their remote isle had not prepared him for places such as this. The ones worshipped here were much newer and younger than the gods he and his followers worshipped. And clearly they demanded much gold from those who served them. Or him? Corann shook his head at the idea of saying there was only one God, though he knew Father Ander believed it true.

Nay, Corann's gods and goddesses needed no resplendent churches or costly vestments. His needed only the awesome places in nature—the water, the sky, the earth, the plants and trees—to find them. They inhabited all of nature and could be found there with no more than a thought or prayer.

The Catholic priest noticed him and walked quickly

to his side. His friend still wore the robes of his calling and carried out his own rituals even while being content at learning his place in Corann's faith. A priest of one or many seemed to matter not to Ander.

"The prior said we could set up our camp in the fields across the river," Ander said. "The abbey owns many manor houses and acres of land around here."

"Did you tell him how many were here?" Corann asked, walking at Ander's side out of the darkened church. He shivered at the cool dampness that seemed to inhabit this God's dwellings. He would always prefer the gatherings in the woods under the warmth of the sun.

"I may have underestimated our numbers a bit, friend," Ander whispered as he nodded at several of his Christian brethren as they passed. "With the recent largesse of the king on behalf of his daughter's presence here, the prior is quite elated at the attention being brought to their abbey and church. Our gift was cheerfully accepted on behalf of our patrons."

Although the consequences of the evil goddess's escape would be felt by all of mankind, the Warriors had decided to keep their intentions out of the view of the authorities. At least as much as they could.

Certainly there would be stories told in Scotland and Orkney about the strange bands of fighting men traveling there. Especially when the unexplainable sights and sounds at those stone circles were reported by witnesses. Father Ander had tried to forestall some of it by sending a letter to his bishop in Kirkwall, but no plausible explanation existed for standing stones that grew and sang . . . or for the otherworldly powers that some people manifested.

"Has Aislinn revealed anything of import?" Ander asked as they hurried back to where the others had gathered.

"She has dreamt . . ." Corann could say no more, for there were too many near enough to hear his words. And no one was more suspicious than those who served this one God. "We will speak anon."

Aislinn had been trained by the best and most experienced amongst their community and was the strongest seer in generations. Some whispered in all time. Her scrying skills were superb and her dreams foretold the future more accurately than anyone in their community. This power took its toll on one so young. The recent death, the murder of her teacher and foster father, had almost destroyed her. Only the support of the others gathered more lately to their cause and her faith in their gods and goddesses kept her strong.

As they made their way through the thriving religious community, Corann thought about his own dreams and prayed they were nothing but his fears put into the imagery of sleep. He saw the small group who'd accompanied them here ahead and waved.

"Well," Ander began, "we are the first pilgrims of the season now that the weather has broken. The prior was quite impressed with your background, Sir William, and your gift."

"As I said, it would come in handily," their leader said gruffly. Though he wore a hood pulled low over his brow, it was unnerving when their gazes met. The red eyes of Sucellus, the god of war, stared back. "Any word of the others?"

"No others from Normandy or Brittany have arrived here since the autumn," Ander reported. "I expect that is how they will be recognized, so I asked about them."

"I do not think they will seek out these sacred places," Corann added. "Smaller ones mayhap," he explained, "like that round kirk in Orphir." Ander shuddered at the mention. "But not like this." He motioned at the huge church behind them. "Filled with godly people who might recognize the great evil who lives within him. Nay, he may be arrogant, but he is not stupid."

"Nay, not stupid," Ander repeated with another shudder. His friend had spent days being tortured and broken at the hands of their enemy, Hugh de Gifford. Ander knew the man's mind better than anyone amongst their group.

"Corann."

He turned at the call of his name. Aislinn approached from the group of wagons and horses with her shadow at her back. Now it was Corann's turn to shudder.

Though he had pledged his loyalty to his own niece, de Gifford's natural daughter, Brienne, Brisbois—the torturer—had spent most of his life in his brother's service. Doing just that—breaking bones and anything else that his brother told him to do. Corann had been the target of his techniques and nearly died. Any and every encounter with the huge brute of a man left

Corann trembling from the painful reminders of his attentions that yet troubled his limbs.

"Aislinn. How do you fare?" he asked as the girl walked to his side. He turned his back on the other, unable to look upon him without revulsion.

"The dreams are clearer now, my friend. And they are closer, much closer now."

She glanced at William, who nodded. Those descended from the gods could sense each other in some way. Aislinn could as well. They thought it because of her priestly skills, but Corann knew better. Marcus had told him much before he'd left to face death on their behalf.

"What do they tell you, Aislinn?" William asked. "Can you tell which of the bloodlines are here? Did the drawings tell us rightly?"

"The prophecy spoke of the caretaker and the bringer of life. The drawings showed the symbols of the earthblood and sunblood opposite of each other in the circle. It seems to confirm who we are searching for here." Corann nodded. "Ander, we will need you to ask about in Amesbury about someone skilled in the healing arts. Especially a woman who aids in childbirth, a midwife." Ander nodded.

"Have Ran and Soren arrived yet?" Corann asked of William. "They may be able to seek out the place more easily."

"An outrider said they will join us in about five hours," William said. "Come. Let us return to our camp and see to our task."

Corann both anticipated and dreaded the coming night. Once the others arrived, they must form a new bond so that they would be connected during their coming battle against the evil one and her followers. The priests who had come from the isle to the west had always been in communion with each other, but that bond had been severed when de Gifford began kidnapping priests to torture information from them. As had been done to Corann.

In his wisdom, Marcus had formed a link only with Aislinn, William the Warblood, Brienne the Fireblood, and William's man, Roger. When he made the decision to sacrifice himself to save Ander, Marcus had been able to close himself off from that link. Now, in his absence, the others must reconnect and bring in the newest warriors—Ran and Soren.

As they made their way to the outskirts of Amesbury, William stopped and nodded for Corann to come away from the others. When they were several paces behind, William spoke.

"I know that it is still so soon, but will you be able to work with him?" the warrior asked him.

Corann let out a breath and watched as Brisbois dogged the footsteps of the seer. "I am trying. Truly I am," he said. "But every time I see him there, I can feel the blows," Corann admitted, rubbing his hands up and down on his arms.

He had not just been beaten by the man; he had been exquisitely tortured by him. Whipped, sliced, and pummeled for days to get information about the other priests. Killed step by step and kept alive by only the demented skill of his attacker. And saved only when rescued by William.

"Brienne swears he is true to her and her alone. She gives her word as his bond, Corann."

When one of the gods' descendants gave her word to a mere human priest, it should be enough. Corann struggled with this hesitation as a test of his own faith. If he was worthy to lead them in this quest, he should be able to accept the fireblood's word and move past his own limitations. "I pray daily for the strength to accept his presence with us."

"In the end, I think it will be our faith, that good should triumph, that will get us through, Corann," William said.

Faith. It would be their success or failure. And after the terrible dreams and seeing his failure in them, Corann knew he must pray and seek guidance.

"I see the pain in your face, Corann. Forgive me for not thinking. Let me call for one of the wagons to wait for you."

He had seen the pain, but misread its cause. Corann decided to use it.

"I am well enough, William," he said, waving off the younger man. "I saw a grove of trees just back there. I wish to sit and pray there."

"And rest your legs?" William asked. Corann nodded. "Should I send someone back for you when the others arrive? I know how Marcus always got lost in his prayers and forgot that others existed."

"I will make my way back."

"You are certain?" William's red gaze narrowed and Corann could swear the man was sniffing the air for some scent.

Without breaking away, Corann nodded and the warrior left him there. He let out a breath and turned back toward the abbey.

The thought had struck him as they spoke about his injuries. Bringer of life. A healer for certain. And one man would be much less obvious than their troop making its way across these lands. And he had hours before the others would arrive. For the first time, Corann felt hope and as though he had something specific he could do.

All it took was a story about needing a midwife for his dear sister to find help and a ride from a local man going north to the village of Lord Geoffrey of Amesbury. A short while later and sooner than he'd thought possible, Corann found himself facing a woman who carried the healing power of the sun in her blood.

Thea had faced the day in a much lighter mood than she'd had in days. It could be the emotions swirling in her heart or the passion they'd shared—she knew and cared not. All she knew was that everything seemed brighter to her.

The sight of her garden, completely prepared and tilled, made her laugh aloud. Tolan must have done it after he left. A way to try out his new abilities mayhap. All she knew was that what would have taken her days to do was done.

She gazed down at her hands, the only part of her

body not covered, and saw the golden haze of her skin. It did not ebb and flow, something different from before, though so far none of the villagers she'd encountered mentioned it.

The other thing that had somehow changed overnight was the way she saw others. At first glance, they appeared the same as they had always been, but she could now see deeper into them. Her gaze could peer through their garments and even through their skin and see the body there.

And the injuries or illnesses. She struggled not to stare as she spoke to her neighbors that morning, the damage and deterioration so very clear to her.

Her visit to old Rigby revealed the results of her previous treatment—the man stood before her without the support of his stick or his wife and took his first unaided steps since his accident. Now, when she looked at his legs, the breaks were healed and the bones strong. Then she sent a burst of heat into his muscles, long atrophied from disuse, to help them grow stronger. His wide smile was all the thanks she needed, but he and Eldreda offered her words and gifts.

As she passed through the village, the cooper told her a man sought help for his sister's lying-in and pointed her toward the southern end of the road to Amesbury where he'd left him to wait. With no one else needing her attentions now, she walked to find the man. She came upon him standing on the edge of the path, in the shadow of the trees. The mark on her arm surged then and she clamped her hand over it as she approached him.

He was neither young nor old and looked like any other man she might meet on the road, but there was something more about him she could not explain. He met her gaze for a moment and then, squinting tightly, he looked away. It took no more than a moment to see the damage in his body. Not a part of him was unscathed, for he was a mess of scratches, tears, bruises, barely healed fractures, and some deeper injuries to his organs. How he stood without assistance, she knew not.

She did know he needed her more than any sister of his did.

"Good morrow," she said, walking closer. "My name is Elethea and I serve as healer to the good people here on Lord Geoffrey's estate. Osbert the cooper said you were asking for me? For your sister's lying-in?"

He nodded without meeting her eyes. He was clearly avoiding looking at her directly for some reason. Though it usually meant fear or even deception, Thea felt neither from him.

"How can I help you?" She waited for him to give her his name.

"Corann, my . . ." He shook his head and stammered, "Corann." His nervousness increased. "I have no sister. I only wanted to speak to you."

"Can you walk to my cottage? It is just down this path, Corann," she said, holding out her arm to him. "I have some ointment that might ease the pain in your leg." And back and neck and arms and stomach and so on. How had he lived through such damage and the pain from it all?

He nodded and accepted her arm and she nearly

cried out as she felt the extent of his injuries and the agony he must be enduring in silence. She did not wait until they reached her cottage where she could use the application of the ointment to hide her new ability—she began sending healing waves into his legs as they walked along. Corann stumbled once as she repaired the bones in his lower legs, and as he did, she noticed that his forearm carried some mark on it when his sleeve slipped and exposed the skin there.

Could he be part of this? Was he another who carried some power in his blood? She thought not, for surely he would have prevented such damage to his body. They reached her cottage, but he resisted entering. She helped him to sit on a log next to her doorway and went to gather a few supplies and brew a tea for him. As she walked away, she felt his gaze follow her and turned to see an expression of wonder in his eyes.

"Who are you, Corann?" she asked, returning to where he sat. Now he did not take his eyes from hers, though she could see he struggled to keep the contact. "What are you?" she asked, now convinced he was something different from anyone she'd met before, and he knew more than others did.

"I am your servant," he said, standing and lowering himself into a bow. She could see the pain it caused him and took him by the arms, raising him once more.

"I have no servants. I have no need of them," she assured the man. "Why would you think that?"

"I serve the bloodlines of the ancient ones," he whispered, bowing his head. "I serve you, a woman who carries the blood of Belenus, the god of healing and life and order. You are the sunblood."

Sunblood. Sunblood?

"Sunblood," she whispered back, feeling the heat surge through her blood, body, and soul in that moment.

It was what she was. There was a name for it.

She staggered back from the man as the heat expanded and escaped her body then, surrounding both of them in its brightness. Corann's body arched and then seemed to absorb the light and heat until she pulled it back within her.

"Corann!" she shouted.

He slid to the ground and Thea was at his side in a moment. Her hand on his chest rose and fell with his breathing, and his eyes began fluttering inside their lids, much as Tolan's had done last night. The man dragged in a gasp and opened them to look at her.

"Praise be!" he whispered. Pushing himself up to his knees, he touched his chest and then his legs and arms. Then he leaned down and touched his forehead to the ground much as she did when she gave thanks in the morning. "Praise be!" he said louder now.

"Corann, I pray you, do not kneel before me," Thea said, climbing to her feet. "'Tis unseemly."

Confused by his words and reaction, Thea wished that Tolan was here. He knew more about these matters than she did. This was an opportunity she could not give up, though, so she touched the man on his shoulder and bade him rise.

"My thanks to you for such a gift as this, Sunblood," he said, his voice filled with awe. "You have healed me. You have made me whole once more." His height now was several inches taller than before—partly because he was not stooped in pain and partly because his bones and sinews were now where they should be. He gazed at her with a reverence in his eyes she found disconcerting.

"Who are you that you know of such things? Are you also one of the descendants?" she asked, pointing at his arm. "I saw a mark on your arm there."

"Aye, I am marked as a priest," he said, sliding his sleeve up and letting her see his. A small stick figure of a man sat there where her own sun-shaped one lay. "I stand for humankind."

"You do not look like a priest," she said, glancing at his garments and his hair. He wore no tonsure as clergy did.

"Not of the One God who some worship," he said, smiling. "We follow the ways of the Old Ones. Those who walked on this earth eons ago. Those whose bloodlines were set up to protect mankind."

The sound of someone approaching stopped Corann from saying more. One of the boys who helped in the fields came running toward her cottage, calling out her name.

"Corann," she began, turning back to him. "I must go now, but I would speak with you more."

"There are others with whom you should speak," he said, backing away toward the shadows. "I will bring them to you."

"Nay, not here." Lord Geoffrey's scrutiny of Tolan made her nervous. Strangers would be seen and word would spread. "I will visit the abbey the day after tomorrow to purchase some herbs. In the morning, after the brothers pray Terce. I will meet you and the others there."

Whether or not he knew of the Christian hours of prayers, Corann nodded and strode off into the woods, heading south toward Amesbury. She took only a moment to watch him walk in long, sure strides, without pain, before answering young William's call to help someone else.

A sunblood. She was a sunblood.

CHAPTER 11

London Road, east of Amesbury

As they approached the town, Hugh opened up his senses, searching for any sign of the others, be they humans or bloods. It mattered not if he found them now or when he arrived at Geoffrey's holdings. From the power emanating from this whole area, the lands to the north and west of Amesbury were filled with likely places. So many stones and circles and henges of all sorts and sizes lay strewn across the lands.

Of course, that was exactly what Chaela's enemies had planned when they constructed their gateways—confuse those who sought them and disguise them from the casual view. So, none of the gateways would be found amongst the known or reported monuments or arrangements of stone. No, those might serve as marking posts or signs, but they would not be the doorways he sought.

Eudes rode to his side and gave him the directions to Geoffrey's estate. Not far now until he reached another of Chaela's faithful ones. As they reached the crest of another rolling hill, it struck him with so much power he gasped aloud at it.

Waves of power. Many beings who carried the blood of the Old Ones. They were here. It was here, too. He smiled, knowing he would never give up his efforts until he freed his goddess. As he turned in his saddle, the burned skin of his back reminded him of his fate if he failed.

Others would feel the wrath of the destructive goddess of chaos, not him, he swore once again to himself, as he sought the place where the power was strongest.

A group of them were south, near the abbey there in the distance, the church spire visible for miles. The others, the ones whose power was just rising, felt like tiny ripples on the surface of a puddle to him now. Untrained, ignorant of their potential, they were to the north.

But the power that left him struggling to breathe was farther away, to the north, along the river that curled endlessly across the plain of Sarum.

Hugh would seek out Geoffrey's keep and refresh himself before selecting a suitable sacrifice to offer to the goddess and to uncover the true circle. He was nodding, dismissing Eudes to lead on, when he felt . . . him.

He was nearby, watching and waiting. Hugh searched across the verdant farmlands and saw nothing but a copse in the middle of the fields. Humans worked them, preparing them for the spring planting, but none of them interested Hugh. He took in and let out a deep breath, focusing on the ripples of power that moved like tiny undulations in the air around him.

Waving Eudes on, he urged his horse across one of the fields toward the trees. Something was there. Some power, but Hugh could not see him. He smiled and nodded in greeting, not expecting a reply. But he knew he'd been seen and that the . . . earthblood felt Hugh's power as he passed. He rode on slowly, staring at the trees until he noticed one that did not bend with the breezes.

He could send his fire at the tree now to demonstrate his abilities, but Hugh would wait before challenging the earthblood. He would learn more in order to bring him to Hugh's side in this battle to conquer all of humanity. And he needed to discover the whereabouts of the other one and win or force them both to help him.

Looking ahead at those in his service off in the distance, he knew he, they, would prevail this time. Nothing in the world around him would be the same again. He laughed aloud and waved at the tree before riding off to catch up to the rest.

It was all falling into place.

His last thought had been to hide from the sight of whatever this creature approaching was. Tolan had been standing in the shade of the trees watching those working this field when something struck him. Not an object, but first a feeling of unease and then wave after wave of. . . something he could not define and had never felt before.

As it grew closer, Tolan stood with his back to the tallest of the trees and waited.

A large troop of soldiers rode over the hill there, coming down the London road from the east, and one man caught his attention. He was different. He was surrounded by an aura like the one Tolan had seen surrounding Thea, except that his was orange, like molten copper or liquid fire.

Then Tolan could feel something probing and pushing at him from the man. The biggest surprise was when the man stopped and turned his horse to face him, as though he could see Tolan there. Looking down at himself, Tolan realized, for the first time, that he was not visible any longer. Not his body. He did not hide against the trees there; he was in the tree.

Shocked, he looked up and found that everything around him had taken on a greenish hue. Then he heard the man laugh loudly and long in his direction.

Could he see Tolan thusly? Or did he see the tree in which Tolan now hid?

How had it happened? One moment a man, the next, with little but a thought, hidden within a tree?

Tolan tried to move his hands and feet and learned the more shocking truth—he did not hide in a tree, nay, he'd become the tree. Unable to comprehend such a thing, he felt drawn back to the man watching him. Whether mocking him or not, Tolan could not tell right now, the man waved at him and turned his horse and rode off to follow the others toward Lord Geoffrey's keep.

He watched until they were too far away to see

before considering anything else. His mind simply could not understand this. The other, the abilities he had to work the soil or to call the plants to it, were strange and awe-inspiring in themselves, but it was incomprehensible—how could a man turn into a tree?

The breeze caught his attention, as did the warmth of the sun shining above. He felt every single leaf that grew on each branch moving in the wind. Though he knew it was impossible, Tolan could feel his feet, or the roots, spread out for yards and yards in every direction away from the trunk.

Disbelief filled his mind and soul. Then, for just a moment, he stopped thinking and simply felt the changes that had taken place in him, wondrous and terrifying though they were. Part of the earth and yet thrust up into the air under the sky. He tried to stretch and saw new branches extend farther and new leaves burst into existence on their tips.

He laughed, though no sound came out.

Extraordinary. Unbelievable. He could think of no word or concept that truly captured what was happening to him or what this experience was.

Or was this a dream? Had he fallen asleep there, lulled by the warmth of the sun and the unseasonably gentle breezes? He looked around him, and every other thing and person he could see seemed true.

Then Tolan realized the direction in which that man and his troop of soldiers had ridden. Toward the keep, aye, but also the village. And if this man had recognized Tolan and his power, would he not recognize Thea's if she crossed his path?

Thea.

With the possible danger to her as his only thought, his body changed in an instant and the man he was took a step and then another toward the road. Turning around, he watched as the earth covered the place where he'd pulled himself free of the soil until there was no trace of any change there.

And nothing for the soldier who was supposed to be following to find when he woke from the bit of rest the hapless guard managed to find each day while Tolan worked in the fields.

As he rushed to the village, he also knew that one question that had plagued him was now answered— there was at least one other person who knew about their power and who carried such a gift within him.

Tolan arrived in the village long after the soldiers had traveled through and entered the keep. Such a large number could not all be housed within the walls, so some remained waiting outside. Tolan wondered about their purpose and if they knew about the secrets he and the man who led them carried.

Night could not come soon enough for him, for he thought their only safe strategy was to put some miles between themselves and this newly arrived stranger. Tolan's attempts to find Thea were unsuccessful. He'd tried not to seem overly anxious, and only when he asked Eldreda about her visit to Rigby did he discover she'd been called to one of the outlying fields to tend to an injury.

With one eye on the keep to watch for movements of the visitors, Tolan oversaw the removal of some dead trees from the edge of one field and managed to quietly arrange for two horses they would need to be readied and left where they could reach them without being seen. Then he spent the next several hours with Kirwyn, both working on some shared tasks and just talking with his son. For the first time, Tolan decided to allow the boy to remain on his own while he and Thea went to Durrington, but he warned Kirwyn not to speak of it to anyone until their return. His son was so thrilled to be permitted this that, thankfully, he forgot to be curious about the reasons he could not come along.

Soon, supper was done, Kirwyn lay asleep in the loft, and Tolan made his way to Thea's cottage. His blood prickled with anticipation—of seeing Thea again, of searching for the truth on his lands and of telling her about the stranger's arrival.

Thea lifted her head and listened. Or rather felt, since she was now aware of small changes in the light and heat around her.

As villagers passed her by along the paths, she could feel the small whorls of their bodies' heat move around her and then dissolve away. When she'd visited several people suffering with fevers this day, she was able to draw it from them.

But the most exciting moment of the day had been meeting Corann. He was proof that others knew what was happening to her and Tolan and mayhap they even knew why. She could not wait to share such news with Tolan.

He was here.

His steps were dogged by another, that guard, but Tolan strode purposefully to her door. She smiled, enjoying the knowledge that he'd declared his feelings for her in such a public manner as he had.

Without knocking, he lifted the latch and opened the door, entering quickly and quietly. The green glow was stronger and brighter now, as hers was. Had he used his abilities as well?

"Thea," he whispered as he walked to her and pulled her to her feet and into his embrace. His mouth was hot and possessive as he took her breath in a stream of kisses. Her body responded and readied for him, but she knew they must leave soon. "I do not like when I do not see you for the whole of the day." Another touch of his mouth to hers and then he stepped back, his hands still on her waist.

"Tolan, I have much to tell you," she said, feeling the excitement swirling within her. The power within her pulsed stronger and brighter when she was with him. The closer they were, the stronger it felt.

"And I, you," he said, glancing at the door. "Can you make me some of that tea that aids sleep?"

"Aye," she said. "For you? Now?"

"Nay, for my shadow," he said. "If he sleeps, he will not hear our movements. We must leave as soon as we can."

"What has happened to cause this urgency, Tolan?" She shivered at the tone of his voice.

"I will tell you more as we ride," he said, pointing to her basket. "The tea now, if you will."

She did as he asked, gathering some herbs from her

basket and pouring some of the simmering water from the kettle over the fire over them. The aroma spread quickly through her cottage as it steeped. She allowed it several minutes to reach its peak before adding a bit of honey to it, to soften the bitterness of the herbs. Tolan watched her every move in silence and waited for the brew.

As he carried it out, she stopped him and added a small crust of bread and a piece of cheese from what she'd packed for their travels. She waited at the open door as he carried out the food and tea to the one hiding in the shadows.

"Denis?" Tolan called out. "Where are you, lad?"

There was a pause before the young man answered, most likely as Denis debated whether he should reveal his position. Whether Tolan's knowledge of him had surprised him or not, Denis acknowledged the call.

"I am here, Tolan," he said as he walked toward the house.

"Here, now, Elethea worries that you are hungry or cold. This is for you," Tolan said, handing the bit of food and tea to him.

"My thanks, Elethea," Denis said loudly, with a nod toward her door. "Tolan." Then he walked back into the shadows about twenty paces from her door.

Tolan waited and watched and then came back inside. She offered him tea of another kind while they waited for the sleeping brew to do its work.

"I met a man today, Tolan. He knew what I am," she said softly when she could no longer keep the news within her. She sat on the stool and sipped her tea. "There are others in the area."

"Aye," he said, sitting next to her on the floor. "A group arrived at the keep today. One of them is like us." He did not sound happy.

"This man, Corann was his name, he said he is a priest who serves those of us who carry some blood-line in us." She thought on the strange words and then noticed that Tolan did not seem surprised by her words. "You knew? You know about this?"

"Aye, Thea, I have known for some time," he said with a sigh. "And I also saw someone like us this morn," he said, again as though admitting anything about this was painful. "Even now he is a guest of Lord Geoffrey's in the keep."

"Did you speak to him?"

"Nay, but he . . . glowed like molten metal in the smith's fire."

"Did he see you?"

He nodded. "He knew I was there." Tolan met her gaze then and leaned in closer. "I changed, Thea. I changed into something . . . else."

She shivered at the very notion that he could be something else, but then so had she when she let the heat and light take over her for that moment with Corann. Thea started to speak, but a noise from outside her cottage stopped her. Tolan stood quickly and walked to the door. Peering through an opening of a scant inch, he nodded to her to look.

Denis lay in a crumpled heap a few paces away

from her door, as though he had been walking to it and had fallen asleep standing there. Which he had.

"Make sure he will be safe, Tolan. I would not want him harmed or hurt because he could not wake," she urged him.

Tolan walked out to move the guard off the path and Thea banked the fire in her hearth, preparing to leave. Gathering up the rest of the food and a skin of water and one of ale, she pulled her cloak on and tugged the hood up to cover most of her. When Tolan returned, she was ready.

"Come," he said, holding out his hand.

She accepted it without hesitation. In spite of her arguments and reasons against marrying this man, Thea doubted not that her future was interwoven with his even as their hearts were. Until they sorted out the changes happening to them, they must work together. What part the others played in this, she knew not. Her place was at his side.

They made their way to the horses he'd arranged and walked them until they were outside the village and away from the cottages and crofts. Mounting, they rode swiftly north, along the road that followed the path of the river. By the time the sun rose in the morning, they approached Tolan's lands in Durrington.

And within a short time, it was clear to her that something was here that was at the center of all the strange happenings. Something . . . or someone lived on Tolan's lands and it was not human or animal.

CHAPTER 12

Tolan dismounted and helped Thea down from her horse. His cousin stood outside the cottage and greeted them.

"Good day, Farold," Tolan called out to him. "You know Elethea from the village?"

"Good day, Elethea," Farold said, nodding to her as he took hold of the reins of the horses. "What brings you here, Tolan?"

"I wanted to show her around the farm," Tolan said. "Before the spring planting." If Farold thought it strange that they arrived in early morn or that they arrived at all, he said nothing. A raised brow was his only reaction. But Farold was both practical and un-assuming—his only concern was that he be allowed to serve as caretaker when Tolan could not be here.

"I am going to the village to bring back some sup-plies, Tolan. I should be back by nightfall. There is porridge in the pot if you have not broken your fast."

Farold nodded and went off, leading the horses to the trough and then leaving them alone.

"Does he work your farm alone?" Thea asked as they watched his cousin ride off toward the village.

"Most of the time," he said. "During planting and harvest, others help him. Come inside now."

The winter's chill still held on tightly here and the cold, moist air covered the ground around them. Their breaths came out as clouds, hot dissipating into the cold. A few minutes by a fire with something hot to eat and drink would be welcome, Tolan was certain.

They had spoken little along the way, both intent on the road ahead of them while traveling under the dim light of a half-moon. Though, truth be told, Tolan could have found his way here blindfolded or in the pitch-darkness of a new moon.

Thea entered and went directly to the fire to stir the pot. She did not first put her hands out to warm them as he wanted to and he realized that she glowed brighter, her heat spreading through the cottage. Tolan walked behind her and wrapped his arms around her.

"This could have some benefits on cold winter days," he whispered as her heat seeped into his cold body.

Tolan dipped his head and tucked his chin between her shoulder and her neck, kissing her there. She was at ease with him touching her as long as they were alone. One day, she would more easily accept his caresses no matter who was there. No matter that she allowed it, Tolan could feel the agitation in her.

"Corann said I am a sunblood," she whispered

without looking at him. "I am *the* sunblood." Now she turned and met his gaze. "What would he call you?"

She was angry. He could feel it rippling through her and saw it as the golden aura flickered around her body. She resented that he'd withheld knowledge from her about their true natures and abilities . . . and his family's ties to the Old Ones. He chose to answer her question for now. Explanations would come as they were needed.

"Earthblood."

The word echoed in the space between them now. He had never spoken the word aloud, nor heard his father or grandfather speak it. But the one who had called to him from the dark woods had.

"Ah, it makes sense, does it not? Your gift with nature, the soil, and growing things. Of the earth," she said. "Why Farold can tend this whole farm by himself . . . or rather the farm can tend itself?" Her gaze narrowed. "You have known your whole life of this?"

"Nay. Only when I reached fifteen years and my blood came alive with it."

"Fifteen? Kirwyn is nearly that."

"I wait to see if he has inherited this . . . affinity with the earth. There is only one in each generation, or so my father and his father before him believed."

"And if it is not him, Tolan? What then?" she asked. A strange expression lit her eyes now. He could not decipher it.

"If it is not him, it will be another of my sons or daughters," Tolan said. There were stories of a daughter being favored with this gift in the past. He knew also that he would have children with Thea. He had no doubt of it now knowing their connection to the Old Ones. It was as though fate had put them together here in Amesbury.

"So you must have children?"

"I want more children, Thea. Like any man does. To help me work these lands and pass onto them for their lives. Do you not wish to be a mother?" As he watched, she steeled her expression first before nodding.

"More than anything in the world, Tolan. More than anything." Her words carried such depth of want and need it nearly knocked him over.

Then Thea turned and walked to the fire once more and the shimmer around her changed. Bending down, she swung the iron hook out and looked inside the pot. Scooping some water in the nearby bucket into a cup, she added it to the porridge and stirred it to ease out the clumps. Then she pushed the mixture back over the flames so it would heat. Tolan walked to the shelf next to the hearth and took down two bowls and handed them to her.

Here, in this house, in this way, he could imagine them together. Loving and living out the rest of their lives here. Tending to each other and to the lands. As though mocking him and his hopes, the earth shuddered then. Thea faced him in shock as the ground beneath them shook.

"Can you feel that?" he asked. She nodded. So it was not just him this time. "It happened when we passed by here last week. And then I heard . . . a voice." He grabbed her hand and led her outside. The rumbling came from the woods once more, as it had done before. "From there," he said, pointing to the large, thick wooded area across the fields near the edge of the river.

"I will bank the fire," she said, turning back. He nodded and went to get the horses. Although not rested, they would be able to take them across the fields to the henge there.

Tolan helped her up and then mounted his horse, touching his heels to its side to urge it forward. The animals grew more skittish with every league closer that they came to the earthen henge encircling the woods. By the time they'd reached the first rise of the henge, they'd slipped off the horses and pulled them along.

"Who built this?" Thea asked as they began walking up the embankment. Higher than Tolan's height, it surrounded the woods like a fence.

"No one knows. Stories of it have been passed down in my family," he said.

"It is like those henges to the west, then?" she asked, walking up the hill of packed earth. "But no standing stones?" They reached the top and could see across the huge area within it. "And much, much larger."

"I think there are stones buried in the center of those trees." Another admission to her. The next in what he thought might be a never-ending chain of words he'd never thought to say. Tolan trusted her. "And more lying buried under this." He pointed at the hill on which they stood.

Her eyes grew wide as she followed the path of it around and around the huge enclosed area before them. It was larger than even the abbey and its surrounding land. She shook her head in disbelief and reached out for him, clasping his hand in hers.

"What is it?" Thea asked him. "What could have been in this place?" She turned and stared at him then. "What is your family's involvement here?"

"We have been caretakers of these lands, Thea." He waved his hand over the lands under their eyes. "We have guarded it and worshipped the Old Ones, bringing fertility and prosperity to all the generations of my family."

She trembled as he spoke and he realized it was that voice again. Not the one from the woods, but the one that felt as though another spoke from within his body. He'd spoken in it before to her, but he could feel it flow like the power he carried in his blood now.

"For eons," he said, "the faithful worshipped in this place and others like it. Festivals to celebrate the plentiful harvests. Ceremonies to honor the gods. Rituals to ensure fertility of man, beast, and fields. All here. Surrounded by the stones. Blessed by the gods."

"Where is it now?" she whispered, yet fearful of him. He could hear it in her voice and see the way her body quivered.

"All buried beneath us and hidden safely out of view," he said. "Until it is needed."

Tolan stopped and listened and felt.

Someone was coming. Not one but many.

On horseback. Charging toward them. Armed.

Led by that man. His power preceded him.

"I feel it, Tolan," Thea said, turning in the direction of those who were coming. "Is that what you felt from him?"

"Aye," Tolan said.

The glow around her became like the sunlight on a cloudless day, so bright that he could not see her body within it. The power of the other one seemed to call forth theirs.

"Thea, it is not safe here. Come," he said, walking down the hill to the edge of the thick, entangled trees there.

Whatever existed beneath or within these lands was powerful, too. So powerful it might block the man's ability to find them. They reached the trees and Thea gasped. The trees were alive, swarming and snarling like snakes at their approach. Tolan shook his head.

"Be not afraid, love," he whispered. "They will not harm you."

At his words, the trees gentled and parted for her. Tolan walked at her side, following the ever-widening path deeper and deeper into the copse. The trees adjusted around them, covering over their heads while moving out of their way. Finally, they arrived at a place close to the center of it and Tolan nodded, pleased that they understood his will.

"They will protect you, Thea. Stay within until I call you."

"But, Tolan, he is dangerous. You cannot face him alone." She touched his hand and then his face. "I cannot lose you."

"You will not," he said, leaning to kiss her. "I will

remain out of sight to see what he does. And I will be back."

"How will you hide? As one of those trees?" she asked as he began to walk away.

"Nay, not this time. The earth is pulling me to it, so I will . . ."

Tolan dropped to his knees as he did during the ritual, but this time he became one with the soil, his body fading and losing itself into the ground. He heard Thea's gasp of shock but continued to move away from her, under the deep roots of the trees that formed the barrier there.

Earthblood, I am here! Come back!

Though it was a woman's voice, it was not Thea's. And instead of coming from above the ground, it came from deep in the earth. As he turned and concentrated on it, he felt the edge of something he could not penetrate. Like a stone wall that extended without boundaries toward the center of the earth. And all he could feel was black desolation emanating from it.

He would come back to learn more about this chasm, but first he must discover the purpose of the man who carried the bloodline of . . . fire. Heat but not like Thea's. This heat destroyed. This heat incinerated with pain and chaos.

Not like Thea's healing light.

Tolan reached the embankment and stayed within it as the troop reached his lands and crossed onto the protected land. He needed to learn more about this man, this invader, so that he could protect Thea and the lands to which his own life had been sworn to serve.

So he waited for his arrival.

Thea watched in wonderment as Tolan disappeared into the earth. His body did not burrow into the ground; it became the ground. She could feel his presence there and as he moved away from her. As she took a step to follow him, the trees closed her path. The branches spread and tangled until they appeared more wall than tree.

When she turned back toward the center of it all, nothing barred her way. She walked along, watching, as the trees opened and allowed her to pass until she reached a huge clearing. There Thea's body began to shake as some force moved over her.

She looked around the site and saw nothing but the open space. Were there stones buried here? A circle of them that held great meaning or power? Thea walked around the perimeter of the field, studying the ground for any signs that others had been here before.

Tolan's family must have visited this place before. He spoke of it as though he had. Wandering to one end, she finally found something—a small stone that seemed to mark the place where it lay. She crouched down to see it more closely and reached out to touch it.

Smooth, worn, and with no signs of carving or decoration, the stone would have fit in the palm of her hand. It wobbled slightly as she ran her fingers over it, loose and not embedded in the ground as she thought it was. So Thea picked it up and held it up to looked at it more closely. It began to make a noise, like the humming of insects and then like the chiming of church bells.

When Thea glanced around her, everything was different.

Where the ground had been empty before her, now there was a smaller circle of eight tall stones to the north and a larger one of more than twenty stones to the south. But they both fit within the huge place surrounded by shorter ones. She tried to count them and lost count. There were so many. Another raised bank of earth lay within the first one and then a ditch, both nearer to her than the stones were. And where the single stone had lain, where she stood now, was the doorway to a small building.

Shaped like a triangle, the sides of it were buried in the ground and its roof was of sod. With a frame made of thick tree trunks and an open doorway into it, it was not a dwelling but seemed more a gathering place. More tree trunks spread out from its corners and opened onto the space before her, guiding her attention to the other circles.

And the people who stood waiting.

Hundreds stood in silence along the walkway between this building and the smaller circle of eight. How had they gotten there? How was she seeing this? They seemed to be looking at her, but when she heard voices behind her, she knew they weren't. Turning and stepping out of the doorway, she saw the small group within. Men and women, all dressed in the same type of white ankle-length woolen tunics, moved in circles around a young woman and a young man.

As Thea watched, the older ones spoke words she could not understand and then laid their hands on the couple. Although shocked, she could not turn her gaze away when the woman was stripped of her garments and led outside to the loud cheers of those watching along the path. As soon as she took her first steps on the path, or was pushed along by the ones behind her, the crowd pressed in closer.

The woman did not seem fearful or embarrassed as those around her began to fondle and stroke and kiss her. To Thea's shock, men rutted with her, releasing their seed within her and passing her to the next one waiting. Thea wanted to stop this, but the woman accepted each man along the path as though she expected such a thing. How many times, how many men's seed she carried in her and on her, Thea lost count.

Drums beat to some enticing rhythm as the woman made her way to the circle. Thea could feel the sound of them in her own blood and she wanted to touch the woman, too. The crowd surged then, rushing forward and bringing the woman into the circle. Stumbling forward, she ran into the center and stood, her arms raised in the air, as she waited . . . for something. The crowd gathered around the outside of the stones, swaying and stomping their feet to the mad sounds of the drums.

As the drums beat faster and faster, Thea's breathing became shallow and quick and she realized that she was aroused. The place between her legs grew wet and her breasts tightened, the nipples becoming taut beneath her own gown. As she watched, for she could not look away, two women and two men joined the woman in the center, stroking and kissing her until she fell to the ground, writhing in pleasure. From the way they moved, their intention was to prepare her but not allow her release.

Thea could feel each touch, each caress, each stroke of their hands and tongues on her own skin, almost as though Tolan was with her, rousing her to her peak. She ached for relief and, within herself, she could feel how close they kept the woman while not letting her body find release . . . yet.

The crowd cried out once more and Thea, now standing within the circle, turned to see the young man being led naked along the same path. Followed by four of the people from within the building who carried bowls, he walked up the path now. He was touched as the woman had been, stroked until his manhood stood ready, but never joined with any of the women who pleasured him. Caressed and suckled, he reached the circle and entered, holding his flesh in his hand and calling out to the woman there. With the help of the four attending her, she gained her feet and waited for him.

Those with the bowls poured out the contents on the two as they stood together. Fragrant oils were spread over their skin and then they fell to the ground, copulating before all. Thea could hear the moans of the couple, of those watching, of those tending to them and she thought she heard herself join in with them.

As they reached that moment, when their releases were nearly upon them, the four others grasped the couple and moved them so that the woman rode the flesh of the man.

As she arched and began to scream out her release, one of the others, one who wore robes of honor, stepped behind the woman, took hold of her by the hair, and sliced her throat open. Thea began screaming then, as the woman's blood poured forth over the man who spilled his seed within her. The woman watched as her life's blood covered the man and the ground around him and then slumped over, silent now in death.

Thea fell to her own knees then and wanted to vomit at such a sight as this. They had killed her. There before the crowds, the woman had been . . .

"Sanctified, by the seed of many and the holy oil," an older man said from next to Thea, helping her to stand. "Her body will now become part of the earth, taking her gift of life and fertility within it to make it new."

Thea turned to look at the man and found it difficult to see him. A bright light shone around him as he spoke.

"He killed her," she argued.

"She gave her life freely, for she believed it was an honor to be offered to her gods in this way." The man's voice was familiar, but she did not recognize it. "Look now." Thea turned her attention back to the center of the circle.

The others had lifted the woman from the man and carried her body to the center and placed it on a stone

Thea had not seen before. The man, covered in her blood, stood near her head, mumbling some words, a prayer, she thought, as the ground began to shake. The soil shifted around the woman's body and then it flowed over her like a wave, covering her completely, swirling away as a wave of water would, until every trace of the woman was gone. The crowd cheered wildly then.

"I do not understand," Thea whispered.

"Cernunnos, the god of the earth and all things that grow within it, was pleased with her sacrifice and has taken her to him," the man explained quietly.

"And him?" she asked, nodding at the young man standing naked and covered in blood.

"He is blessed by the gods now, Elethea. His seed will be spread among those women who seek a child and they will produce many offspring who will serve their gods."

The young man was led away, back down the path to the building and taken inside. Women began forming a line outside, and as she watched, the first one was called and ran inside.

Spread among many? These women would couple with this man and bear his children. She turned back to the man beside her to ask another question and saw that he was walking toward one of the tall stones. Once he reached it, he turned and smiled at her.

He was outlined in brightness, like the sun. As she looked at each of the other stones, she noticed richly dressed men and women before seven of them and the man in the robes before the eighth. Each of the seven glowed as a different color surrounded their bodies—yellow like the sun, green as the plants, orange like the molten metal, silver, turquoise, red, and blue. They changed then, growing to the size of the stones before melting into them. Only the man, the priest, remained there, staring at her.

Then, in the next moment, all of it was gone. Thea stood holding the small stone in her hand, alone on the empty field where nothing stood now. But now she stood in the spot that had been the center of the smaller stone circles. She tossed the stone there to remember the place. Wandering across the area, she found no other trace of what she'd seen built there.

How long had she been caught up in this . . . vision? Surely, it had been that, a glimpse back into the past of this place and into the practices the people had followed to keep their gods satisfied. And if it was that, then those seven men and women must have been the . . .

"Old Ones," she whispered. The ones Corann and his people served.

She needed to tell Tolan what she'd seen here. She ran to the place where she'd entered, but the trees had closed it to her. Each time she tried to walk into them, they grew closer and more tightly together. It did not seem to matter to them that she needed to leave. They were going to keep her within until Tolan returned to her.

Shaking now, she sat on the ground, tucking her legs under her to wait. Some time passed before she felt the tremors below her. Tolan was here, in the earth, moving toward the place where the circle had been. She could feel him there, searching for something deep within the earth.

As she watched, he rose from under the ground, a being of soil and plants molded into the shape of a man, with glowing green eyes that watched her. He took the first step toward her as a creature of clay and dirt and she fought the urge to run.

This was Tolan. She knew it. She felt it, recognizing him in her own marrow and bones. With each step closer to her, he changed more and more and by the time he stood before her, he was a man once again.

A man who looked at her through the glowing green eyes of a god named Cernunnos.

CHAPTER 13

Hugh could feel it miles away.

Just as he had felt the presence of the earth-blood in the field as he rode into Amesbury.

For a few moments during their ride here, he had also been aware of the second one—the sunblood—before losing both of them to the greater force. The circle was there. He laughed aloud then as he kicked his horse's sides to spur him on faster. The others, including Geoffrey, followed along in silence.

How had Geoffrey not recognized the two of them? This Tolan's abilities with the land should have been so obvious. And the woman, Elethea, and her skills with healing. Both so plainly in sight and plainly carrying the powers of the Old Ones. But the bloodlines of all the followers had weakened so much that even the faithful could not tell when they were in the presence of power.

His father had warned him relentlessly about these

weaknesses that would challenge him in this quest. It had all come down to this time and this generation being the last one strong enough to break open the barrier holding Chaela in her prison. After this, there was no guarantee that there would be enough pure-bloods born and capable of opening the gateways.

"How much farther?" Eudes asked as he rode at Hugh's side.

"Several miles," Geoffrey answered.

Hugh did not need to know the distance; he felt it there, the waves of power getting stronger with every league covered.

"Should we stop—" Eudes began, but Hugh cut off his words with a glance. His commander and half brother dropped back, understanding there would be no more delays. They passed a man riding toward Amesbury, but Hugh dismissed him without interest, feeling nothing from him as they passed.

The tension within those following him grew and Hugh could feel it. Some had traveled with him from the beginning, but others were new to his service, having joined him back in Brittany. They had no idea of what was to come, and the anticipation of finding the circle made his own blood race with excitement.

Finally, there ahead of them and visible, he saw the huge, dark, thick forest of trees over a low hill. A small cottage sat just off the road there, in the middle of some of the most fertile land in England, just as Geoffrey had told him it would be. It was his home, the house built by and lived in by generations of his family before him—Tolan the earthblood.

Now he kicked the horse, anxious to get closer and to find the circle. The animal had a mind of its own and slowed and bucked as they approached the embankment that encircled the woods. Finally, he stopped fighting it and dismounted, tossing the reins to another to see to.

He gave no orders, Hugh simply walked up the hill and knew that the small troop of men would follow him—Eudes would make certain of it. He nearly lost his footing as he reached the crest of it and peered over at the huge expanse of land within it.

Hugh smiled and laughed again. He had not stumbled; the ground under him had shifted, trying to throw him down. The earthblood was at work here . . . now. Geoffrey had revealed Tolan's family history of holding this prosperous land for generations, going back almost a thousand years that they knew. Small-minded men like his cousin could not comprehend the true length of time that Tolan's ancestors had lived here, taking care of these lands and protecting this circle and its secrets.

Well, the time was here for Tolan to be part of the bigger mission and to be part of the future of the goddess and her followers. Coming this close to the trees, Hugh knew he would never penetrate this barrier with the earthblood's help.

He threw some fire at the trees. They wiggled and snarled like living things before drawing closer to each other and tighter, preventing anyone or even his flames from getting inside.

"Bring an ax. Bring all of them, Eudes," he said as

he walked down the hill to the living barrier. Each of the ten men there took their axes and followed him down the hill to the edge of the trees.

There was no sign of damage from his fire. That was not good. They should be singed or burnt, but no, no changes. Cernunnos was a powerful god, one of the most powerful, and clearly this descendant and his work had the blessing of the god. And eons of attention to make the spells and protections strong.

"There," Hugh said, pointing to what looked to be the likely place to create a gap. "Cut them down."

The men were some of his strongest warriors, though all were human, and Hugh could tell within minutes that this would not work. He walked along the perimeter of it, toward the river, and saw no breaks in it. If anything, it grew tighter with each pace he took in its direction. The grunts of those trying to cut a path in went on and on and Hugh allowed some time to pass before giving up.

"Cease!" he called out. With a wave of his hand, he sent them back to their horses to wait for him. Only Eudes remained, ever watchful. Hugh crossed his arms over his chest and studied the place.

"A sacrifice, my lord," he offered.

"Nay. Not now."

These lands were protected against just that. This earthblood was exceedingly strong and had been using his powers for some time. This was the first time Hugh had encountered a bloodline that had kept the faith as his own had and prepared for this time. The Norse priest, old Einar, had tried and failed, but this one . . . was very strong. He might not know the extent of his powers or have been using all that he could, but he was more experienced than any of the others had been.

A worthy opponent in this challenge. When Hugh forced his cooperation to open the gate, it would be even more satisfying.

If they were unable to hack or burn their way in, the only other choice was to use the earthblood to open a path. And for that, Hugh must give the man a good reason.

Hugh crouched down and touched the soil at his feet. Aye, there was power here. Living here and flowing. And it came from not one or two sources, but three. The circle was the strongest pull he could feel there. The earthblood was the second.

And the sunblood was the third.

He laughed then. The two had already made a connection—that was why their powers had grown lately. Not only the pull of the goddess and the circle beneath this ground.

Standing, Hugh brushed the soil off his hands and smiled.

He'd underestimated the ability of that kind of connection between the stormblood and his mate, the waterblood. He'd been faced with the same kind of choice when the product of his love for the only woman in his life who had mattered stood before him. But his life had been guided in this task of freeing and serving Chaela for so long that, to him, there had been no choice.

Oh, he had given himself a moment or two of reflection and remembrance, but no real choosing had occurred.

The rewards she promised were unfathomable. His future would see him as her human consort and the father of a new generation that would bring about the chaos and destruction Chaela had sworn against humanity. Even now he shivered at the very thought of what it meant.

Nay, no need to make a choice. He would force this earthblood to choose, though. Hugh strode back toward the rise of earth and faced the entire wooded area.

"I know you watch and can hear me, Tolan Earthblood," he began. "I wish to speak to you directly. In your human form. I will be at Geoffrey's keep, waiting for you. Come to me so we can parley as equals. We both have much to gain as friends or to lose if we become enemies."

The only reply he received was that of a slight swirling in the ground around him. Hugh smiled. The earthblood heard him.

Hugh walked up the embankment and down to where his men and his cousin waited. Mounting his horse, he nodded at Eudes, who led them back toward Amesbury. Then Hugh rode to his cousin's side.

"Tell me more of Tolan and his lands."

Tolan remained part of the earth until they left the area. They rode past his house without pausing and did not stop along the way back to Amesbury. Wanting to ensure Thea's safety, he took no chances. Once he felt them arrive at the keep, he moved through the ground, almost as he moved when swimming in the river or a lake.

Under the ring of trees that seemed to ease as he passed them. He could feel Thea in the middle of it and went toward her, until that voice spoke to him once again.

I wait for you, Earthblood. Come to me now.

It was difficult to resist the draw of her, so he let himself follow along, deeper and deeper and farther into the center of the circle. Until he reached that black place and could go no farther.

Find a way to release me. The sunblood will help. Ask my faithful. You must free me from this prison.

Tolan stopped, listening and trying to locate the one speaking. They were behind this barrier, and as he spread out through the ground, he could not find a breach in it. Then he felt Thea's distress and went to her immediately.

He rose from the soil, and her face lost all its color. As he moved forward, he realized that he yet remained part of the earth. With each step, he pulled his human body back into form and finally stood before her a man. Now, though, his vision was tinged green around the edges of it.

"You resemble him," she said, her voice trembling. "But I know it's you, Tolan."

"Whom do I look like?" he asked, holding out his hand to her. He could feel her trying to control her fear. "What happened to you?"

"I . . . saw . . ."

He caught her just before she crumpled, lifting her in his arms and carrying her out through the trees until they reached beyond the embankment. He knelt and placed her on the ground and sat with her head on his lap. Touching her cheek, he found it cold and clammy now.

"Thea," he said softly while stroking her cheek. Her eyes fluttered while closed and then she opened them, staring in confusion at him.

She reached up and touched his cheek, stroking it as he had hers. "You . . . changed."

"Aye. And you fainted. Inside the trees."

When Thea shifted to sit up, he placed his hand across her to keep her there. She might be awake, but her color was pale.

"Just tell me what happened," he said. She relented and lay back against him. Holding her felt right. Protecting her did as well.

"The trees led me inside, to the clearing," she began. "I do not understand how it is so huge there and yet none of it can be seen from out here."

"Nor I," he agreed. He took her hand and entwined their fingers. "And then?"

"I walked around it, looking for anything, a sign of something. And I found a stone, about the size of my hand, and picked it up." She took in and let out a deep breath. "Then I was someplace else."

"You left the clearing?" he asked. He could move through the ground, but she could not. Or could she, moving as the sunlight did?

"I did not move and yet everything was different.

One moment I was in the clearing and the next I was . . ." She pushed herself up to sit and turned to face him. "I was seeing the circles as they were long ago, Tolan!" Now her face flushed with excitement. "It was a vision or dream, I know not which."

"What did it look like?" He had his suspicions, having traveled underneath the area and having seen the buried stones around the whole of it.

"There was another embankment," she began, pointing in the distance. "And stones, stones not taller than me, stood all around it." She stood now and he did, too. "Two smaller circles of taller stones stood within the larger one. And there was a building." Now her cheeks turned red, like a rosy blush.

"Can you show me?" he asked. She glanced around and he knew she was looking for the others. "They are gone. We are alone." He held out his hand and in a short time they were standing in the clearing once more. She led him across it to a place nearer the river's side.

"The river came up higher," she said. Boats were moored just over that rise." She walked a few paces and pointed again. "The building sat there. A wooden structure, laying half-buried at the end of the path." He followed the movements of her hand as she explained the way things had looked to her.

"There were two circles built here, Tolan."

"Two? Where?" he asked, watching as she peered across the clearing as though seeing them now.

"One to the north and one to the south. The northern one was smaller, having eight tall stones, while the other had twenty. They walked along a path here, to reach the smaller circle." She grew quiet then and the blush was deeper. What had she seen?

"Who walked here, Thea?"

The words poured out from her in a rush, the story so detailed he had to believe her. A ritual of fertility and sacrifice to the Old Ones. He'd heard stories of such from long-ago times but had never had the explicit details that she described. The part he'd not heard before was about the seven beings who became the stones at the end of it all. Four men and three women. Surrounded by colors like the ones they could see around each other.

"Who do I resemble, Thea? You said it before you fainted."

"Cernunnos. The one who was pleased with the sacrifice and took the woman's body into the earth." She stared once more at his eyes and he knew they remained green even now.

"My ancestor," he said. The name had been whispered for generations.

"It is so difficult for me to take it all in," she said at the end of it all. "At least you have known about this."

"Not all of it. Much has been lost in the mists of time. My father told me he thought this began thousands of years ago." He pulled her closer and put his arm around her shoulder. "We should go."

"What do we do now, Tolan? This, all this, and the knowledge we have is for some purpose."

As he looked in the distance, it began as a whisper. At first, only he noticed it. A few moments later, Thea turned to the place where she'd said the smaller circle lay. Then the sound became a voice. The same one who'd spoken to him several times now.

Earthblood. Sunblood. Heed my call!

"What is that?" Thea asked. "Where did it come from?"

Free me! Save me!

"From under the circle, buried deep there in the earth," he said.

"Who can it be?" Thea turned and then walked toward the place she'd seen in her vision. The eight stones had disappeared beneath the ground there. She pointed. "Can you uncover the stones there?"

"I could," Tolan replied, hesitation clear in his tone.

Free me! the voice cried out again.

For a moment, all Thea could see was the body of the woman sacrificed to the gods, naked, covered in her own blood and the seed of many men, being taken into the ground by the god Cernunnos. Was she somehow alive there? Her soul remaining long after her body turned to dust?

"Is it the one who was sacrificed here so many years ago, Tolan? Could it be her crying out?" She knew even as she said it, it could not be the same one.

"Nay. I think I know who calls to us," Tolan said. Shaking his head, he held out his hand once more to her. "And I think we should leave here now."

"Who is it?" Thea asked as they walked swiftly to the edge of the trees.

Stop! Come to me now! The voice was so loud, her ears pained her as it continued to scream.

They began running then and Thea struggled to

keep up with Tolan's long strides. Soon, they reached the end of the trees and, as they ran, Tolan leveled their path so she would not have to climb the tall rise to escape.

Their horses stood grazing in the distance and Tolan let go of her to retrieve them. Soon, they made their way back to his cottage, surprised that no one stood guard or had disturbed anything there. Tolan wordlessly took down two cups and filled them from a jug—of wine—before holding one out to her. Only after they'd emptied their cups did he speak.

And when he'd finished, she almost wished she could go back to the ignorance in which she'd lived only a short time ago.

CHAPTER 14

William stood back in the shadows watching, as Corann brought the woman toward him and Brienne. 'Twas decided that the three of them would speak to her first before bringing her to their encampment.

"She is frightened," Brienne said, leaning against his side and sliding her hand into his. He nodded.

"Were you not?" he asked, kissing his mate's hand. "I know I was when I discovered the truth of my nature."

"Frightened? I think not, Will," Brienne said. "I cannot imagine a warrior of your experience being frightened. Nervous mayhap. Uneasy, certainly. But frightened?"

"I thank you for your confidence in me, but to learn that nothing about you or your world is what you believed nearly had me soiling my breeches."

She laughed softly and the sound surrounded him.

She was his life. Part of him that he'd found and claimed without ever realizing she was missing. He would risk anything and everything for her.

"A warrior, every warrior, knows fear, my love," he continued. "Experienced warriors accept it and do their duties in spite of it. The best warriors use their fear to spur themselves on in battle—"

"Here now," she interrupted. "She comes."

William watched as the color surrounding this woman, Elethea of Amesbury, changed. Rather than being an even aura, it sputtered and ebbed and flowed. Fear, he suspected, made it change so. Brienne released his hand and moved to stand in front of him. They'd decided, especially with his new appearance, to have Brienne greet her first.

"My lady . . . ," Corann began.

William smiled as the man fumbled over how to introduce them. Only he held the title of sir and he carried royal and noble blood in his veins. Brienne carried the noble blood of her father but was raised as the daughter of the village blacksmith. The priests, however, were too discomforted by addressing them by their names and always searched for some honorific because of who or what they were now.

Descendants of the gods and goddesses they worshipped.

"I am Brienne of Yester," William's mate said, stepping forward and offering her hand to the . . . sunblood. "I am a fireblood." The expression on the woman's face, which had been nervous but welcoming, was now shadowed with fear.

"Another fireblood?" she asked, glancing from Brienne to Corann.

"You know of the other?" Will asked, stepping closer. At the sight of him and, more likely his eyes, she took a step back away . . . and into Corann. Brienne stepped between them and gave him a dark glance.

"The other one is my father, Lord Hugh de Gifford." Brienne offered a soft smile to the woman, seeking to ease her fears. "He is not one of us."

"And I am . . . ," Will said as he offered his own hand in greeting, "I am William de Brus, the warblood." He felt the warblood trying to surge forward but held him back. This woman did not need to see that part of him yet.

"My husband," Brienne said.

The sunblood stared at him, meeting his gaze and searching it. The color around her calmed and became like the sun on a midsummer's day.

"My name is Elethea," she said softly. "Though you most likely know that from Corann."

"Aye, my lady," he said, bobbing his head in acknowledgment. "I did tell them your name."

"I am not of noble blood, Corann. I am not your 'lady.'"

"They, the priests, are not at ease with us, Elethea," Will explained. "For generations they have been raised to worship their gods and give reverence to their descendants, to those of us who carry the bloodlines. To address us by name is difficult. But they are working on that." He looked over at Corann, who looked no more at ease now than Elethea did.

"You are surrounded by blue, but your eyes," she began, staring at him once more, "are red?"

"A recent change," he said simply. "The warblood is here with me all the time. He sees in the red haze of war and blood."

"And the blue?" she asked. She shook her head. "My apologies for asking such things. This is all so new to me and I do not understand so much of it." Will smiled at her.

"We all understand, Elethea," he said. "We are all so recently called to rise and still have so many questions. We each seem to know parts of it or have only small bits of knowledge. Together, though, we are stronger." She nodded and a tentative smile lit her features then. "When the warblood truly rises, he is like a berserker of old. And like those ancient warriors who painted their skin blue, he is blue. So I carry his true color in my bloodline."

"Will you come back to our encampment so we can speak of this more openly?" Brienne asked. William's wife understood that standing on the edges of an abbey with its fine church and its many worshippers was not the best place to discuss such heretical things as other gods and the powers they passed down to their descendants. "It is just over across the river there. We will bring you back here whenever you wish."

Will doubted in that moment that she would come with them, though even showing up here to meet with Corann showed her interest in learning more. That did not guarantee she and the other one would join their cause and act against Hugh and the others who followed Chaela's plans, but it was a good start.

"I have many questions," Elethea said. "And would like to know more." She looked from Brienne to him and then to Corann before nodding her assent.

"Come, then, and we shall try to answer yours and learn more about you," Brienne said.

Will took up a position behind the others as they walked back to the river and the place where they'd be able to cross the river. Though Ran had offered to open a path for them across the rushing waters, Will and Corann urged caution at exposing their abilities here and now. Through the warblood's eyes he peered around the area as they moved away from the abbey, seeking any signs of danger or deception.

Elethea appeared to be much as he and Brienne and Ran and Soren had been at first encounter with each other—curious, nervous, and excited at finding others of their kind. Will lifted his face and sniffed the air for signs of threat, another ability the warblood gave him. Sensing none, he followed them to the boat and across the river.

Brienne spoke quietly to Elethea the whole way there, asking about her family and the village in which she lived. All things that were familiar to both women. Will's wife was trying to put this stranger at ease and was preparing her to meet the rest of their group.

Will looked past the three to those who now gathered waiting by their tents. Soren and Ran, outlined by the color of their powers, waited and watched.

Father Ander and a few of the other priests were close by. And his friends Roger and Gautier were nearest to him. Glancing for the one William thought would be the most curious, he found Aislinn and her guard standing behind the other priests.

The young woman had walked in a sort of confused grief since they arrived here. Without Marcus to guide her and to counsel her, Aislinn seemed to have lost her heart. She had asked them to wait before making their connection once more and he feared she did not wish the others to feel or sense her overwhelming loss. She raised her head then and he caught her gaze, offering a smile to acknowledge her pain.

In that moment, he noticed something he'd not seen before when looking at her—she seemed to shine. Not every moment, but at times, as she moved or as she looked off in the distance, he could see a distinct silvery brightness to her. He glanced at Brienne and saw her fiery outline. Elethea carried the golden yellow glow of the sunlight around her. Turning back to Aislinn, he saw it once more.

Did he only notice it now because he looked through the warblood's eyes? At the times when the warblood had risen before, they were in the middle of a battle or in danger and he'd not had time to pay attention to much else. Had it been there all along?

Or was Aislinn destined to play a much bigger role in their endeavor than they all suspected? Raised as a priestess and gifted with powerful gifts of prophecy and the sight, Aislinn had helped him and Brienne close and seal the first gateway they'd found. The young woman had helped them locate the second one and had foretold of the third.

When the drawings of Soren's grandfather had been read, the last two connected were the marks of the beast and the moon. A priest did not stand in the eighth position, so the four of the bloodlines had discussed its possible meaning. Now, seeing this change happening to Aislinn, Will was certain she was more than a seer. More than simply the priest to pray the words.

More than any of them understood.

Will turned his attention back to Elethea and walked forward to Brienne's side so that they might all talk with her. And discover more about her powers and that of the other one they had not yet met.

Thea stared in amazement as the people from the encampment came out to greet her. They stood in smaller groups around the area, some clearly warriors and others whose skills were not so apparent. But two took away her ability to breathe.

The man was tall and blond, the body of one who worked with the land clear in his stature and muscles. He gazed at her and she could almost imagine a storm swirling around him. The woman at his side was also blond and tall, taller than most women she'd seen, and she glowed with a turquoise aura. Remembering the vision she'd had, she thought that she knew which of the gods were their ancestors.

Though Brienne of Yester had put her mind of ease, Thea worried still over being here and saying too much to them. Tolan had wanted her to wait for him, but she convinced him to see to the safety of his son and cousin and she would see to this. Though he looked ready to argue with her, he acquiesced and went on his own way . . . and she met Corann at the abbey.

"This is Ran Sveinsdottir and Soren Thorson, Elethea," Brienne said, introducing her to the two. "They come from the island north of Scotland—Orkney, the lands of the Norse." Elethea accepted their greetings and nodded at each of them.

Brienne's warrior husband joined them then and stared at her again. Glancing to the others, she realized that both of the men's eyes had the eerie appearance of glowing as Tolan's did now. But did everyone see it as she did? Corann approached then, standing up straight and walking with ease, and bowed to her.

"I would introduce you to Father Ander," Corann said, tugging the shorter man closer. "He is also from Orkney, though he is one of your priests." Startled by the description and to find a Catholic priest in the midst of all this, she nodded at him.

"God works and brings others to His endeavors in mysterious ways, does he not, Elethea?"

"Clearly, Father," she said.

"Come this way and we can speak," Corann said, walking at her side as they moved through the camp. "These are our other priests. They have all come from the island I mentioned to you and will serve however we may."

When the group of about fifteen all looked at her with awe in their gazes and bowed, Thea did not know what to do. They believed her part of their gods. They believed she had powers. From their expressions and words of greeting, she thought their faith in her might be more than her own. All she knew she could do was somehow heal people. But they seemed to think she could do more.

"You are feeling well, Corann?" she asked. Observing and visiting those she helped was part of her duties, and this was the first time she'd seen someone so completely healed. As they walked, she opened to her new skill and observed him. All of the injuries and damage she'd seen there before was gone. Healed. Every part of him whole now.

"I am," he said with a smile and a nod. He appeared younger now, as though his pain had aged him as well.

Corann stopped now before a young woman, and before Thea could greet her or speak a word, the woman dropped to her knees and touched her forehead on the edge of Thea's gown.

"Sunblood," she whispered.

The pain that this young woman carried within her cried out to Thea. It took but a glance to tell that it was physical pain borne out of profound grief and loss. Before she knew what to do or say, she reached down and lifted the woman to stand. Suddenly, she knew her name was Aislinn and that she had lost the only man she considered her father. And his name was . . .

"Marcus gave his life in service to us and is blessed forever for his sacrifice, Aislinn," she said in another's voice. Her body heated and changed then, light bursting forth as she held on to this woman. "Remember him well. Honor his memory by remembering all he taught you." The rest was for her ears only, so Thea leaned in and whispered, "Aislinn of Cork, Marcus believed in you when he took you in and raised you. You are also blessed and will stand against evil. Be strong in this. He is always in your heart and in your soul."

When Thea released her, she realized that everyone was staring at her and Aislinn. Some, those without power, shielded their eyes as though a light too bright to watch had been shining there. Aislinn . . . how had she known this woman's name? Aislinn's eyes, now the color of moon glow, stared at her now and nodded at whatever words Thea had spoken to her. Stranger still, Thea did not recall everything she'd said.

The pain was gone from the young woman now. Oh, grief remained, for her loss had been great and terrible, but that would take time.

"Praise be!" Aislinn whispered before stepping away and moving aside.

Silence, a complete silence in which only the sounds of nature around them were heard, descended on the whole encampment then. She looked around and found shock, astonishment, and reverence in every gaze that met hers.

Sunblood. Praise be. The healing power of the sun. Belenus.

The words repeated and followed her every step until they reached a small clearing at the other side of the camp. Only the four others said nothing and watched her with compassion and understanding in their eyes. They trod the same path on which she and Tolan were embarking—from a simple person to something else. She could never imagine herself as a god or even one descended from that. When their small group that now also included several of the warriors stopped and a stool was offered to her, she asked her first question.

"Who was Belenus? I heard that name as I passed them by." She looked at each of them and then Corann answered her.

"Belenus is the god of life and order and healing. His touch is seen to be that of the sun's light on everything around us."

She nodded and thought on this knowledge. It made sense with everything she knew from Tolan and had experienced herself. But Tolan did not know much about the ancient ones, who had long since been relegated to a group of deities and had lost their individual names by his own ancestors. Cernunnos he knew. The other names he did not.

"Are you are each descended from others?" she asked.

"I am waterblood, from the goddess Nantosuelta," said Ran, the Norse woman.

"And I stormblood. From Taranis," Soren, the Norse man, said.

"Sucellus, the god of war," William de Brus said. "Warblood."

That left only Brienne, his wife.

"I am a fireblood, like my father and the goddess

he worships," Brienne said softly. "Saying her name upsets the priests, so I avoid it."

Thea could feel the fear in those listening and understood.

"Do you know the earthblood?" Aislinn asked. Everyone looked at Thea with an air of expectancy. She'd agreed with Tolan not to share more than was necessary, but they already knew his power.

"How did you know there would be an earthblood here?" she asked back.

"There were drawings made by my grandfather that showed your symbol and that of the earthblood's," Soren said.

"And the prophecy speaks of a caretaker and a bringer of life," Aislinn said. "If you are the bringer of life, then the earthblood is the caretaker."

"That is logical," William added.

"Not that logic always works in this, William," Father Ander said. "Sometimes it is with faith alone that we must tread along."

"Do you know the earthblood?" Aislinn repeated her question.

"I do," she said on a sigh. "I know the earthblood."

"And does he know you as well?" William asked. Thea understood why he'd asked it of her. Though peasants and villagers might be fully aware of the nobles they served, it was very possible that it might not be the same way round.

"Aye," she said. Brienne knew first, Thea saw it in her expression. Then Aislinn and Ran. The men, well, they were being men and did not.

"We should meet with both of you," Brienne said. "There is much to discuss and plans to make if we are to defeat my father."

"You would do such a thing? Against your own father?" Thea asked. "None of the gods I saw were . . ." She had let her inhibitions go lax and had spoken of something better not shared. The others glanced one at the other until the Norse woman spoke.

"When I touched the stones at an ancient circle, I saw a ceremony. A fertility ritual," Ran said.

Thea could not stop herself from touching her hand to her heated cheek at the memory of what she'd seen and felt.

"It ended in sacrifice."

Thea nodded, not trusting herself to speak.

"The gods with whom we share a bloodline were capricious and demanding," Soren said. Though Corann bristled, he continued. "They demanded service and sacrifice back when they lived here among us and even now."

"Sacrifice?" Thea asked. Surely not.

"We have lost many, in this battle against evil. Some died in the fighting, but others were sacrificed or offered up their own lives," William said. "My father," he began.

"And mine," Ran added.

"Friends and loved ones," Brienne said. "My mother, I suspect, was a victim of my father's aims."

"And faithful followers," Aislinn said.

"Your Marcus," Thea found herself adding. She'd seen the man's death in Aislinn's pain.

"If my father succeeds and he releases the goddess, thousands and thousands more will die." At Brienne's words, the priests began to chant, soft and low, but clearly praying that it would not happen. "So we must do everything in our power to stop him . . . and her."

Thea met each of their gazes then, the ones who carried the bloodlines, Father Ander, Corann, and the soldiers, and knew they spoke the truth. She knew they were trying to save humankind from a terrible evil. One that even Tolan's ancestors had been warned about and one that the circles on his lands kept away . . . or within. She nodded. "His name is Tolan."

CHAPTER 15

They'd arrived back in Amesbury village before dark and in time to stop Farold from returning to the cottage. Once he'd made arrangements for Kirwyn and Farold to hide from sight among various barns and outbuildings, he and Thea had sought their own refuge and slept for a few hours. Though his son initially argued, Tolan convinced him to follow his instructions for two days before leaving his hiding place and seeking him out.

The night passed in a flurry of furtive discussions and bouts of bed play. As though they both accepted that the next days would be dangerous for everyone they knew and loved, Tolan could not stop touching her. Even after she had drained him and he had exhausted her, he kept his hands on her body, drawing her close through the night, memorizing every inch of her. What he would remember most were the words spoken between them—a vow of love that he would hold on to until after they faced this reckoning ahead of them.

Tolan could not deny it—he had a terrible feeling about how this would play out. If he believed all the stories told to him over the years, this was not simply a family tradition but a war waged between good and evil. And he and his family had been and would be part of the eventual outcome.

By the time the sun rose above the horizon, they were on their way to the abbey, taking a circuitous route to avoid being seen. Thea convinced him that there would be no danger in meeting with the man on the sacred ground of the abbey, and Tolan trusted her judgment. So they decided together that she would meet with Corann and discover what she could about the others while he accepted the *invitation* issued by Lord Geoffrey's guest to learn what he could.

Thea going separately worried Tolan, but it could not be helped. And, though Geoffrey might speak her name, Tolan did not want the fireblood to see and know her yet.

She might be safe longer . . . .

Even now, as he approached the gateway in the wall surrounding the keep, he thought on the way Thea's brow gathered in close as he explained the history of his family as he knew it. Never did she scoff or mock. Her questions were logical and probing and made him think on things long-ago forgotten. Stories told by his grandfather's father. Bits of tales about the battle between good and evil.

He could not be certain if finding her was part of

some larger plan of the Fates or the gods, but he was thankful he had found her, for facing this challenge with her at his side made him feel as though they could win.

Tolan rode by the group of foreign soldiers who'd arrived with the fireblood. They did not react to his approach, so he passed by and nodded to the guards above the gate. He'd traveled this path countless times in his life and yet this time it was all so different. He noticed the other men camped within the walls now. He tried to count the number of the soldiers as he went through the yard. Too soon he was at the steps leading into the keep.

He felt the fireblood then, an awareness or disturbance in his thoughts, and his body told him of the other man's nearness. With each pace he took, the sensations grew stronger. There had been an awareness of Thea and yet it was completely different from what he now felt passing through him. Tolan cleared his thoughts of her and made his way into the great hall.

He had expected someone who looked less like a man, like a demon of some sort, and he was wrong. The man sitting in Lord Geoffrey's chair at the high table looked like most noblemen Tolan had encountered or seen in his life. Well, if truth be told, this man was wealthier and more powerful than any he'd seen.

The blast of heat came out of nowhere and Tolan struggled to remain upright in the face of it. By no change of expression or movement of his body did the man give any sign that it came from him. The fireblood's eyes glowed with an unholy light for a few moments and then the heat dissipated and his eyes changed to what most would see—except that they were an unusual amber color.

Tolan walked closer, waiting for another attack, but none came and he soon stood below the dais before the two nobles. He paused before meeting the man's gaze and bowed as he would be expected to do. He waited then, hands clenched in anticipation.

"Tolan," Lord Geoffrey called out. "Come. Have you broken your fast?"

A warm welcome was not what Tolan had expected. He shook his head and climbed up the five steps to the table where the men sat waiting. Finally, he raised his gaze.

"Lord Hugh is my kinsman from Normandy," Lord Geoffrey said, waving Tolan to a seat on his right. "He said he encountered you on the road north of here."

"My lord," Tolan said, bowing once more before accepting the proffered place. "I thank you for this consideration."

Once he was seated, the servants brought him a bowl in which to wash his hands, a custom he knew. Then a trencher and a cup of ale were placed before him and soon filled with a hearty porridge and several others dishes. The conversation was light and mostly about farming as Lord Geoffrey touted Tolan's abilities to his kinsman. There was a short discussion about the fecundity of his lands over time and even some murmurings about making an offer to buy them. Lord Hugh added a few well-placed questions about the length and breadth of Tolan's lands, but otherwise allowed Lord Geoffrey to continue talking. Finally, after they'd eaten, Lord Hugh made his move.

"Cousin, I wish to speak to your man . . . alone," he began. "With your permission, of course."

If Lord Geoffrey thought it strange, he gave no sign of it. Rather, Tolan suspected this whole meeting had been arranged step by step well in advance of his arrival in the hall this morn. And that Lord Hugh was the one in control of all of this, including his cousin.

"Certainly," Lord Geoffrey said. "I will wait on your return here."

Lord Hugh stood and so did Tolan, for it was a practice and a courtesy first learned as a child. Tolan waited for him to walk past and then followed him, anxious now to learn the truth of this matter. But, instead of going into one or another of the chambers leading off the hall, or even going outside into the yard, Lord Hugh led him up the stairway and high into the north tower. Soon, they reached the top and Lord Hugh opened the door that led to the battlements of the keep. The guards there saw who had arrived and left, pulling the door closed tightly behind themselves.

Tolan watched as the nobleman separated himself and walked around the perimeter, stopping several times to peer off into the distance. Was he preparing himself to attack Tolan again? How could he battle fire and heat? Certainly not by becoming a tree or plant. So he would have to change into something of the earth. His gaze had begun to fringe with green when Lord Hugh faced him.

"I did not expect to find another descendant whose family had kept faith with the Old Ones."

Whatever he had expected, these words surprised Tolan. "My lord?"

"Come, now, we can dispense with the disingenuous words, can we not? My family has passed their faith down through countless generations, as yours has. If they had not, neither of us would be where we are now."

"And where would that be, my lord?" Tolan asked, crossing his hands over his chest.

"Our blood has risen. Our powers are growing. We are preparing to open the gateway so we can worship our rightful goddess." Lord Hugh raised an eyebrow, challenging him to disclaim his words.

"I was raised only to protect the lands, my lord. I know nothing of a plan to open a gateway. Or of the goddess you speak of."

And he spoke the truth—he did not. The stories passed to him had told only of good and evil. Of protecting all the lands but especially those now possessed by his family. Of waiting for *the time to come*.

"I think you speak the truth," Lord Hugh said after studying him for a few moments. "Then let me tell you of our history and the great quest that lies ahead for us and our kind."

Could he speak honestly with him?

By the strength of the spells placed on the lands that were held by his family, Hugh thought Tolan would have been fully versed in their ways and practices. The knowledge of their true natures and the extent of their powers. The worship of the Old Ones and their warnings.

Instead, this man appeared to have gained use of his powers without being fully taught. The fertility of the lands under his care could not have occurred by luck or offhand chances. As his cousin had explained, the records kept for hundreds of years demonstrated Tolan's family's successes here on this land. Hugh had no doubt that it went back and back even further to times long before records, long before Normans or Saxons, before the ancient Romans.

So Hugh chose his words carefully now, knowing this was one way of getting everything he needed with nothing but a conversation.

"Our ancestors worshipped the old gods who existed since the dawn of time. You know that much," he began. "But when one goddess, Chaela, questioned their ways and their excesses among their human followers, she was attacked. Only by banding together did the others overp—imprison her. She lies in an abyss, deep within the earth and yet existing in another place. As her descendant, I seek a gateway to that prison."

"And that is what lies on my lands? Beneath the soil?" Tolan asked him.

Hugh kept to the truth as much as possible, for it was far easier than concocting and keeping to too many lies. "Aye. There are four of them, each surrounded or disguised by a circle of standing stones," Hugh explained. "Is there a circle within the barrier?"

"More than one," the earthblood answered. "But buried deep beneath the surface now."

"Have you seen the circles? Walked among them?" Hugh asked.

"Nay," Tolan said, shaking his head. He glanced off in the distance. "I think I may have when I was a small child. I think I did. . . ." So this one's father or grandfather had held enough power to move the earth? He must succeed with this man.

"Opening any of them would free her," Hugh said. "But two descendants of different bloodlines must perform the ceremony to open a gate."

"This is the first one you have attempted, then?"

Hugh tried to practice the patience he'd learned at his father's hand. He could feel the strength within this one and knew this earthblood could conquer lands and destroy cities with the flick of his hand. Mountains could be leveled. Palaces brought to ground. And Hugh desperately wanted him at his side and not against him. After all, Cernunnos had created the prison with but his thoughts alone and surely he could destroy it the same way?

"Nay. We have tried two others, but the descendants of the other gods sealed both of them first. They do not know that in the eons that have passed, Chaela has learned the lesson the Old Ones meant to teach her in this. She is ready to take her place here among them as they wanted her to do so long ago. As the descendant of Cernunnos, you have the ability to open this gateway."

Tolan watched him closely as he spoke, so Hugh

kept a placid expression on his face. He must convince not only the earthblood but also the sunblood to aid him in this. Geoffrey had spoken of Tolan's connection to the village healer, and Hugh knew she must be the other one he sought.

"How is this done?" Tolan asked.

"A ritual where blood is spilled on the altar stone and then poured onto the barrier to break the spell that holds her within it. Worry not on that, Tolan. I need you and the sunblood to agree to help me, to help the goddess, to restore the balance that should exist among those with the power over all things on earth."

If Hugh had not been watching carefully when he mentioned the sunblood, he would have missed the slight narrowing of Tolan's eyes. But he saw it and it confirmed everything he had suspected after questioning Geoffrey about this man and his connection to the woman who carried the blood of Belenus in her. If Tolan had claimed the sunblood as his mate, that would explain the strength of their powers now.

And it gave Hugh a weapon to use against him if needed.

Once again, their ignorance would play against them and he would exploit it if necessary. Though, as Hugh watched this one consider his words, he almost hoped Tolan would join him of his own accord. That would allow Hugh to show the earthblood the full extent of what lay dormant within him even now. He'd had the same hope with his daughter and had begun that training with her, but it had been a complete failure.

This did not have to be.

Having the abilities and powers of the earth and sun, the two most powerful of all the ancients, at Hugh's side—and Chaela's—would make them invincible. He could not stop the shiver of anticipation that moved through his body, nor the torment that followed from his back.

"I will think on this, my lord," Tolan finally said.

"Call me by my given name, Tolan. We are equals in too many ways to fall back to the expected courtesies of those who will serve the gods once more."

Hugh held out his hand now in greeting, as he would to those of the highest status in the land. Tolan hesitated for only a moment before grasping it in return. The earthblood wanted what Hugh and the goddess offered. He wanted . . . more. As the man stepped back and turned to leave, Hugh called out to him.

"Two days, Tolan," he said. "I need an answer in two days."

"Why?" the man asked.

"The others gather to the south and prepare to destroy the circle you protect. We must open it first or they will."

The earthblood's eyes widened and he nodded. Hugh watched him walk away, feeling the waves of power coming off him. Tolan had no idea. Simply no idea of what he truly carried in his blood. And Hugh intended to keep him ignorant for as long as possible.

At least until Chaela once again walked the earth.

To make that happen, Hugh understood now that he would need a means to his end—something or someone to use to ensure that Tolan and his sunblood cooperated. Hugh walked to the edge of the battlements and watched as Tolan mounted his horse and road through the gates toward the village.

There was the sunblood herself, but Hugh could not risk harming her. Holding her would gain Tolan's attention. But Hugh needed something to bring him to heel like a well-behaved bitch. For that, he needed someone else. Someone who could not fight back or defend himself against Hugh.

Hugh smiled as Tolan disappeared into the heavily wooded village.

Someone like a cousin . . . or a son.

Hugh did not bother to send soldiers to follow Tolan now, as Geoffrey had done. He knew where the man would eventually turn up. From the curiosity in his voice and in his questions, Hugh suspected that Tolan would try to uncover the stones next.

Then the true battle would begin.

CHAPTER 16

Thea waited near the abbey for Tolan to meet her.

She'd spent most of the morning in the encampment across the river, and, true to their word, they brought her back here when she asked. Though they seemed guarded over some matters, she was surprised by how much they had shared.

Whether they were right or misguided, she could tell that they believed they were on the side of right in this situation. Thea had felt the pain suffered by the losses they'd mentioned.

Their need was plainly spoken—they asked her to bring Tolan to them so that they could all work to defeat the goddess whose followers threatened the future of everything she knew. Though convinced by what she'd witnessed within the circle—that all of the ancient ones worshipped as gods were both good and bad—the stories told of the one called Chaela were more than that.

But they told of a power out of control and driven by a hunger that would not be appeased or satisfied until anyone who threatened or questioned her was destroyed.

They spoke of an inherently evil creature who held nothing sacred except her own desires and aims. Even the Catholic priest agreed with them.

So, did it mean that the fate of everyone alive and those yet to come sat in her and Tolan's hands? How could that be possible? How could the two of them, raised in a village, now be so important in all this?

As though her thoughts had conjured him, Tolan walked toward her, the reins to two horses in his hand. He smiled at her and nodded. Even from here, she could see that his eyes glowed, as those of the other men had. And she knew now that most everyone could not see them do that. Only those of power or those who were marked with one of the signs could.

Tolan reached her and pulled her into his embrace. She would never tire of being held by him. Or kissed by him. Or being loved by him. No matter what came in the days ahead, she would treasure every moment. And she knew in her heart and soul that she would do whatever was necessary to protect him. She drew back and reached up to touch his face, caressing his cheek.

"I find that any separation is too long to be away from you," he admitted. Glancing around at where they stood, he smiled again. "Come. Let us get away from here."

She grabbed his hand and tugged him to stop.

"They wish to speak with you," she said, nodding

back toward the river and the camp. "They asked me to bring you there."

"You spoke with them?"

She nodded.

"You spoke of me?"

Another nod.

"Was that wise?" he asked.

"Tolan, they knew so much more than we do," she explained, nodding once more. "I only gave your name. I did not share anything else about you. Only about me."

She'd spent time with their wounded and suffering. A terrible battle with the human followers of Chaela had resulted in many injuries and some deaths. Thea could help the battered and bruised and did so for them.

"There are four of them there," she said. "Can you feel them?" She waited and watched as he closed his eyes and breathed in deeply.

"Many more than the four," he said. "Dozens and dozens, like those Lord Hugh has with him at the keep."

"You met him?" She shivered at the thought of someone who would forsake everything good, including his own flesh and blood, to carry out this war. "What is he like?"

"A nobleman. I did not expect him to appear so . . . human after feeling the power he has. And with him controlling fire, I expected . . . a demonlike creature."

She shuddered at the thought and crossed herself. "His own daughter fights against him, Tolan."

He startled at that, surely thinking of him and Kirwyn being opposed to each other. And the seriousness of such a thing. Tolan stood in silence for a few moments, his body tense and his eyes glowing. "Take me to them."

She nodded and they walked hand in hand toward the river. The others stood waiting for them there, watching as they reached the bank. Instead of using the boat tied there, Tolan led her and the horses into the river. Without Tolan's seeming to exert himself, the ground beneath the flowing water rose until they could make their way across it.

When the horses balked, he tugged their reins tightly and led them the final steps. Thea turned back to look where they'd walked and saw that the river flowed deep and fast as it usually did. He smiled then and squeezed her hand. As they reached the group of four, his smile disappeared.

"Tolan, this is Sir William de Brus and his wife, Brienne." She nodded at the tallest of the men and the lovely black-haired woman beside him. William offered his hand in greeting, carrying all the bearing of a nobleman, and Tolan accepted it.

"You look familiar to me," Tolan said softly, examining Brienne closely. Her flame-colored outline shone brightly then.

"You have met my father, no doubt," Brienne answered curtly. "We have the same coloring." Though she might have meant the color of their hair and eyes, it was also true for the coloring that outlined her body.

"Lord Hugh?" Tolan asked. Then he nodded, realizing that this was the daughter of whom Thea had spoken. "I have met him."

As Thea watched, William began to change, growing taller, wider, and more muscular . . . and blue! The changes and the growling sound that he made scared the horses away. Thea understood how they felt.

"William," Brienne said, placing her hand on the warblood, "all is well. We knew Hugh would seek him out." The warrior transformed once more, turning back into a simple man, though his eyes remained red.

"What did he say?" William asked, his voice somewhere between speaking and growling.

"We know what he said," Soren said, stepping forward to greet Tolan. "He told you a tale of a wronged goddess and his attempts to free her."

Tolan nodded.

"What other lies did he try to woo you with?" Soren turned and spat on the ground as the winds began to whip around them.

Clouds that had not been in the sky before gathered overhead. Thea glanced above and, with a thought, pushed the clouds aside to let the sunlight pass through once more. The others turned to her and Tolan raised an eyebrow.

"This is Soren Thorson and his wife, Ran," Brienne added before Tolan could answer. "They are from Orkney."

"So you are the four who sealed two of the gateways?" Tolan asked. The four nodded.

"Along with the help of the priests and my men," William added. "And not without a terrible cost. Hugh will sacrifice anyone who stands against him or help anyone who does."

Thea could see Tolan considering their words and knew that 'twas not his custom of doing things to immediately accept or deny another's words or request. He would listen and think on it and decide. They had done that together before they'd gone off separately, and she knew they would again when he finished hearing their reasoning.

The next hour passed slowly as the other four answered every question he asked—about their powers, about the ritual needed, and about their lives before and after finding out their true nature and their history. Many of them were the same ones she'd just asked, but they did not seem bothered to repeat their knowledge to him. Finally, when the bells of the abbey across the river chimed out that it was time for the holy office of sext, Tolan stood and thanked them.

Although the others seemed willing to let him, them, leave, Corann walked closer and spoke to them.

"What will you do?" the priest asked. The tone of his words was more challenge than question.

"I need some time to speak with Elethea about this. It involves her risking her life as well as my own and I will not become part of it until I know the truth."

"But, my son," Father Ander said, "they have spoken the truth to you."

"And Hugh has spoken his," Tolan replied.

Soren charged Tolan then, and as Thea watched in horror, the warblood rose again to his astounding and terrifying height and strode across the clearing toward them. Corann grabbed her and tugged her aside, clearly fearing the worst. In that moment, though, it was the

Catholic priest who stood his ground, stepping between the three men and shouting until they stopped.

"William! Soren!" he yelled. "Be at peace, my friends!" Father Ander pushed and pushed, even at the huge war-blood, until they all stepped back. "Peace, I say unto you."

Out of breath from fighting all three, the priest pointed at each of them and motioned for them to remain away. When he caught his breath, he sighed.

"Each of you had to make your own decision over this quest. It must be freely chosen and knowingly entered. Give them a chance to contemplate what they have heard," he advised. Everyone stepped back then and accepted the priest's admonishments.

"I do have one more question," Tolan said as the horses were brought to them. "If this ritual requires a priest and none of yours will help him, where does the fireblood get the one he needs?"

"We know not," Corann said. "Unless there are more like Ander, people raised near the stones who did not know of their place in this?"

"Are there many of those?" Thea asked. She'd never thought about the necessary priest, either. Surely the fireblood would.

"Until Einar and Ander, we thought we were the only ones of the priestly calling. Only those born on the island were raised to know the ways of our faith," Corann explained.

"And me." Aislinn stepped forward as she spoke. "I was not born there."

The priests watching all drew in their breaths at

the same moment, resulting in a loud gasp. Every one of them turned to the young woman. Her words had been either a shock or something forbidden for her to say. What had she revealed?

"So there may be more priests than we know of, Corann," Aislinn finished.

"Pray to the gods, he does not find one to do his bidding, Aislinn," Corann said.

Tolan reached out to Thea and she took his hand. Whatever they did, they were doing this together. Thea had no doubt of their decision, but Tolan wished to speak to her about it and she was pleased. Jasper never asked her opinion or gave her a choice in any matter affecting her. To be valued and to have her thoughts taken seriously meant so much to her.

If only . . .

They rode north in silence. She knew their destination without a word spoken. With a glance, she kept the clouds away and the day warm and sunny. She could not move the earth or become other things, but at least her gift would keep the day a good one for traveling.

Geoffrey paced the length and breadth of his chamber again. He'd lost count of how many times he'd completed the twelve paces north to south and the fifteen paces east to west. It mattered not.

Nothing mattered now.

He was a dead man.

His cousin did not forgive or forget. He mostly did what he wanted and everyone did as he said or got out of his way. They had grown up as boys on the family estates in Normandy and Brittany, and Geoffrey had been brought into the family's true endeavor as a boy.

And Geoffrey had understood his place and he had accepted his role in their ancient faith and plans. When ordered to move here and marry, he had done so without question, and he'd taken over the lands that his family had held for untold generations.

When his cousin had sent word for him to be watchful, for the time had come for the rising of the bloodlines, he had been. He'd noticed something different about Tolan years ago and suspected he would play a part in this. When Hugh had demanded he search for a circle of standing stones, he went. He traveled for weeks and weeks using everything and everyone at his disposal to try to locate the one.

He'd even taken Tolan along, hoping he would give some sign of his knowledge. Geoffrey should not be held accountable if the man did not.

He stopped his pacing and drank deeply from the cup on the table at his bedside. Rich wine from the vineyards in Brittany filled his mouth and refreshed his dry throat. But it would not help what he would face when his cousin discovered the secret he carried.

Walking to the branch of candles near the door, he tugged the sleeve of his robe up and gazed on the mark that would mean his death. Not one like his cousin's, showing that he carried the blood of the fire goddess within in. Nay, that would have been a sign of the truth of his life—he worshipped her, as did every other male in their family.

Nay, he was marked as something else entirely. His skin had burned and blistered into the form of a man, sketched in small streaks.

The mark of the priests.

The priests who worshipped Chaela's enemies.

He thrust his fingers into his hair and held his head, moaning out in pain and fear. Falling to his knees, Geoffrey tried to think of a way out of this terrible predicament.

He could not and would not betray his cousin or their family, especially not when he knew the consequences of such betrayal. Geoffrey had watched with his own eyes as Hugh had called forth his power and burned men to ashes with a word or a glance. He shook now, unable to control the fear at his fate.

So caught up in his misery was he that the door opening caught him unawares. He jumped to his feet and faced Hugh as he entered the chamber unbidden and uninvited.

"What ails you, Geoffrey? Your cries can be heard down the corridor," his cousin said, staring at him. "Should I call that healer from the village?"

He'd already told Hugh about the woman who shared Tolan's bed, the one he'd been watching for years, and who gave every sign of being a bloodline. Her abilities had soared recently and her outrageous successes were being spoken of through the village and the keep. And when Tolan suggested marriage to her, Geoffrey intervened as he knew he must.

"Nay," he said, shaking his head as he stood before the man who would speak a word and end his life.

Geoffrey could not see a way out of this now and the place on his arm burned again to remind him of his fate. How did one throw oneself on the mercy of someone who had none?

"Hugh. Cousin. My lord," he finally said, "I have always been faithful to you and our family and our goddess. You know this to be true," he added, bowing low. "I beg you. . . ."

"What have you done, Geoffrey?" Hugh said through clenched teeth as he pulled him up by the front of his tunic. "What is this about?"

The chamber grew hot and hotter still as Geoffrey's cousin glared through narrowed eyes at him. The hand that held his garments in a choke hold glowed red and heat poured off it, aimed at Geoffrey's chest. He must speak quickly if there was any chance at survival.

"I swear it is not something I chose. I did not. Hugh, I would not."

"Tell me now. What is this about? What is not your fault?"

"This, my lord," Geoffrey said as he held out his arm and showed his cousin the newly burned area there.

Sheer and utter silence slammed down around him, and the only sound he heard was that of his own labored breathing. Nothing moved. Hugh did not grasp him tighter or release him. Hugh's gaze then began to shift back and forth, from Geoffrey's arm to his face. Over and over until Hugh suddenly released him and he fell to the floor. Geoffrey remained there as the strangest expression fell over his cousin's gaze.

Geoffrey had once seen a man being treated for a palsy by the brothers at the abbey. The man had gone into strange and unusual fits. One moment or for several minutes even, he remained completely still, almost statuelike in his bearing. Then, without warning, the man would drop to the ground, rolling and contorting and frothing at the mouth like a madman.

Was that affliction now in control of Hugh? Geoffrey watched without moving or speaking to see if Hugh would fall into the convulsions next. He did not. Instead, he did something even stranger. Hugh began to laugh.

He laughed loud and hard, bending over at his waist without regard to his appearance. Guards appeared at the door to inquire, but Geoffrey waved them off from where he lay. He thought he might not die this day, though he dared not draw attention yet.

The laughs turned into choking coughs and then loud gasps of what seemed to be pain as his cousin tried to regain control over himself. Hugh's breaths were sucked in deeply and exhaled forcefully and followed by grimaces of agony. Several minutes later, he climbed to his feet and motioned for Geoffrey to do the same. His reprieve over, Geoffrey stood and waited.

"You have no idea, do you, Geoffrey?" Hugh said, not really asking a question. "None at all."

"Nay, my lord."

"This," he said, taking Geoffrey's arm and pointing to the figure there, "this is a better thing than anything you have ever done in your life."

Geoffrey frowned and looked more closely at it. He

thought his cousin would rather it be the mark of the flames, like the one Hugh carried on his arm. That would mean Geoffrey could help his cousin in more effective ways.

"Now you are second in importance only to the earthblood and sunblood. You can carry out the ritual and speak the words to open the barrier. Your name will be proclaimed as the one who freed the goddess." Hugh had begun to glow in shades of fiery orange. Geoffrey blinked several times, but it did not go away.

"I am? I will?" So confused by this turnabout in his life, he nodded in acceptance of whatever Hugh said. Hugh reached out and took Geoffrey by the shoulders.

"We needed one who carries the mark of man, a priest, to open the gateway and now we have one." Hugh smiled, the first genuine one Geoffrey ever re- membered seeing on his cousin's face. "This changes everything."

"It does?" he asked, trying to grab ahold of any- thing that would make sense.

"Aye. I have been struggling to find a way to bring one of their priests to our cause, but they are willing to die rather than help us. I have delayed pressing the earthblood and sunblood into it because I did not have a priest."

Geoffrey was intelligent enough not to mention the large hole in this plot, that he had no training and had not the knowledge of how to complete the ritual. If Hugh thought this was a good thing, Geoffrey would not argue it or ask questions. If it meant staying alive, he would do whatever Hugh asked of him. Not many could claim to be in Hugh's favor, so Geoffrey smiled and nodded. "Aye. Now you have a priest."

Hugh let out another barking laugh and strode to the doorway, calling the guards back in. He gave several short, direct orders to the men and then nodded at Geoffrey. "Now we can force Tolan to cooperate. He will not have a choice at all. Not once I have his son in my custody."

Tolan valued nothing more in his life than his son, Kirwyn, and everyone knew it. As Hugh strode out, Geoffrey hoped Tolan would capitulate quickly and do as Hugh commanded. Geoffrey had seen the results of resistance to Hugh's plan and will, and none had been less than deadly.

The only thing that might keep Tolan's son alive was Tolan's cooperation. For once, as Geoffrey left the chamber to follow his cousin, he was thankful that he'd never had a child who could be used as Hugh's pawn.

Gods help the boy.

CHAPTER 17

He did not wait very long before the need to hold her grew too strong to resist. Tolan slowed his horse and waited for her to stop at his side. Reaching over, he lifted her easily onto his lap.

Though surprise shone from her dark brown eyes as she met his gaze, she did not hesitate to accept his arms or his embrace.

He loved that about her. She was open to him in a way he'd never expected, considering her recent past. He'd seen people who had been beaten and abused and they rarely trusted anyone and they especially did not accept physical contact. If she shied away from others, he'd not seen it. And once she had accepted him into her life and her bed, she never had resisted his touch.

Tolan was about to urge his horse on when he realized that the only thing he knew for certain after all the shocking revelations of the recent days was . . .

Her.

He loved Elethea in a way so different from what he'd felt for Corliss. And on the morrow or when they faced this great evil, he knew he might lose her. He slid his leg over his horse and dismounted. Once on the ground he helped her down and took her in his arms.

"Thea, I know that you do not wish to marry me," he began.

"I do not wish to marry, Tolan. It is not you." She reached up and placed her fingers over his lips to stop him.

The same argument again, but it would not, could not, stand this day. Tolan released her and walked a few paces to give her some room for this discussion. "I know what Jasper did to you, Thea. I know that you nearly died."

Her face lost all color at his words and the golden shimmer surrounding her shifted and quivered.

"I am not him. I would never raise a hand to you," he promised. "You know that." She nodded but did not look certain about anything at that moment. "But there is something else stopping you in this. It is not that. So tell me what it is," he said.

"Tolan," she said, shaking her head. "Let this go, I pray you."

"If I believe everything we have heard this day, and I suspect more of it to be true than not, then we face terrible danger. I want to face it with you at my side."

"I will be at your side," she assured him. "I will be there through whatever comes." Her promise was not enough.

"I want you as my wife before we take another step, Thea." Tolan met her gaze and saw the fear there. "Tell me what holds you back. Tell me."

He watched her struggle right before his eyes. The usually assured woman disappeared and the cowed woman he would witness in the village after one of her husband's fits of anger appeared now. Tolan had forgotten how much he hated it. He'd hated it when it had happened—in spite of having no standing or right to a concern about her at the time. And he hated it now, for it marked the success of her husband's attempts to break her.

"Tolan, I am not worthy to be a man's wife," she whispered. The defeated tone in her voice hurt to hear.

"Not worthy?" he asked. "You who saved Linne and brought Medwyn safely into this world? You who healed old Rigby and their priest? You are not worthy?" He wanted to take her in his arms and kiss her until she relented, but she must take this step of her own volition.

"I know that you value your son more than anything in this world, Tolan," she began. "And I know it is important for you to have more children, for the caretaking of the lands and now to pass on this power we know exists."

"Aye, I want children, Thea. And so do you."

"I want children so much it hurts to look at them in the village. It tears me apart when I help to birth or bury them, Tolan." Now she walked toward him and he clenched his hands into fists to keep from touching her.

"But I cannot have a baby. I cannot give birth to the

children that you want and need." Thea reached across the space dividing them and touched his cheek. "No matter how much I wish it, it cannot happen."

The devastated expression in her eyes told him that this was the true reason for her refusal. Whatever damage Jasper had done, this was the terrible result to her. One that apparently even her skills as a healer could not treat. He would not burden her by arguing over it or asking more questions of her.

The question that mattered now was whether it made a difference to him. It took less time than he thought to come to the answer to that.

Thea watched him ride away, stunned by and yet not certain of what had just happened. He'd walked to the horses, handed her the reins of hers, and mounted his. A mumbled demand that she remain here was all he said. Looking around the place where they'd stopped, just north of the abbey's lands but not yet near their village, she found a large rock near the edge of the woods and sat on it.

Her heart ached then, reminding her that she knew what his reaction would be long ago. It was why she dreaded having to reveal her failing to him. Though she knew she could never be the wife he needed, a part of her felt lighter somehow at having released the secret from within.

He'd not responded at all. He'd just watched her with those gleaming eyes as she spoke the words that ended any possibility of a future between them. And then left.

At least now there was honesty between them. At least they would face the dangers ahead understanding that they could not be together if they survived. And she would treasure whatever time they had together for the dark, lonely days later.

Leaning back against the trunk of a tree behind her, she tugged her kerchief from her head and closed her eyes. God's truth, she was weary. What with the nights with Tolan and the miles they'd crossed and the things that had happened to her and them, Thea thought a few minutes rest would not be amiss while she waited for Tolan's return.

The next thing she remembered was hearing the sound of approaching horses. Rubbing her eyes and trying to wake, she saw three horses and riders galloping toward her. Fear filled her for a moment until she recognized Tolan leading the two others. It took only another minute before he reached her and slowed to a halt, waiting for the other to arrive.

Father Ander. Corann.

She stood to greet the priests as they climbed down from their mounts, and she noticed that her hands shook now, with her not knowing what to expect. Tolan walked toward her, and this time he took her in his arms and kissed her, claiming her in a most inappropriate manner before the two holy men. She regained her wits and pushed him away.

"Tolan!" she said while nodding to Father Ander and Corann. "Why did you bring them here?" She had an insane thought at first. However, she did not dare to give it credence.

"The others wanted to come, but I did not want too many witnessing my shame," he said. "If you refuse me again."

"What others?" she asked, watching as something like merriment entered his gaze, though it remained green. She knew his goal now and held her breath, her heart pounding against her chest.

"To be honest, Elethea," Father Ander said, "most everyone at the encampment wished to be here."

"Especially William, Brienne, Soren, and Ran," Cor-ann said.

"And Aislinn and Roger and the rest of the priests," Tolan added. He walked to her and took her hands in his, leaning closer so the two would not hear. "I want to marry you, Thea. Be mine?"

Her heart soared at his words. He knew her truth and yet would still commit to marriage with her.

"But, Tolan—" she began to explain.

Now he placed his fingers on her lips to stop her words. "Be my wife, Elethea. Be at my side as you are in my heart."

He knew the moment she accepted, for the light around her became blinding. Father Ander and Cor-ann shielded their eyes from it, but Tolan did not look away. He would memorize this expression for all time.

She did not feel worthy of him.

That had been her excuse to reject his previous proposals. She believed she was less a woman and less a marriageable woman because her ability to bear children had been beaten from her. She did not consider the amount of courage it had taken for her to survive her brutal husband and take back control of her life.

"I will be your wife, Tolan," she whispered to him. She rose and kissed his mouth. "If you are certain?" she asked again.

"I am."

"Ah," Father Ander said. "Do you wish it to be a Catholic ceremony? Or should Corann bless it as his people do?"

He looked at Thea for her opinion and she nodded, understanding what he wanted.

"Both?" he asked.

Father Ander and Corann exchanged a few words and nodded. Tolan had been told that these two had recently stood witness at the marriage of Ran and Soren in Orkney, a marriage that had been delayed more than two years because of mistakes and betrayals and mistrust.

"What do we do now?" she asked.

"We marry."

Within a few, quiet minutes they spoke their vows to the priest in their own faith and then accepted the blessings of another. Now she was his, to love, to claim, to protect.

And all of that must begin soon. He asked for a moment with his new wife and took her hand, leading her off so that their words would be private.

"We will help them?" Thea asked before he could speak on the matter that faced them. "I have not met Brienne's father, so you must tell me of him before we commit ourselves."

We. He liked the sound of it.

"He presents himself as though he would ally himself with us, Thea. But even I could sense the evil and deception at his core." Tolan shook his head. "I think that we must help the others, whether or not we understand all this or not. We must stand against evil."

She shivered then and nodded. "We must."

Tolan took her hand and turned back to the priests.

"We will join your cause," he said. "We go ahead to Durrington to uncover the stones. Bring the others and we will seal the gateway."

The two men stood still then, as though listening to something. Then they nodded in unison.

"We have a link forged between us, as the priests learned to do many generations ago. We told the others that it is time," Corann explained. "They will meet you there, though Ran and Soren can get there sooner."

"All of you are . . . ?" he began. A link?

"In your thoughts?" Thea asked. "Between you?"

"Aye, in our thoughts," Father Ander said. "Not all of us—all of the priests used to be so connected, but Hugh discovered it and used it against them."

Corann looked away then and Tolan suspected he had been used against them. It would explain the broken bones and other injuries that Thea had spoken of.

"So now only a few of us are so blessed," Corann said softly. "Those of the bloodlines, Ander, myself, and the warrior Roger." He glanced away again and once more the priest nodded. His tone now became lighter. "Though the humans have a more difficult time learning the boundaries of such a thing." Corann smiled then, as did Father Ander. Then their faces darkened and a shudder passed through them.

"Brienne asked if there was anyone who needed protection," Corann said. "She said her father would use whomever he could against you."

"Kirwyn," Tolan and Thea said at the same time.

"I must go to him," Tolan said, releasing her hand.

"Nay!" Father Ander said. "You must not return to the village now. Seek your lands and uncover the circle."

"William will seek him out and take him to the encampment. He will be safe there," Corann said.

Tolan told them where Kirwyn and Farold were hiding and also gave them instructions that his son would recognize as his own, so the headstrong boy and their cousin would accompany them to safety.

"Which of you will guide us through the ritual?" Thea asked. The priests looked at each other and then back at him and Thea.

"Neither," Corann answered. "Aislinn is the seer. 'Tis for her to do."

"I thought you said you helped to open the one in Orkney, Father?" Thea asked.

"Aye. But I was not called to do it, I was forced." Father Ander shrugged. "According to Marcus, the priest who led them here, Aislinn is the one prophesied to seal the gateways."

Marcus was their leader until he'd sacrificed himself to save Father Ander. Now Corann stood in that position, though clearly he was learning the way of leadership while healing from his horrendous injuries. The two turned once more to leave, but Corann called back to them just before they urged their horses forward.

"Aislinn thinks that Hugh will know the moment you uncover the stones. So wait for us to be there."

"By dawn," Tolan said. The priests nodded and rode away.

Tolan stood at Thea's side and watched them ride back to the camp where the others would be preparing to travel north.

"They value her," Thea said, "and obey her commands."

He'd seen the huge guard who walked only a pace or two from the young woman. No one else in their group had a guard such as that. And no one else in their group spoke to him.

"Then we should do as she says," he agreed.

Before he was ready to leave this place, the place where they had spoken the words that joined their lives and hearts to each other, he needed and wanted to consummate those vows.

She walked into his arms and lifted her face to him as she always did. He touched his mouth to hers, slanting his head and slipping his tongue inside hers when she opened. He felt her hands slide around him, caressing his back and pressing her body and its curves against him.

"Husband," she whispered against his mouth as she met his gaze. Her eyes shone like sunlight, and her body warmed in his embrace. Leaning back, she smiled. "I never thought to use that word again in my lifetime, Tolan."

"I am gladdened that you chose me for it." He kissed her once more, wanting to be inside her now. Unfortunately, they did not have time for this.

"A few minutes, husband, is all we need." Had she heard his thoughts? Or was his desire so obvious?

"More like an hour's time." He challenged her assertion that he would be spent in only minutes. Though given the right circumstances, he would only last through several deep thrusts into her before spilling his seed. She did that to him.

"Half that, at the most," she murmured, moving her mouth down to his neck and then along his jaw, kissing a path along the edge of it.

He did not remember actually agreeing, but all it took was a thought before the trees began to rearrange their branches around them, forming an enclosed bower and shutting them away from any possible prying eyes. The grass grew thick on the ground, filling it in and making a soft place upon which they could lie.

"A handy skill," Thea said, stepping back from him. "My contribution seems small in comparison."

The air around them warmed until the chill of the outside was gone. 'Twas a comfortable place in which to spend their short time together.

"A valuable one, though," he acknowledged.

Then Tolan held out his hand to her, offering himself once more, and he waited for her reaction.

CHAPTER 18

Married.

Married to a man she loved.

Married to a man who held within him great powers of unimagined consequences.

All things that would never have been even considered possible just a few weeks ago. When Thea thought about all the other changes, she simply could not take it all in. So, for now, she looked at the man standing before her and then took his hand.

In spite of everything she did not know—the coming hours and days, the fight against evil, their futures—she knew that she loved him and he had given her back the piece of her heart and soul she thought were gone forever. And for that, she would do whatever she had to in order to keep him from harm.

A shiver raced through her then, one not of passion but of fear and foreshadowing.

He frowned then. "Is aught wrong?"

"Nay," she said with a shake of her head. "All is quite well."

She untied her cloak and he took it from her, tossing it on the now-mosslike grass within their bower. Thea waited for a moment to see if he wished to undress her. When he stared at her with those eyes, she felt her own power surge and fill her body and soul.

Thea unlaced the ties on her gown and took it off. His gaze did not move from hers. Her shift was next and then she stood before him in her stockings and shoes. Her body felt the touch of his gaze then, and when it moved to her breasts they tingled. Lower, the place between her thighs ached when he stared there.

And grew moist.

She lost her thoughts as he undressed then. She wanted to touch him, and follow the lines of muscles down from his chest, down over his belly to touch the flesh that now stood. Thea licked her lips and swallowed to ease the dryness in her mouth as she imagined that hardness in her mouth and between her legs. Her body trembled then and he smiled as he tossed the last of his garments aside and stood naked before her.

A tension built between them, their breathing the only sound within this privacy. Her body grew hotter and hotter still and the glow of it surrounded both of them now.

"Taste me," he said gruffly. "Have me, Elethea." She met his passion-filled gaze and smiled as all sorts of pleasurable things came to mind. "Then it will be my turn to have you."

Her body understood the promise of his words, for her breasts tightened and ached, as did the flesh between her legs. She wanted his mouth on her, tasting and kissing and licking and biting all the places that now throbbed for him. But first, she would give him pleasure.

Closing the space between them, she reached out and touched his chest, her fingers teasing his male nipples as she wanted hers teased soon. Thea leaned closer and kissed her way over the strong muscles of his chest. She nipped over his belly and slid her hands between his thighs and cupped his flesh.

His indrawn breath spoke of her success. Then his hands in her hair, stroking and loosening it from its braid, told her what he wanted. She knelt before him, kissed the lines of muscles that ran down from each hip to his engorged flesh. Then she tilted her head and took him in, inch by inch, hearing his groans and feeling his hips thrust with each suckle. When she had him fully in her mouth, she slid away, pursing her lips tightly. The moans that escape his clenched jaws gave her satisfaction.

He hardened more, his hips thrusting as they would when he entered her, pushing his flesh deeper into her throat. His sack tightened and she knew he would spill his seed. Just as she grasped his cock with both hands and suckled him harder to bring him to satisfaction, he lifted her up by her arms and kissed her mouth.

His hands slid under her, holding her higher and tighter against him. Thea felt him open her cleft and she rubbed against the ridge of hard muscle, wanting him inside her. Wanting him to thrust in deep and hard and fast and hard.

"Ah, you do not like to play it fairly, do you, love?" he whispered against her mouth.

He knelt with her in his arms and then laid her down on the mossy ground. Tugging her hands from around him, he spread them out above her, making her back arch and her breasts thrust up. He kissed her openmouthed, thrusting his tongue into hers until she suckled it as she had his cock. Leaning back on his knees, he met her gaze, his becoming a deeper yet brighter green now, and said one word to her.

"Stay."

Before she could nod, vines grew from the surrounding trees and branches and entangled themselves around her arms, holding her as he'd placed her. He smiled wickedly and nodded. A moment of sheer and complete panic filled her as memories of other times and of another man flooded in. The vines disappeared in an instant.

"Look at me, Elethea," he commanded in a voice that was more than just his own. "I am not him. You are not the one he preyed upon any longer. You are more."

Her body filled with power and she allowed it free. The light filled the bower and beyond, bursting into her veins. She nodded and allowed him his way. Slowly this time, almost as though he was caressing her skin, the vines approached and slid over her arms, wrapping around them and entwining until she was once more in his possession. Never too tight, the vines seemed to move with her as he touched every inch of her body, inside and out, with tongue and lips and hands. Then he lay at her side, kissing her mouth and thrusting his hand between her legs.

"I think I have prepared you well, my love," he boasted now. His hand opened the folds of her heated flesh, and his fingers entered. She lifted her hips to take him inside. "Ah. Quite well." His thumb stroked hard against the sensitive bud of her flesh and she screamed.

"Nay, Tolan! I want you inside me," she said, panting and trying to resist the wave of pleasure that threatened with his every move. "Inside," she heard herself beg him. His hard cock rubbed against her hip and she ached more.

"I like bringing you to pleasure with my hand," he taunted. "I can do this"—he touched something and she moaned—"and watch the flushing rise in your breasts."

Thea tried to slow her breathing, to slow the onslaught that was rising in her body, but he destroyed her best efforts with nothing more than a movement of his fingers and a few words. She grabbed hold of the vines around her hands and fought to slow down.

"Or this," he said, sliding three fingers into her woman's channel and stroking her deeply as that damn blessed thumb of his pressed once more.

Her body broke free of any control she thought she'd been exerting, and pleasure poured through her in an instant. Everything that had tightened within her burst and her body shuddered and shook as he pushed her on into bliss. Tolan continued to urge her on and on with whispered words and slowing touches until her body was spent. She lay there, unable to move, as that languorous feeling of satiation permeated every inch of her.

Only when her arms moved did she open her eyes to see him kneeling once more over her. The vines were there, but now her arms were at her sides. When she shifted them, the vines loosened to allow the movement and then gripped her as she lay back.

"Interesting," she said, meeting his gaze.

"They keep you where I want you," he said with a hint of male exultation in his voice now.

"And what about where I want you?" she asked before realizing her error. It simply spurred him on and he moved his fingers to remind her that he still touched her intimately.

"Here?" he asked, sliding his finger along the throbbing flesh until they glided softly but slowly over that engorged part of her. She arched against it, marveling that her body could even move or respond.

"Or here?" He kissed her mound and then moved lower, using his knees to open her legs widely. Thea watched his face as hunger and arousal filled it. When he licked his lips and lowered his head, she lost herself.

Blood and heat rushed from between her legs and through her, into every part of her as he loved her with his mouth. Thea arched her hips to open herself to him and he laughed against the throbbing flesh. The feel of it echoed through every muscle in her body.

She did not think he could arouse her any more, but then his thumb slipped into her other opening and she screamed out in pleasure. The pressure of it as he thrust into her with his tongue brought on a wild and screaming release. Then, when she was certain she could take no more, he climbed between her thighs and slid his own flesh into her.

It hurt from the overwhelming arousal and his attentions. It ached from too much pleasure so quickly. And yet when he filled that place deep within her, she could not imagine him not being there.

She watched the intensity in his face as he seated himself as deeply as he could inside her. He did not breathe. The muscles of his arms and legs coiled in tight control as he waited for her.

Thea let out a breath and he moved deeper. She gasped as he slid almost completely out of her and then back in. Each one's flesh sliding against the other's in a glorious friction. Instead of hurting now, her channel clenched his cock, trying to keep it in deep. Each slow movement of his brought out a louder and louder gasp that became a moan as she found herself once more on the precipice of release.

"I love you, Elethea," he whispered against her mouth as he kissed her then. His tongue sought hers and touched. "Now you are mine," he swore just as he thrust that final time.

Her body answered and held his flesh as he spilled

his seed within her. With a few soft grunts, he found satisfaction as she did once more. Tolan collapsed on her then, tucking his head under hers and resting on her breast. When the vines had disappeared, she knew not, but she caressed his hair and his back as their hearts and bodies calmed.

"As you are mine," she whispered.

How long it had taken, she did not know. Glancing up at the sun and its place in the sky, she guessed more than a few minutes and less than an hour. That made her smile. No matter the passage of time, it was her stomach's loud growling that roused Tolan.

"Do you never eat?" he asked, pushing his hair from his face and glancing at her belly. When it rumbled again in answer, he laughed. "Come, I have food in our bags."

He rolled from her side and she felt the absence immediately. Thea watched him dress, not moving from her place on the ground until he finished and held out a hand to help her to her feet. If she wobbled a bit, she would blame it on him and his wonderful attentions to her.

He helped her dress and then the bower disappeared, the vines and branches withdrawing back into the trees within seconds, and they were standing by the road as their horses grazed nearby. As though none of it had happened.

"Thea?" Tolan said, tugging her to face him.

When she looked at him she realized that the

golden light that had filled and warmed their private bower was not gone. Now her vision was framed in it.

"Your eyes glow now," he said, pulling her closer and searching her gaze. "Sunblood. My sunblood."

She could feel it in her blood now. She was called to this just as he was. And now she saw everything in the light of the sun.

There was no going back now.

"Aye, Earthblood," she said, feeling the presence of another within her. "My earthblood." Their joining had strengthened her in some way that she did not understand.

It took little time for them to eat and be on their way—north to whatever the Fates, and the gods, had in mind for them.

It had taken several hours, but Geoffrey's men and his own had found the boy hiding in one of the many barns on the extensive farms that Geoffrey owned there. Another man, one the boy called his cousin, was with him and Hugh recognized him as one they'd passed on the road the other morning. When he'd sensed no power, Hugh had ignored him, but now—now he might serve a purpose.

Studying the boy, a young man almost of age, from where he sat on the dais with his own cousin, Hugh noticed the resemblance to his father immediately. He had not yet attained his full height or girth, though he was a strong and able lad from the looks of him.

He was curious, for he continued to snatch quick

glimpses of Hugh as he'd been brought into the hall. Hugh's cousin, trained well to his humble status, never lifted his head.

"This is him, my lord," the soldier called out, pushing the boy forward. Hugh stood and the guard backed away when the boy did not. Courage, too?

"What are you called?" Hugh asked, walking down the steps.

"His name—" Geoffrey began to speak, but Hugh cut him off with a wave of his hand.

He wanted to hear how this one presented himself. Did he know of his father's abilities? Their bloodlines? Or if he carried it?

"I am called Kirwyn," the boy said. "Son of Tolan."

"I have met your father," Hugh said as he walked closer. "How many years do you have?"

He studied the boy, trying to assess his age . . . and whether or not there was power within him. There was no way to know until the boy came of age, and it certainly did not always travel from father to son or mother to daughter. Over the generations, it had become less certain a thing, as Hugh had discovered.

His own father had sought out and planned marriages and breeding within their family in order to produce those who would carry the power of the fire bloodline. Sometimes, as with himself, it had worked splendidly, but for his twin and his half brothers, not so well. And his own efforts to breed a son or daughter to carry down his power had failed through the usual method of marriage and yet succeeded in the bastard daughter he'd produced outside marriage.

Brienne would be the first one he would destroy when he freed Chaela and claimed full power from her.

Some betrayals could not be forgiven.

Turning his attention back to the boy, Hugh noticed he did not squirm or shuffle under scrutiny. Interesting. But he had also not answered his question. With a bit of force, he asked once again, more to learn how the boy would react, for Hugh knew his age already. "I asked, how many years have you?"

The boy grimaced then from the pain Hugh was sending into him for not responding to his question. Kirwyn surprised Hugh by blinking and shaking off the pain before lifting his head to meet Hugh's gaze.

Very interesting.

"You, boy," Geoffrey called out, motioning to one of the guards. "Show respect to my cousin and do not raise your eyes to your betters."

Before Hugh could intervene, the nearest guard lifted his hand and struck the boy across the face. The blow, with the strength of the guard and the weight of the gauntlet he wore, forced the boy to his knees. Hugh watched as Tolan's son wiped the blood from his cheek and pushed up to his feet, daring a peek at Hugh as he did.

Bold. Not so stupid as to look directly at him . . . not yet . . . but not willing to play the fool as his cousin did next to him.

What he would not have given for a son like this one! Neither of his own brothers, the one with whom he had shared a womb for nine months or the one who now commanded his army, had the mettle of this one. Hugh walked over and stood directly in front of Kirwyn now, opening his own senses up to search for any sign of power.

"Look at me, Kirwyn."

The boy met his gaze and Hugh searched him as he had his own daughter. Not forceful enough to hurt him unnecessarily, but using his own to find a glimmer of the earthblood there in his human body.

"How many years have you, Kirwyn?" he asked again, this time softly. He heard his cousin's gasp of surprise. It was true that Hugh did not ask twice, let alone a third time. However, this one was different somehow.

"Ten and almost five, my lord," the boy replied, already holding his gaze longer than most could.

Ah. The time of power rising.

Hugh looked deeper and found it there. A small kernel waiting to burst into being. Green, like his father. Potential for a great being lay there in his core. Hugh pulled back and met the boy's gaze then.

"Where is your father?" he asked. He put his hand on Kirwyn's shoulder. "And there is no cause for you to lie to me." The boy narrowed his eyes and then nodded, accepting his words.

"I know not, my lord," he said.

"Does your cousin there know?" Hugh asked, nodding at the man who had not raised his eyes from the floor before him.

"Nay, my lord." The man shook harder, but the boy never wavered.

Hugh made a decision in that moment unlike any

he'd made before in his entire life. He would take this boy, once the goddess was freed, and train him himself. He might not be an earthblood, but Hugh knew how to wield the power that came from the gods. In the new order of things, Kirwyn could be a valuable ally.

"I know where your father will be," he said, taking the boy under his arm. "We shall go there and meet up with him."

Kirwyn nodded and Hugh led him up the stairs. They would finish their noon meal and then ride north to Durrington and do the goddess's bidding.

"Come, eat," Hugh invited the boy to the table. He looked at Hugh and then at Geoffrey, who was near apoplexy, his face drawn tight in shock. "Sit."

Hugh's original plan was to force Tolan and his sunblood, whom he'd now mated with, to open the gateway or lose his son. And he might yet have to do that. But he would accept this other possibility. It all depended on the value Tolan placed on his son's life. Seeing the boy now, he thought it would be a high enough one to force his compliance.

He questioned the boy as they ate and knew by the end that Kirwyn was an intelligent lad who heard and saw much more than he was supposed to. He was kind, too—a trait Hugh would rid him of quickly—for Hugh found him stuffing half-eaten crusts of bread into his tunic when he thought Hugh was not looking. For the cousin who remained standing before them but who threw longing glances at the sumptuous food on the table.

"Feed him," Hugh called out.

A guard led the cousin to a smaller table there and a servant placed food before him. The only reason Hugh allowed it was to keep from distracting the boy from answering his questions.

Geoffrey once more reacted in surprise. "My lord?"

"Eat your supper, cousin," Hugh ordered. "Worry not over my actions."

Just because his cousin was now needed would not stop Hugh from killing him once his task was done. He had never realized how annoying and sycophantic a man his cousin had become.

Eudes entered the hall to say everyone was ready, and Hugh nodded. He was not . . . quite . . . ready.

"So, Kirwyn, tell me of your father's lands in Durrington."

By the time they did mount up, Hugh understood more about Tolan, his freely held lands in Durrington, and his son.

Strangely, he hoped he would not have to kill the boy to make his point. Oh, he would if it was necessary. He would sacrifice—and had already done so—just about anyone to complete his mission to open the gateway. But somehow he understood that he would not enjoy killing the boy as much as he would some others. With a glance at Geoffrey, he called the order out to his half brother.

CHAPTER 19

Tolan took the horses and smacked their rumps to make them run away. He turned to Thea and held out his hand. They approached the raised embankment, which he leveled before them. Just as they crossed it, the winds above them began to swirl and blow. A wave flowed up from the river Avon and stopped before them.

One moment wind and water, and the next Soren and Ran.

"It took you long enough to get here," Soren said, glancing at both of them.

Ran elbowed her husband before nodding at Thea. "Soren, they have mated."

Soren glanced at them and then nodded. "They have. I hope it makes you stronger together than you are separately, as it helped me and Ran when we faced it."

Tolan kissed the back of Thea's hand. They would be stronger together. He knew it.

"We tried to enter, but neither of us could," Ran said. "I can be the water in the ground, yet something stops me from getting inside that."

"I tried to open it with winds. It did not budge," Soren added. "I think that only the bloodline or lines that hid it so can expose it."

Tolan looked over at the twisted trees of the forest and began to open them up. It took effort to unwind them from their tight knots and time, too. Longer than he'd expected it to. These must have stood for centuries and grown stronger with each earthblood who reinforced them. They could bend to allow him to enter, but to banish them completely would take hours.

"How long until the others arrive here?" Tolan asked, walking closer to the writhing trees.

"Let me see," Soren answered before disappearing into the air around them.

A few minutes passed and Tolan concentrated on his task. Thea spoke quietly with Ran, waiting to help in whatever way she could. Then Soren was with them once more.

"Both groups travel here," he explained. "Our people come from one direction. The others from Amesbury."

"How long, Soren?" Tolan called out.

"About three hours." Soren walked to his side. "I can try to slow Hugh and his men down. But . . ."

Tolan faced him and did not like the look on the stormblood's face. A glance at the waterblood showed the same dark expression.

"Hugh has your son."

The words hung out in the air around them and Tolan could not think. He felt Thea's touch and wanted to sink into her and cling to her. He did not want to think about his son in the hands of a madman who controlled and could become fire.

"William and Roger went to get him as he said they would. By the time they arrived where you'd hidden them, Hugh and Geoffrey's men had found them and taken them to the keep."

"I am sorry," Ran said, tears streaming down her face.

Tolan shook his head and faced them all. "You speak as though he is dead. You said Hugh has him. Did you see him? Does he live?"

"Aye, he rides with Hugh. He is alive."

Tolan had so many thoughts running through his mind that he could not focus on one. His son was in terrible danger. Hugh was ruthless and would stop at nothing to open this gateway. Tolan could not help this evil be unleashed on the world. His son would be killed if he did not.

"Tolan, what can we do?" Thea whispered to him.

"The only thing you can do is seal this gateway," Ran said softly. "I know the high cost, but the price is the rest of humanity."

"My son is—"

"Your son will be as dead as my father is, Tolan," Ran said bitterly. "He may be alive now, but when Hugh gets here, he will kill him if you do not do his bidding."

"Ran." Thea began to argue with the Norse woman. Tolan shook his head and turned back to the task before him.

Tolan could not even think of sacrificing his son. The possibility simply could not be considered. So he pushed it all aside and did the only thing he could to give himself more time—he pushed with all his strength to clean this thicket away from the land beneath it. It was a slow process, for the living hedge resisted his efforts. Then he felt Thea behind him and she wrapped her arms around him, infusing her warmth and power into his body.

With a burst of strength, he pushed the twisted woods away and out, clearing it yard by yard, over the next hours. Finally, as darkness fell, so did the first layer of protection over the stone circles. Thea used her power to light his way as he walked around the perimeter removing the last bits with a fling of his hand.

Now they could see the huge area in the open. The embankment ran around the whole perimeter, higher on the hillside and lower toward the river's edge. Though he could not see any stones, Tolan could feel them. And he could feel that black abyss within the ground there.

"It is huge," Thea said. "When it was covered, I could not imagine how big it was." She walked at his side, still touching his arm.

"Aye." Tolan studied the land before him and felt for the stones around them. "This was not built at the same time as the smaller circles within it."

He pointed out the raised earth and then it began

to shudder and quake. Bit by bit, the soil shifted, rolling in waves away from the raised places. The earth rumbled and Tolan held on to Thea so she would not lose her balance as the stones rose.

One by one, they came from their hiding places, pushing up until each one was exposed. He heard Thea counting under her breath and smiled. He did not need to count, for he knew their number. One to mark every day of the year.

From where he watched, the stones erupted on each side of him, most likely as they had been hidden eons ago, until a complete circle stood where the hill had just minutes before.

"This is what I saw," Thea said as she walked over to touch the nearest one. "Look! They are all different heights and shapes, but none are taller than I am."

Some of the stones were no more than large boulders rolled into place. Others were taller and thinner, more like columns. Some carried the marks of shaping tools, while others seemed untouched in that way. Each of them reflected her light back, sparkling in shades of gold in the unusual sunlight Thea created.

"Tolan." Ran called his name and he turned to face her. She called him back to things he did not wish to think about. Soren stood at her side. "What will you do?"

"What can I do, Ran? How can I condemn my son to a death he does not deserve? How can you make me choose?"

"My father faced the same death, Tolan. I wanted to save him. I bartered to save him. But I knew what I had to do when the choice had to be made."

Her father had lived a full life. From what they'd told Tolan yesterday, Ran's father had been at the root of the betrayal and lies that had split Ran and Soren apart. Ran's father was not Kirwyn. Kirwyn was innocent of this. Tolan could not lose his son. Not now. Not this way. Not . . .

. . . not when he would have no others.

Tolan looked at Thea then and knew she was thinking the same thoughts. The misery on her face said it all to him and most assuredly, it spoke of her part.

The question of whether or not Kirwyn had inherited his power was moot now. It mattered not to him. Kirwyn was his son, his only son, his only child. Tolan would rather offer himself up than let his son die.

She'd warned him not to marry her. Now, married and more, mated in the ways of the Old Ones, they shared an unbreakable bond of faith and love. Aislinn had told him that they'd be unable to produce any children outside of their union who would carry either of their powers, for only descendants of the gods could mate and create more of their bloodlines. Warriors of Destiny, as she called them, were born and not found or made. Only those called to be priests and serve the Warriors seemed to be spread all across the areas surrounding the gateways.

Thea watched his sorrow and misery and knew part of it was because he knew as she did that children were not possible between them. This would be a death sentence for his family, his bloodline, and his son.

All because she had given in and accepted his soft words and his love.

A boy who played no part in this battle of good and evil would pay the ultimate price, and it would destroy Tolan as sure as this evil minion would.

"How can you ask such a thing of him?" she asked Ran and Soren. "Losing a parent is expected, but to lose his only child?" She turned back and saw the stark horror of it on Tolan's face. "If you would sacrifice his son, how are you any better than the bloodthirsty gods?"

In her reasoning mind, she understood the necessity of losing one over losing humanity. But as she looked at the man she loved, her heart could simply not take it in.

So, what choice did he, they, make? For she had sworn to be at his side, and that was where she would stay, no matter what happened now.

"I pray you, just wait for William and the others. Speak to them before you make any decisions," Ran begged.

That was when the noise began.

A terrible screeching sound came from under the ground around them. An inhuman, ungodly voice screamed out in rage, and the sound of it made Thea clutch her ears with her hands. But that did not stop or even lessen it. It was as if the sound was under and in and over and around them at the same time.

"She is here." Soren's voice trembled then and Thea glanced at him.

Thea knew of whom he spoke and she could not say

the name, either. Not because of the priests, but because her voice would not put a simple, human name on such a terrible, fearsome being. The ground shook then, rumbling in waves outward from the place where Thea had witnessed the ritual in her visions. When the howling started, Thea fell to her knees in fear.

Tolan stood alone there, his stance wide and sure as he shifted with the waves in the ground. As she watched, his legs merged into the earth and he rode it as a boat on a sea did.

"Would you release that into the world, Tolan? I pray you to see reason," Soren said.

"Leave him be!" Thea screamed out against the constant roar in the earth.

She climbed to her feet and went to him. She did not want to think about the possibilities of the monstrous thing in the abyss he'd mentioned getting out, but she understood the horrifying thing they were asking.

"Tolan?"

He stood stone-faced and stared at the earth.

"Can you hear me?"

The roar continued around them and she called over it. He gave a curt nod to acknowledge her presence there but said nothing else to her. She watched him there and could feel his heart breaking apart. They must do something. All the others were coming soon—the Warriors and priests and men as well as Hugh and his followers.

She knew when he'd made a decision, for his body turned to that creature she'd seen here before. One of earth and plants that could walk like a man. Who was also a man. "I will uncover the circle. I must, regardless of my decision."

For a moment, Thea was confused. The noise, the terrible groaning and roar that had overwhelmed them, stopped. Gone. Complete and utter silence covered them now. The usual sounds of night in this area— night birds, insects, animals on the prowl—ceased.

She looked to Soren and Ran and found them staring at Tolan, both in disbelief and surprise. They could each take the form of their power as Tolan did—even Thea lost her human body when she shone like the sun—yet it was still a shock to see it the first time.

Tolan looked at her and then disappeared, sinking completely into the ground. She could feel him moving away from them and toward the smaller of the two circles enclosed in this henge. The silence changed to something else now, not the screaming or the roar but a whisper.

Thea could not make out words being spoken. She moved toward the location she knew and watched and waited. Soren and Ran kept their distance, even moving away, as Tolan began his work. They'd said they could not enter the area around the circle, though Thea had no trouble approaching it.

Seconds turned to minutes before she saw the ground shifting where the stones had stood and would stand once again.

Ran had explained that she and Soren had used their powers together to uncover the circle of stones lying beneath the waters of the loch near Stenness in

Orkney. Combining storm and water, they had blown away the water and debris covering it and raised it from the loch's floor.

"Did it take you this long?" she shouted to them. From the stern expressions, she did not believe they would answer her at all.

"Nay!"

Since they could clearly not approach her, she walked to where they stood watching.

"These lands, this area, is heavily protected from both under and above the ground. Tolan's family has been spelling it for centuries, mayhap even from the beginning," Ran said. "That is what Corann and Aislinn believe."

"Are they close?"

"Aye, but not as close as they are," Soren said, nodding behind her. "Get back where he cannot get to you," he warned.

Thea ran back to the area nearest the circle and watched as a great troop of soldiers rode past his cottage and up over the embankment to the area now cleared of their protective thicket.

And there at the front rode Tolan's son.

In the grasp of a man whose power could be felt even at this distance.

"Sunblood!" Hugh called out to her. Kirwyn frowned as he met her gaze.

"Aye," she replied, sending the light out around her, lighting the entire plain so that all were seen.

"Call your earthblood to you. We have much to discuss."

CHAPTER 20

Trapped.

He was trapped as surely as the stones were in the ground.

If Tolan opened the gateway, he saved his son but humanity lost its battle. If he sealed it, the fate of his son was sealed by that act.

The problem was, he'd known enough noblemen, even those without power like that of the one holding his son. Noblemen who saw to their own needs and wants and plans without any regard for anyone else. And this one, bolstered by the power in his blood, was so much worse.

Tolan knew that there was a great chance Kirwyn would die and that hardly anything Tolan did would influence this Hugh de Gifford. He believed everything the others had told him. He did.

So, once he merged with the earth, he traveled back to them. They rode as fast as they could toward

Durrington, but Tolan knew that the others would arrive first. The only thing he could do was take his time uncovering the stones until the Warriors arrived and rescued his son.

He rose from the ground before them and waited for the warblood to approach. As Tolan watched, William leaped from his horse and became that being with every stride he took toward him. By the time they faced each other, the blue-skinned creature of war was taller than any man Tolan had ever seen and more fearsome than any wild animal. His sides heaved as he stood between Tolan and the others, glaring through his red eyes with hands that were now a sword no man could carry and a battle-ax.

"You cannot do this, Earthblood," the warrior growled.

"I will not sacrifice my son," Tolan answered in a voice that came from the earth beneath him. "I will not."

The warblood rose and towered over him. Tolan did not respond in kind, but he waited for attack.

"Will," a soft voice said from behind the warblood. Brienne crept around and tugged on his arm. "Withdraw," she whispered. The warrior slid back into the man before Tolan, only the glowing eyes of the warblood remaining now.

"We understand, Tolan. We do. But you must know that my father will kill your son whether or not you open the gateway. He does not have mercy within him. Even for a child," she explained.

"I cannot take that chance, Brienne," Tolan said.

His voice shook as he became a man once more. "I will not."

Tolan wanted to be the one to defeat this evil one, to seal the door of her prison once more. He'd heard her there, felt her attempts to escape. He'd sensed the madness, not reconciliation that lived within her, and knew what it would mean to free her. He met the gazes of those who had brought this fight to his lands and then looked at the warrior.

"No matter which side I choose, I must uncover the circle. I go there now to begin." He raised his hand when they began to argue. "You have until I finish to rescue my son."

Silence met his words.

"When he is safe, then we will seal the gateway and end this."

Roger, William's second, was the first one to act. He walked to William and began to lay out a plan, a strange combination of strategies to deal with both their human and more powerful adversaries. They had done this before and Tolan knew it was Kirwyn's best chance at survival.

"Soren has shown us the lay of the land there," Roger said. "The only way to approach is from the hillside to the west. If he"—Roger nodded at Tolan—"can keep the embankment high there, my men can move into place." Humans without power were difficult to sense.

The others among the group with battle experience offered their own suggestions, but Tolan did not need to be here for this. He needed to check on his son and then do the thing only he could do. . . .

And he needed to speak with Elethea.

Tolan saw the guilt on her face when they realized the demand made of them and he understood that she blamed herself. She defended him to Soren and Ran out of that guilt.

If the worst happened to Kirwyn, he would never have another child. Never be able to pass his bloodline and power down to a new generation to face whatever would come of this.

Unthinkable, but true.

But this was not her guilt to carry, 'twas his for not protecting his son more carefully. For not making a decision sooner. For failing.

"I know that you are linked," Tolan said to William and Aislinn. "I can hear what is said from within the soil. Tell me what you need of me and when you need it. I will do what I can."

Tolan walked to William and took the man by the arm. "I must save my son," Tolan swore. "But I do not want the being in that prison released and will do everything in my power not to allow it."

"Except seal it now."

The stark words sat there for a moment between them before Tolan spoke. "You will understand when you have a child." Then he walked away and returned to the earth.

He would not sacrifice his son.

He crossed the miles back to the circle, passing by Hugh's men. Tolan could see Kirwyn riding behind

Hugh, looking unharmed, though scared. His cousin Farold fared as well farther back in the group of riders. As Tolan moved by them, Hugh called out to him, startling him.

"You are there, Earthblood," Hugh shouted. "Your son and I will meet you at the circle."

Tolan rolled under the surface, causing the earth to quake and shudder. Hugh's horse and many others reacted skittishly. Some reared up and others cried out in terror. The last thing Hugh said unnerved him.

"You see, Kirwyn," Hugh said to his passenger, "I told you your father was powerful. He can become the earth and move through it."

Tolan felt his heart breaking then, knowing that Hugh had revealed the story of their family to his son. Not him. He would not be the one to speak of the power and their duty to the lands here. Their secret had been shared with him by one not of their bloodline. He roared out his sadness and fury then, and it made the ground around him and throughout the plain quake and rattle.

He moved faster back to Durrington and found her there. Shining like the midday sun, she faced him as he left the soil and stood before her. This time, she opened her arms and welcomed him.

"This is not your fault, Thea," he whispered against her mouth. Stroking her face and pushing her loosened hair away, he kissed her again and again. "I see it there, just as I did when Jasper did his worst to you," he said. She shuddered in his embrace now, but he shook his head. "That was never your fault and neither is this."

"But if something happens to Kirwyn—" she began.

He pressed his lips to hers to stop her. "If something happens to my son, that is not your guilt to bear."

"Tolan, I cannot—"

Tolan took her mouth in a fierce kiss then, stealing her breath and making her stop her words. "I think that these gods have some plan in place. If Kirwyn dies or survives, if we do, there is some purpose to this." She nodded in agreement. "We need a plan of our own. Neither of us can do this alone. It is either both of us together, in accord, or neither. So what say you?"

She pulled away from him just as the din of the riders began. Glancing over to the large heavily armed group growing nearer and then back at him, Thea spoke. "We must do what we can to defeat this evil one and those who serve her, Tolan. But I cannot do that at the cost of Kirwyn's life."

"The Warriors will try to rescue him. We will do whatever we can. But if it all fails and the only choice is to . . . open it? What say you?"

"Save Kirwyn," she said.

He changed before her and sank into the earth, seeking the stones buried there. First, he raised the height of the embankment all around the perimeter, pushing the stones now seen up higher until they appeared like a huge fence around the site. It would not stop Hugh, but it would slow them and make his men more vulnerable by thinning their lines for the Warriors.

As it turned out, uncovering the stones was not an

easy task. They were buried deep and anchored there by some sort of powerful, binding spell. Pieces of memories floated through Tolan's mind then of his grandfather walking this area and singing or chanting words Tolan could not remember now.

Like with a web woven tightly from many directions, Tolan needed to cut the ties on each one before the earth would move away from them. He lost track of time. He lost track of everything going on above him. He concentrated on each stone, one at a time, until they were free and ready to move.

Tolan climbed from the earth and faced the circle.

Hugh's men were spread around, inside the embankment, but not near this. Tolan heard the approach of the Warriors and felt the stormblood above and the waterblood trying to seek a path through to the stones herself. Then he saw Hugh and Kirwyn, standing together between the raised stones watching him.

He turned away from them and commanded the earth to move.

Every sound ceased as the first stone rose through the ground and took its place there. Even the mad whispering from the abyss stopped as though the evil within wanted nothing to interfere with his task.

Thea had told him of eight stones, but there was an altar stone there near the center of the arrangement, too. By the time he'd brought the second one to the surface and stood it in its place, he was sweating. His breathing grew labored by the third and he had to pause after the fourth one was in place.

For the first time in his life, it seemed that the earth

was working against him in a task. Always, when he asked of it, it delivered, whether life to barren fields or a bountiful harvest or anything asked. Now, as though it knew this was wrong, the earth fought him. Thea joined him there, outside the stones, but not even her presence or the strength of the sun she bore within her helped.

"Tolan," Hugh called out to him. "I would speak to you now."

More to give himself a chance to consider this challenge and to give the Warriors time to ready their plan, Tolan nodded and walked, as a man, to where the fireblood held his son. He tried to remain calm. He must think quickly in order to save his son.

"Kirwyn? Are you well?" he asked, stepping closer to his son.

Hugh stood with his arm draped over Kirwyn's shoulder, holding him before him as both a prize and a hostage. Kirwyn gave a nervous shake of his head rather than speaking.

"We spoke so plainly before, Tolan, and I found it refreshing. So I wanted you to know what choice you face in this moment," Hugh said.

"I know what my choices are, de Gifford," he said bitterly.

"Ah, but I think you do not."

Tolan met the fireblood's gaze and then followed it to his son. Studying Kirwyn for a minute, Tolan gasped as he recognized it—his son carried the earth's bloodline within him. He would have the same gift, the same power, over the earth as Tolan did.

"More, I think," Hugh said. "Such great potential within him."

"Have you told him?" Tolan asked Hugh. How much had the fireblood revealed to his son?

"Much of it," Hugh admitted. "I was so pleased to find that he carried the bloodline that I spoke of it. But, Tolan, we can train him together. There is still so much you do not understand about your own powers." Hugh leaned in, whispering his words so only the three of them were privy to them.

"And with Chaela's presence, our own powers will increase, for she is not a bloodline but a goddess, able to grant her favor to those who serve or friend her."

"So, if I do as you wish, you will spare my son?"

"Spare him? More than that, Tolan. I will teach him how to use the power within him. I will place him, and you and your sunblood, at my side as the only goddess comes back into the world."

Tolan asked the final question, one to which he already knew the answer. He would not look at Kirwyn as he did so. "And if we do not?"

Hugh laughed aloud then. "I think we all know the answer to that, Tolan. Though, after meeting your son, I think I will regret his loss." Kirwyn trembled then but did not cry out. Brave even at his age. Tolan was proud.

Hugh nodded to someone nearby and Lord Geoffrey pulled Farold out into the open space between the stones above and the plain behind them. Before Tolan could speak, Hugh lifted his hand and pointed at their cousin.

"This is what you can expect if you do not open the gateway."

Nothing else warned of the man's terrible intention but the act itself—Farold began to burn. Flames crept up from his feet and, within seconds, had engulfed him in fire. The screams of the dying man and the smell of his burning flesh surrounded them, and Tolan could not stop it.

"Do not, Ran Waterblood," Hugh called out to the unseen woman. "He will be dead before you can stop me." He returned his hand to Kirwyn's other shoulder.

Minutes that seemed like hours passed until Tolan's cousin actually died. With a last scream, his body disintegrated into ash.

"I think you have something to do?" Hugh said, nodding to the stones behind them.

"But we have no priest to pray the ritual," Tolan argued.

"Worry not, Earthblood. I have things well in hand," he said, squeezing Kirwyn's shoulders.

Tolan met Kirwyn's gaze then and smiled at his son. As he walked away, he hoped that William and the others had a plan, for he was out of ways to keep the worst from happening.

CHAPTER 21

Thea stood at his side as he strained to raise the stones.

Tolan had worked silently ever since he watched his cousin die. Her power might heal, but she could not bring back the dead, so there was nothing Thea could do. She hated this helplessness and watched and waited for her opportunity to do . . . something.

Though the sun had risen into a watery sky earlier, she shone her light at Tolan to give him strength. But, try as he might, he seemed to be fighting the earth itself. Or mayhap he had used so much power that he had less to use now? Raising the embankment, uncovering the outer ring of hundreds of stones—she could not imagine the amount of power that all took. When the eighth one stood in its place, Thea held her breath.

"There is another," he said as he pointed near the center of it.

A flat, tablelike stone seemed to float through the

ground and in the air there. Two shorter ones positioned themselves under it and it stood there. An altar. This was different from what she'd seen there, but it mattered not.

Tolan turned to face her then and nodded. "It is done."

For a moment everything and everyone around them stood still in utter silence.

For a moment.

Then a battle cry rang out and mayhem broke free all around them. The men who fought under William's command swarmed over the embankment, which Tolan seemed to be controlling, lowering it level before their path. While she watched, Roger led them in spreading lines across the wide-open space where they would fight with Hugh's soldiers.

Thea thought that Hugh's men looked ill-prepared for the onslaught, but not a one gave ground or ran. The battle on the ground was not the only fight, for she saw William in a form that her human mind could not comprehend—growing taller each second as he strode across the field searching for Hugh.

Though she'd heard about each of their forms, nothing prepared her for the sight of this berserker or his mate, Brienne, who changed into living fire. Though shaped like her human body, she burned like the brightest flames Thea had ever seen. Hotter than even the blacksmith's hearth, she moved across the area toward her father as well.

Bolts of lightning struck the ground around them as Soren began his attack from the sky above. Winds buffeted the soldiers, too, as he moved like a storm through the fighting, knocking down Hugh's men as his wife doused fires that Hugh began throwing at their own men.

In the midst of the chaos, Thea saw Aislinn making her way, with the large guard at her side, toward the circle. Once they got Kirwyn to safety, she would enter the stones with them and pray the words that would seal it forever.

Then all it took was a boy's cry to bring everything to a standstill.

Kirwyn screamed in agony as Hugh took hold of his hand and turned his own to flame. Their hands melted together and Thea felt her stomach seize and roll at the sight and sound of it. She began rushing there, for now there was something for her to do. She could heal this. She knew it.

"Go to the stones, Sunblood," Hugh called out, meeting her gaze across the distance. "Come one more step and it will move up to his arm." As though to prove it, Hugh inched the fire past the boy's wrist, sending him into agony. "When the gate is opened, you can see to him with your healing touch. If you or your mate continues any closer, there will only be a lump of melted flesh left when I finish with him."

She would heal him, but for now she obeyed the fireblood and backed her way toward the circle, never turning away from the horrifying sight.

"Halt!" Hugh called out, his gaze on the ground in front of him. "You see, I can control this, Tolan. I can make it go quickly." The flames burst out of Kirwyn's skin now and the boy's howls made her skin crawl.

"Or slowly to prolong it." And he did just that, pulling the flames back now and making their joined hands glow like hot metal instead.

"Take Geoffrey to the stones now," Hugh ordered.

"Why Geoffrey?" Tolan asked as he rose before his son and his tormentor and stared at Hugh. He reached out toward Kirwyn, and Hugh smiled as he nodded.

"Geoffrey carries a mark of his own," Hugh explained. He nodded at his cousin, who pulled back his sleeve to reveal his arm to one and all.

"Jesus, Mary, and Joseph!" Thea turned and saw the epithet had been uttered by Father Ander. The Catholic priest was closest to her then, one of those trying to get Aislinn into the circle.

As they'd told her, once the three—the two of the bloodlines and the one marked as priest—entered the circle, it would seal them inside it until the ritual was completed . . . or failed. For if the ceremony, which was different at each circle, began and a mistake was made, the circle and everyone inside it would be destroyed.

"Tolan, take him to the circle and begin the ritual," Hugh said loudly. "Once the gate is opened, you can have your son back. As I promised."

Kirwyn had fainted, a blessing, Thea thought, but Hugh did not release him or his hand.

It took Tolan only a moment to nod and walk toward Geoffrey, their lord. How had he been marked as a priest of the Old Ones? If he was related to Hugh, should he not be a fireblood? It made no sense until she thought about Father Ander. He'd had no connection to the other priests until his mark had risen. And he had no knowledge of the ritual needed.

But Soren had. His grandfather had, unknowing to him, taught him the words in the songs of his childhood.

Since she had no inkling of her own power or connection to the Old Ones, Thea had no idea of what words would be needed within the circle. Tolan had been raised by believers. Mayhap he knew?

As she watched, his body turned to soil and wrapped itself around Geoffrey, before sinking into the ground beneath them. The earth swallowed up Geoffrey's cries of fear, though Thea could feel their approach where she stood. Soon, Tolan thrust up from the ground and dropped a coughing, wheezing lord at her feet.

"Tolan! Thea!" William called out to them. "Do not do this."

"I have no choice," Tolan said quietly and with a sad tone of resignation. Truly, what else could they do?

"One to open, one to close," Soren called out. "There is always a choice, Tolan!"

The other bloodlines approached from all directions, but Tolan did not give them a chance to stop the three of them. With a tilt of his chin, he forced the earth beneath their feet into a wave that spread out from the circle and knocked everyone to the ground. Grabbing her hand, he pulled Thea with him as he shoved Geoffrey into the stones. With one last glance back, she stepped with him between the stones.

* * *

A white flash of light surrounded the circle now, swirling around it, preventing them from seeing out and the others from seeing in. It stopped them from passing through the stones as well. Tolan released Geoffrey and walked around the inside of the circle, looking and listening for some sign of what they must do. When he tried to get a glimpse of what was happening without, he could see only shadows, some moving, some still. Pressing his hand between the stones did no good. The light was some kind of barrier of its own now.

The altar stone gleamed sheer white now in the light and caught his attention. Tolan walked to it and beckoned Thea over. Lord Geoffrey stood where Tolan left him, with shock and fear covering his face. He tried to speak several times, pointing at Tolan and murmuring unintelligible sounds.

Tolan guessed that the journey through the ground might have upset the lord's sensitivities somewhat. He could feel the man as he tunneled through the ground, holding on to enough of his own form to protect Geoffrey as they moved through the soil there. It was a strange and yet terrifying moment, being in the ground, part of it, for Tolan, too.

"Tolan?" Thea asked as she walked inside the circle. "This was not here when I saw this place. The sacrifice was laid there." She pointed across the clearing to a different spot.

"Sacrifice?" Geoffrey stuttered out. "Another sacrifice?"

Tolan strode over to him and grabbed him by his tunic, pulling him up close. "Have there been others?"

"Aye," he said, shaking his head several times.

"When?" Tolan asked, tossing him back onto the ground.

"All his life, he has worshipped the goddess. Sacrifices were part of that," Geoffrey admitted.

"Like my cousin?" Tolan asked, remembering the terrible sight.

"Aye, though it was worse for any woman chosen."

Tolan did not even wish to think of the depravity that could be involved, but he did see Thea shudder at the words.

"So, what do we do here, my lord?" Tolan asked, infusing the title with sarcasm. "If you are marked, if he sent you in here, you must know."

Tolan did not take his gaze from the man who'd ruled his life, but he did walk to Thea and pull her close, entwining their fingers.

"He said we must spill our blood on the altar stone. And we must break the altar so that our mixed blood flows . . ." Geoffrey stopped and looked around the area, searching for a place. "He said the barrier is in the center there."

"And then?" Thea asked.

"Then she will be freed from that place."

"Come," Tolan said, approaching the center of the circle with Thea at his side. Geoffrey remained next to the altar as though afraid to move near the center.

"Is this the area you could feel but not penetrate, Tolan?" Thea asked.

Tolan looked into the ground and nodded. Even now he could feel the outline of it. It ran deep into the earth, so deep he could not reach the bottom of it. "It is surrounded by stone or something so hard that I cannot even sense through it."

"Hugh said Cernunnos created it with a thought," said Geoffrey.

Tolan and Thea turned back to the nobleman. His ancestor was so powerful that he could carve this immeasurable abyss with a thought?

"What more do you know of it? Of what we are supposed to do?" Tolan asked, stalking back toward Geoffrey.

He threw his hands up before Tolan, ready to fend off any blows. Used to having guards to protect him had turned the lord soft, so all Tolan would need was one well-placed punch to take him down. But if they were to open this barrier and Tolan was to save his son, he needed this man.

"You must know more!" Tolan shouted. "He is burning my son inch by inch. What must we do?" He ran his hands through his hair, trying to figure out the rest of it.

"If a priest is needed, there must be prayers? A ritual of a sort?" Thea asked softly. "My lord, do you know these prayers? Or are they here somewhere to be found?"

Geoffrey pointed to the altar stone, and Tolan realized the man had been searching it the whole while.

"Is it there?" Tolan asked.

"I cannot see anything now, but Hugh said to mark it with blood and the words will show."

"Then do it!" Tolan yelled.

He and Thea watched as the man pulled a small dagger from his belt and tugged back his sleeve. Holding his hand out, Geoffrey made a quick slash, deep enough to make the blood flow freely. As it dripped, he spread it over the surface of the altar. The pristine white stone seemed to reject the blood at first, but then the droplets filled in channels cut into it.

These were not words in their language, for Tolan could read and write and recognized none of them. These slashes and cuts were not familiar to him. Another language?

"Do you recognize these? Are these Norman or Breton? Latin?" he asked Geoffrey. Tolan's skills at letters was basic and he knew nothing other than the language of this area. Geoffrey shrugged and shook his head.

"We are missing something," Thea said. "It must be a combination of things. These words, the blood, and something else." Tolan thought on her words. "Your family passed down a great power to you, Tolan. And the stories of the ancient past. Is there anything they told you that referred to this place or this ritual?"

Tolan could remember bits of his grandfather's old stories and prayers and those, too, from his father, but what he remembered most clearly was the songs. As they worked the fields, his grandfather would sing songs of the earth and the plants and the . . . stones!

"Thea, I think you are right!" he said, pacing around the altar stone trying to pull those memories. "There were prayers I heard as a child. And chanting, hours of chanting as we worked the fields." He rubbed his face. "I thought they were like the waulking songs used by the women to keep up their pace in their work, but now I wonder."

He began to hum one of the tunes he did remember. Memories of warm summer days in the fields grew stronger, as did the sound of it. His grandfather would begin it, his father would add his voice, and then Tolan would wait and join in when they told him. The melody and words woven together helped the lands, his grandfather explained.

One song to open the furrows and one to close them.

As the sound of the song echoed around them, a vibration began under their feet. Then, coming from the center of the circle, a stronger motion started and it felt as though something was beginning to shudder inside the earth.

"Wait, Tolan." Thea grabbed his arm and tugged. "Do not sing it!" She pointed at Geoffrey and the altar. "If it begins, it must end correctly or we are all destroyed, along with the circle. Be certain before you begin."

As though a last warning, a scratching noise followed by something that sounded like a large animal panting emanated from within the barrier. Tolan swallowed deeply, his throat dry with fear now as he, as they, contemplated releasing *that*.

"He will kill the boy," Geoffrey said. "And everyone else out there if you do not do this." The nobleman lost the color in his face then, telling Tolan that worse was coming. "He will raze the village and burn the fields, too. No one will survive and nothing will grow here for generations, Tolan. His fire cannot be withstood."

Tolan must have worn a mutinous expression, for Geoffrey continued with his warning.

"You, she, the others do not have the power that he has. He has honed it under the tutelage of his father, who learned it from his. He has practiced it for his whole life, since it rose in his blood. It would take you years to gain the ability to wield it that he has now. And you, we, they"—he pointed with his chin outside the circle—"do not have that kind of time."

His hopes to avoid this dashed, Tolan glanced at Thea one last time. She would do as he asked to save his son and the others, no matter the risk. Her smile, on trembling lips, spoke of her love and her agreement. Tolan closed his eyes and thought of the last time his grandfather had worked the land with him. He thought about the huge, strong man whose hands dug into the ground and turned it. He remembered watching the earth begin to churn and the furrows appearing as they made their way through the rows.

He opened his eyes and looked for one final time at the woman who was sun to his earth. Whose heart and soul held his own. And offering up one last prayer to the Old Ones for forgiveness and strength, he began to chant.

CHAPTER 22

"Pray for us sinners, now and at the hour of our death. Amen."

"Father, could you not choose another prayer?" William asked the priest as they stood outside the circle, unable to get in or stop the abomination that would be released now.

"Do you think they will open it, then?" Brienne stood at his side and he could feel her warmth there.

"Aye," Will said to them. "Look there." He turned his gaze on her father and watched as the fireblood continued to hold and torment the boy. They'd tried everything they could to free him and break the hold de Gifford had on his father, but to no avail. "Tolan believes his son will be safe."

"Corann, what do we do then?" Soren asked. "What do we do if the goddess is freed? What will she do?"

No one spoke for several seconds and then Brienne did. She'd encountered the goddess in her father's secret chamber and had shared only bits of that with him or anyone.

"She will rise as an unholy creature and will seek vengeance against all those who kept her prisoner," Will's mate said. He tamped down the warblood's need to protect her, for there were other problems to face first.

Father Ander murmured his favorite prayer once more, under his breath, and William suspected that most all of them, save Corann and Aislinn, joined in silently now.

"So we will be her first targets?"

William needed to understand what could happen and prepared his men and the rest for it. Nay, what would happen, for each passing moment spoke of Tolan and Thea's compliance with Hugh's demands. He was an experienced warrior, partaking and winning a number of battles against human enemies while serving his king and liege lord. And though the warblood gave him superhuman strength and abilities, sometimes it was the human warrior who could see patterns and make plans better.

"She may not attack the sunblood and earthblood, believing them to be allies," Corann said. "You heard the fireblood's words—he wants both Tolan and his son at his side." William scoffed, but Corann continued. "Cernunnos was one of the most powerful of the Old Ones, William, and Tolan's family have kept to the faith, making him stronger than most of you. Belenus was another and though the sunblood is unpracticed, she will be of great value. So, to keep them with him would give him a huge advantage in the coming times."

Coming times? From the sound of this, none of them would survive to live in the coming times.

"I do not believe they will stand at Hugh's side," Aislinn whispered. "They are forced to this by . . ." She glanced off in the distance as the boy whimpered now in ungodly pain from de Gifford's burning touch.

"Anyone who can pray the ritual or prophesy will be her first targets," Roger said, spitting on the ground. "You said there is still the fourth circle to deal with, Corann? So those who will know where to find it are in danger?"

Even if the worst happened here this day, even if the goddess was freed, there was still a fourth gateway. One that she would need to destroy to protect her from the possibility of ever being returned to the abyss where she'd spent the last hundreds of centuries. And it was, as Aislinn and Corann explained, the last remaining place where the goddess could be captured, if they knew how to do it.

Will did not wait for more. "Roger. Brisbois. Take Aislinn and Corann to safety."

Aislinn began to argue, but William would hear none of it. She was too valuable. More than a priest, she was the most powerful seer among all of them and she had some destiny that none of them understood yet. Marcus had revealed that much before he died at Hugh's hands, so now it was William's and the others' responsibility to see that the young woman survived—whether or not she agreed mattered not at all.

"Corann, you may stay. Aislinn, go with them now," he ordered quietly. "Roger, give the order to the men as we'd planned." Roger nodded at him and escorted Aislinn away from the circle, with Brienne's uncle at her back. He faced the priest and spoke, not mincing words or possible outcomes for what would happen.

"You need to do what you can, Corann. Now and in the coming hours, for I fear we may not be enough to do battle with this goddess."

"Brienne, you must protect those you can from the worst of her attack. She will go for those humans who cannot fight back, won't she?"

"Aye, she will," Brienne said. "I pray that what I saw in the abyss was a mirage, a false vision projected to keep us unaware. For if she comes into this world in that form, I fear . . ." She said no more, but the shudder that made her whole body tremble said more. If a fireblood feared the goddess . . .

"What should we do?" Ran asked, touching Will's arm then.

"Water and storm to fight fire," Corann interrupted. "Protect the others."

"Mayhap they will have a change of heart and not open it?" Brienne asked, though none of them believed it would be true.

Something happened then, something Will could not describe as anything other than a shift in the ground around them. It took only one glance at Hugh's glee-filled face to know it was not good. In fact, it was bad. The air grew still and the white light around the standing stones pulsed brighter and brighter until he had to look away. When he looked back, it was the war-blood who now stood in his place.

"Prepare!" he called out in a growling command.

His blood flooded now with the need to fight, and so he stalked off toward the groups of soldiers readying for the attack. He paused before his mate and lifted her up to him. Closing his eyes, he inhaled her scent and rubbed his face against her cheeks and neck, marking her with his.

"You will have a care, Brienne," he whispered to only her.

He could not lose her. He could not. He whined out in a moan that came from deep within him, from that place that feared she was in danger. That she would not . . . He leaned his head back and growled his fear loud and long into the air. Her hand, touching his cheek softly, stopped his anguish. He gazed into her eyes and saw her love for him there.

"Aye, William. You have a care, too, my warblood."

He placed her carefully on her feet and then ran off to take his place near the circle. He raised his weapons in the air and screamed out his battle cry once more.

And then he waited for the coming fight.

Thea could only stand and watch as Tolan began humming some melody she'd never heard before. His voice grew stronger and he added some words to it, chanting in a pattern like what the monks at the abbey did during Matins. But these were not the words the monks used. They were guttural sounds, primitive in some way that her blood recognized.

Heat built within her and she could not contain it. Bursting forth, she lost her form and became like the sun there in the circle. She could see and hear as though still a person and she watched as Tolan approached the altar and Lord Geoffrey.

As he sang, the carvings on that stone grew deeper and more precise and the blood filled in the etchings. Geoffrey stared at them until his eyes rolled back into his head and he grabbed hold of the edge of the altar. Rather than preventing him from seeing, somehow, not only could he see what was written there but he could also now read it.

Geoffrey spoke then, a language she did not understand and yet she could. The words were about the Old Ones, the gods who'd been worshipped eons ago and who had left behind their descendants. It called on the earthblood and sunblood to sanctify the altar anew and open the barrier.

A terrible wave of pain struck her, taking her breath away and filling her with such fear and trepidation that she could barely think or watch. Tolan's voice rose, the chanting becoming some kind of chimes that echoed around the stones.

Nay, not around the stones. The stones themselves now chimed in chorus with Tolan's chant. Louder and louder, Tolan and Geoffrey sang and prayed, one and then the other, as the chiming became screaming. But it was not the stones screaming. It was the being that lived in the abyss underneath their feet.

Then that thing began scratching the barrier, a dreadful sound of claws or talons scraping along stone that made Thea's blood go cold. What was the goddess, truly? Thea wanted to look in the center to see if she could see anything and yet the sound made her unable to look.

Though both Geoffrey and Tolan stopped their song and prayer then, the sounds echoing across the circle grew louder and louder. Tolan nodded to her and held out his hand for hers.

"Tolan," she whispered. "This is our last chance."

"For my son, Thea. For my son."

His words, his plea broke her heart and she nodded at him, pulling her power back inside her body and holding out her hand to him across the altar stone to him. He grasped her wrist with his upturned hand and nodded at Geoffrey. Serving as priest, the man sliced across their wrists while saying another prayer she could not understand.

Watching in disbelief, Thea saw that the blood that flowed from her veins was golden in color and shimmered like the sun as it poured onto the surface there, mixing with the deep red blood there already. Tolan made a fist and added his, green and glowing, into the other two. The bloods swirled there, mixing and yet remaining separate.

This was the point from which they could never turn back. If they dipped the marks they each bore into this puddle of blood and painted the stones that held the same marks with it, the gateway would seal. If they destroyed the altar and the blood drained onto the barrier, it would break and release hell on earth.

Time itself seemed to hold then. She could see

nothing but Tolan. She could hear nothing but the beating of a human heart somewhere within her. The blood bubbled and boiled there before them and then . . .

Tolan reached out and, using a hand of stone, crushed the altar before them.

The three-colored blood poured onto the ground and ran down the few yards toward the center slowly. She watched as the first drops ran over an edge she'd not seen before and splashed onto the barrier she knew was there. Tolan met her gaze for a second before turning to watch. Geoffrey backed away as the cracking sound began.

Like the sound of a breaking eggshell, but multiplied thousands and thousands of times, the barrier broke. Steaming air rushed out of the chasm in a gush, spreading over the circle and out. Suddenly, the light was gone and she could see those outside.

She thought there should be screaming now. Or wailing. Or pleas for mercy. Instead, nothing broke the silence as they watched something begin to rise from the steam.

A talon appeared over the edge, followed by another grasping near the same place. Thea had seen hunting birds like hawks and falcons. She'd seen huge owls with their deadly talons that could pick up their prey and bear them away. But the talons sliding along the ground there before her were larger than anything she had ever seen.

Then wings were revealed, unlike those of any bird she knew. Sliding, almost crawling along the ground, gaining purchase and a hold as the creature hoisted its head and body out of the earth. It could not be and yet it was.

A mythical creature of legend. A deadly beast of fire and destruction. Chaela the goddess was a . . .

Dragon.

Thea looked at Tolan and shook her head, taking one, then another step back. He grabbed her by the shoulders and pulled her more quickly away until their backs were against one of the stones standing guard around the now-opened gateway.

Like a ghastly version of a newly born colt, the creature shook itself as it half dragged and half crawled out of the abyss. Once it was completely out onto the ground, it peered around and found them.

Was this their last moment? Would they die for their sin now? Would the others be killed by this demonic being that they had unleashed?

The dragon stretched its arms and wings out over the circle and almost covered the whole area of it. Scales of black and red covered the expansive wings, and the talons appeared dipped in gold. Its head reared back then and Thea saw the huge fangs in its mouth. But that was not the worst thing to happen.

Nay, the worst was when it screeched out a horrible, earsplitting cry and then let out a blast of fire. Thea watched in shock as the beast smiled and looked on its enemies, its deadly intent clear. It inhaled then, filling its lungs with air, and spewed flames over the stones and into the field where the others watched in horror. A sound that could only be described as jubilation followed as though it was well pleased with its abilities.

Then the dragon stood and took a step and then another, reaching the stones. It took but one more step for it to breach the circle, and as Thea stood frozen in fear, it began its attack.

Corann could not tear his eyes away. After decades of praying that this would not happen, he was witnessing it himself. All their planning and preparation and yet they had failed. The goddess was free of the barrier that held her in the abyss and was now turning her glowing amber gaze on the countless soldiers and priests surrounding the circle.

This was his nightmare come alive. He searched within for his faith so that they could cast protective spells that might strengthen the warriors and those fighting. And he found none. His fear was so paralyzing in this moment of greatest need that all he could think was of the terrible mistake Marcus had made in choosing him to lead.

Then he felt the hand of the priest Ander on his arm.

"Marcus chose you, my friend. He believed you could lead us in this grievous time."

Corann found himself surrounded by the other priests, the ones who had followed their calling from the island where peace had reigned for their entire lives. Now they most assuredly faced their deaths and yet they turned to him.

As he witnessed the first attack and as many fell before her fire, Corann sought the spell that would protect them all. In his memory, he heard Marcus singing it and he closed his eyes and began to sing the melody. The words, he could not find or remember. Ander and the others joined in, waiting for him to add the power into the spell with the words only he would know.

More died in his moments of hesitation and he could only think of simple words—save us, O gods of all, save us. He repeated the words, closing his eyes and hoping to find the ones he, they, the world needed when the air around him heated and the priests made no sounds at all.

When he dared to open his eyes, the hellish gaze of the dragon stared into them. Like living fire, its eyes were the color of molten copper and its breath was fetid and hot against him.

"Priest," it whispered, "I am free." A woman's voice, partly human and partly something else, spoke from within the beast. "And now you all will die."

It inhaled deeply, preparing for a killing strike, and he heard Ander mumbling his prayer. Would the gods forgive him this failure? Would he forgive himself for not being to protect those who'd put their faith in him?

The dragon lifted its head back and began to exhale.

CHAPTER 23

Tolan watched as the creature prepared to unleash hell on earth. At first, Tolan could not believe what he was seeing, for the only place where a thing such as this existed was in stories and legends of old. But then, if the Old Ones were only known through the same, Tolan should not be surprised that a dragon had just crawled up from the earth.

Giving him and Thea and Geoffrey nothing more than a glance, the dragon turned its sight on those outside the stones. Those who had stood and did stand against it. Those who called themselves the Warriors of Destiny and the humans who fought alongside them. To Tolan's absolute horror, the first wave of fiery death was aimed at those most vulnerable. The dragon took out a line of William's fighters, killing at least ten men with one breath of flames.

"I have to get Kirwyn," Tolan said. He pressed

Thea against the stone and bade her to remain. "Stay here."

The dragon crawled across the land, regaining its strength and mobility as it headed to other groups gathered around the circle. Tolan ran toward the spot where Hugh stood watching it all, the fireblood's laughter heard above the screams of terror and death. But then something caught Tolan's gaze and he turned to see the creature advancing on the priests. Corann and Ander stood before them, the only thing between the small group of praying defenseless ones and the destroyer poised to kill them.

With only a thought, Tolan thrust up a wall of earthen clay before the priests, protecting them from the first blast of its deadly breath. The heat of it baked the clay as in an oven instead of the people standing behind it. They scurried back away, but the dragon rose now, lifting itself off the ground with a few flaps of its huge wings.

"Soren!" Tolan called out. "Stormblood!" he yelled, and pointed.

A strong burst of wind hit the dragon, knocking it from its path and its intent and sending it tumbling to the ground. It rolled several times before screeching out its fury and rising once more. The stormblood continued to pummel the beast. Each time it stood or tried to rise, the winds would take it down, pushing it to the earth.

Then rain poured in torrents on the beast, creating a thick cloud of steam whenever it breathed its fire. It screamed out in frustration and turned its gaze to other targets.

With the two fighting its every move, Tolan turned his own attentions from the beast and back to reaching his son, who remained in Hugh's grasp there up on the ridge between the stones.

"Kirwyn!" he yelled as he moved the earth to flatten the embankment around the area. Though the move made Hugh stumble, he never lost hold of Kirwyn. Reaching the place before Hugh, Tolan rose and faced the fireblood. "I did as you said. Now release my son."

He tried not to see the agony on his son's face. Hugh's hand still merged with his own and Tolan could not imagine the pain of such a thing. Now Hugh turned to face him and nodded.

"Is she not the most glorious thing you have even seen, Tolan?" Hugh laughed again, nodding at the creature who was trying to escape from the assault of the stormblood and the waterblood. "She has not fed for a long time so is not at her full strength. But even their bloodlines will not help them when she does."

"Hugh," Tolan said again, prepared to beg if need be to get his son out of the clutches of this dangerous man.

"'Tis done here now. We can leave these to the goddess," Hugh said. "She will take care of them and grow stronger. Then we will set the world on fire and make it as we want it to be. Come."

Hugh released his fiery grip on Tolan's son, and Kirwyn stumbled. Tolan took one step and Hugh shouted to stop him.

"He has much to learn, Tolan. As do you," Hugh said in a calm voice. As the battle raged on around them, Tolan only knew he must free his son. "At the goddess's side, we will rule," Hugh said.

Tolan would not do that, nor allow his son to be so tutored, and his resolution must have shown in his expression, for Hugh shook his head. "I can still kill him, Tolan. Doubt it not."

"As I could kill you, my lord?" Kirwyn said softly.

Both Hugh and Tolan noticed the dagger at the same moment. Deadly sharp. Kirwyn held the point of it at Hugh's neck. His hand shook, for it was his left one rather than his right, and from his pain-ridden condition.

"Drop this weapon, Kirwyn," Hugh said. His tone was like that of a rebuking father rather than someone in fear of his life. All it would take to kill him would be one twist of that dagger in his neck and yet he seemed almost patient with Kirwyn.

"You will not use me against my father again," Kirwyn hissed through clenched teeth. He raised his hand, threatening to push the weapon into Hugh's neck. "I will kill you before I let you use me to force him to your bidding again."

Fierce pride warred with terror at the sight before Tolan. His son was braver than even he was, and Tolan wished he had known that. Now, though, Tolan must stop this. Hugh could kill the boy in an instant, and yet he did not.

"You see, Tolan? He is stronger than you thought and will grow stronger, too."

"Nay!" Kirwyn said. "I will not be your pawn."

Kirwyn's arm shook badly now and Tolan would

not be able to get there quickly enough to stop either thing from happening. His son bent his hand at the wrist and started to push the dagger in. The moment seemed to last for hours until an unseen guard thrust his sword through Kirwyn from behind.

Blood sputtered from Kirwyn's mouth as he looked at Tolan in surprise and disbelief. He began to fall and Hugh caught him, exchanging a momentary and inexplicable glance with Tolan. As Tolan ran to them, Hugh lifted Kirwyn in his arms and tossed his son to him.

He cradled Kirwyn to his chest, tears pouring from his eyes as his son forced a breath in and out. Blood poured from the deadly wound and from his mouth.

"Kirwyn," Tolan whispered. "Son."

Kirwyn's chest rattled and he took his last breath. His eyes, the blue-green color that was part of him and Corliss, now stared sightlessly into the smoky sky above.

"Nay!" Tolan roared.

He could not be dead. He could not die. Kirwyn was his only child, the only thing left of Corliss. His son. Tears poured down his cheeks as he rocked the boy as he had many times before. When he was sick. When he was teething. When he was hurt. Tolan walked the floors of their cottage for many hours soothing whatever hurt his beloved son.

Now . . . nothing he did could fix this.

He screamed out his pain and wrapped himself around Kirwyn, taking him into the earth beneath them. Mayhap the earth itself could save him? Mayhap his power over it could bring Kirwyn back to life? He burrowed deep and far, praying to the Old Ones for their help. Praying for their blessings.

Praying for their forgiveness.

Tolan stopped, holding his son close, and knew the truth of it—the gods would not give favor to one who had betrayed them.

His son was dead and evil had been let loose on the world.

His son was dead.

The guard was dead an instant after the boy died.

With but a glance, Hugh killed the guard and motioned for Eudes to gather their troops. The goddess would destroy the others and then take flight, seeking a refuge to regain her strength. And Hugh would follow her.

Even if the others could survive her attacks, their ranks would be decimated and they would not be able to do much but gather to lick their wounds. And stand by uselessly as Hugh fulfilled the work of countless generations in bringing about the reign of Chaela.

Hugh watched as Tolan caught his son and realized he was dying. A strange sensation filled him then, one he had not allowed himself to feel in a long time.

True regret over such a loss.

The boy had such potential, but more than that, he was bright and inquisitive and someone Hugh would have found joy in teaching. Mayhap his death was a better thing, for allowing some kind of tender feelings to build between them might create a weakness in Hugh as it had in the boy's own father? Hesitation could not be allowed in following the goddess, so this removed any possibility.

Within seconds, Tolan had engulfed the boy and taken him underground, as he had Geoffrey. Did he think he could bring the boy back to life? Restore him somehow with his own power and that of the earth from whence he drew it?

It would not work. Hugh had tried it before, using the power of his gift to raise the dead. So he knew Tolan would fail.

Eudes brought Hugh's horse and he mounted, searching within and without the standing stones for his cousin. Geoffrey had succeeded beyond Hugh's expectations, in both finding the necessary words and conducting the ritual to open the gateway. Both Hugh and the goddess owed him much.

"Can you see Geoffrey?" he called out to Eudes as they rode north. "He is supposed to bring the sun-blood to us."

He'd most likely expected too much of his cousin in this regard. With Hugh's promise to draw the earth-blood away, Geoffrey was to bring the woman to him when the confusion could cover his actions. Without the earthblood to protect her, it should be a simple, though not easy task. And yet Hugh could see his cousin within the circle near the woman. Hugh rode closer, intent on grabbing her when Geoffrey pushed her outside the stones.

He stopped just a few paces from the stones, gaping at the abyss now that was still opened into the earth. When he had been allowed a glimpse at the place where the other gods had imprisoned Chaela, his human mind could not conceive of such a place. Now, seeing the chasm and the sheer size of it, he could not imagine it existing, let alone being created by a single god's thought alone.

At the sound of the sunblood's screams, he looked into the circle and saw her struggling with his cousin. Geoffrey was trying to drag her, and when that was not successful, he pushed her back against one of the stones. He only got one chance before she fought back.

In an action even Hugh did not consider, Elethea exploded with the light of the sun, losing her body's limitations and surrounding her attacker with light and heat. Hugh knew she healed with such a power, but this time it was something different. Geoffrey glowed brightly for a moment as she held on to him and he screamed in pain. The shining light that filled him began to grow dull with each passing second until it went out.

Hugh's cousin was dead. His body remained like an empty husk before her until she pushed him away, shaking her head as though she did not believe what she'd done. He knew immediately what had happened. Just as she was the healing and life force of the sun, she could also take that life force from someone.

Hugh laughed and called to her then, holding out his hand for her to come to him. "Elethea! Come with me now!"

She looked at him in horror and backed away, from his cousin's body now at her feet, and from him.

At Eudes's call, Hugh knew he had no more time to

wait for her. This would not be their last encounter, and he would get the opportunity to invite her to join him. That would be the last offer he would make to her before he and his goddess destroyed her and any left standing against them.

Hugh shivered in anticipation of conquering this one and the Norse woman and then he answered Eudes's call and rode west.

To Wales.

The dragon's unholy gaze fell upon Aislinn when it could not reach the priests. With Tolan gone, the war-blood knew not when he would return, or if he would at all. The boy died right in front of his father, and Tolan had gone to earth. Now the most valuable of their allies was under attack.

Brienne! William called out to his mate. Looking across the wide expanse, he saw her following Hugh and knew she planned to fight him. But the seer, the daugh-ter of the moon, needed her help now. The fireblood in her seemed stronger somehow. Once the goddess was freed, Brienne had done things he'd not seen before.

Now she could travel through the air without need-ing a source of fire to target. Will watched as she flowed much like a current of air across the plain toward him. He began running toward Aislinn when Brienne passed him. Charging the beast himself, the warblood turned his hands into war hammers and pounded into her side. Startled more than hurt, the dragon smiled and inhaled and aimed her foul breath at him.

The fireblood that was Brienne's father had burned

him once. During their battle to close the first circle, Hugh had attacked him with the flames. He was certain the dragon's would be fiercer and more dangerous than that. He drew more strength from his powerful blood and prepared to feel it.

The next moment, Brienne spread herself like a shield before him, her fire protecting him from the dragon's fire. He could feel her straining to keep a barrier between him and the goddess and he reached out and touched her with his hand. Rather than burning him, it strengthened him and her, for she pushed her flames back against the dragon, sending the creature flailing away, screeching in pain.

Only a moment later, it reared back and sent a wide burst of fire across the area, catching more of William's men. Once more, the creature sought out Aislinn, knowing the young woman was at the heart and soul of any plans against her yet. She flew up into the sky, fighting off the push of the winds, and swooped down at the woman. The warblood changed his path, too, running to once more throw himself at the beast.

Aislinn's guard pushed her to the ground and covered her with his body just as the dragon flew over them, taking the brunt of the attack. Then Brienne formed above them, shielding them. But she could not be both places at once, and the dragon knew that. From her position above them, it spewed fire in many directions until it could not. The warblood took advantage of that momentary weakness to call out his order.

"Attack!" he growled. "Now!"

After so long defending against the evil one, it felt good to him to begin an offensive plan. Using all their powers and all their strengths and weapons at hand, the Warriors and the humans beat the dragon back away. And as Brienne had suspected, the beast was weakening from so long a confinement without sustenance. Finally, with swords and crossbows, with winds and water and fire and brute force, they chased her out of the clearing.

Sensing the immediate danger was done, the warblood sank back inside and William spoke. "See to the injured and the dead. We must make plans as soon as we can."

"Should I follow her?" Soren asked.

Looking off in the distance, in the direction that the dragon had flown, William knew it would be easy enough to track her. He shook his head.

"Unfortunately, she will be easy to find," he said as Brienne walked to his side. He took her hand and kissed it. "My thanks for coming to my aid."

"And mine, my lady," Brisbois said. His voice startled everyone, for he never spoke first or freely among them. De Gifford's former torturer nodded at the niece to whom he'd sworn fealty and bowed.

Will felt Brienne's discomfort and looked away for a moment at the stones. Elethea stood there, alone, leaning against one of them. He nodded at her and Brienne walked over in that direction.

"Bring the injured together," he said. "Set up some tents over there and gather our supplies." He pointed to a place outside the embankment. "We will see if Elethea will aid us."

"Are you certain you want to ask her?" one of the men asked. "She helped open the gateway."

Will could not deny her guilt, but he could not be certain he would not have made the same decision if faced with a child of his and Brienne's being held hostage. "She remains behind when she could have gone with de Gifford and the goddess. Which of you can say you would not have chosen to protect your child if forced to it?" He met the gazes of those around him and nodded. "We will need her help and Tolan's, if he returns."

Will walked off after Brienne and caught up with her as she reached the standing stones. She stopped and did not enter.

"I can still feel the goddess's evil here," she said as he now escorted her in and to where Elethea stood.

"The chasm remains open. She spent endless centuries in there," he said. They reached the sunblood, who stared at the ground before her and did not speak.

"Elethea?" Brienne said, walking toward her. That was when they noticed the body there.

"Is that Lord Geoffrey?" Will asked, crouching down closer and examining the body.

A nod was all the response he received. Reaching out to touch the corpse, he found the skin now in thin, dried layers like husks of corn left out in the sun. But whatever had been inside this body had withered and died. All it took was a touch for the whole thing to collapse in upon itself. The flakes were caught by the breezes and carried off like ashes on the wind after a fire.

Watching her now, Will recognized the expression on her face. Her brown eyes glazed over and her skin was pale. She wore the look of someone who had killed for the first time. He'd trained men for battle and knew that the first kill left them marked by it. 'Twas not his place to speak about it with her—Tolan should do that—so he did the thing he could—he tried to distract her to another task.

"We have many injured, Elethea. Would you heal them?"

She startled at his words.

"You would ask my help? After . . . this . . . all?" she asked.

"Aye." Will did not embellish it. A simple request and a simple answer was best at times like these.

She looked from him to Brienne and then at the place where the body had disintegrated and nodded. "I will help."

Brienne wrapped her arm around Elethea's and began walking in silence at her side. As she passed him, he asked the question.

"Do you know where Tolan is?"

She shook her head. "Not here. I cannot feel him any longer."

They walked to where the injured had been placed and he watched as her hands glowed. He left her there with Brienne and Aislinn and went to see to his men. Some hours later, as the sun reached its zenith, she yet moved among their numbers, laying her hands on one and then the next and the next.

But when evening came, she was gone.

CHAPTER 24

Thea lost count of those she tended that day. She moved from one to another, guided by Brienne and Aislinn and a few of the other women who oversaw such things in the camp. She did not speak to anyone or even meet their gazes, for she did not wish to see the hatred and loathing that would be there for her and Tolan.

Other than accepting a cup of water and a crust of bread, she did not stop the whole of the day. She asked no questions and did not remain with anyone too long. But mostly she stayed that busy to avoid thinking on what she and Tolan had done.

Oh, their actions had been for a good reason, the best really, but the results were catastrophic—an evil goddess in the form of one of the deadliest creatures possible now roamed the lands. Kirwyn died in spite of their attempts to prevent it. Tolan had disappeared into the earth.

And she had murdered someone.

To anyone watching, it would have appeared as though she defended herself against Geoffrey's attempts to take her to his cousin. And that was how it began.

Before her anger rose.

And her loathing for what they had done together.

When she reached out and grabbed Geoffrey's arm, at first to push him away, it became something else. In her mind, she knew they had sinned. If she accompanied Lord Hugh to the goddess, Thea knew she would do worse things than she'd done here today.

She felt Geoffrey's life within him—the beating heart, the breathing lungs, the pumping blood and more—and wished for it to be gone. She sensed his own light shining within him and snuffed it out like a candle, drawing all the heat and warmth from it until it sputtered out and died.

As he did.

She turned onto her knees and vomited in the grass there. Her stomach clenched and she retched long after the meager food had left her. When she sat back, someone handed her a wet piece of cloth and she wiped her mouth with it.

"I have been told by one of some skill that you should rinse with this but not swallow it right now," Aislinn said, offering her a cup of water. She followed the instructions, knowing the truth of them.

"Who is the skilled one?" she asked, looking up at the young seer.

"Enyd," Aislinn replied. "One of those who traveled from the island with us." Aislinn looked in the distance where the priests had gathered. "She is the tall woman, with pale hair."

"Well, she is well learned if she gave this advice."

Their trite conversation at an end, Thea watched as Aislinn prepared to say something of import to her.

"The others have told me that they can feel the others of the bloodlines. More their mates, but also the others." Aislinn met her gaze then. "Can you sense Tolan? Is he . . . alive?"

Thea closed her eyes and tried to find him. He was not nearby. Or was he . . . dead? Nothing. It was as though all the lands around them were as empty as her own heart was right now.

"I . . ." She could not speak of him.

Aislinn laid her hand on top of Thea's in a comforting gesture, one she would have done to those she helped or healed. But the kindness was too much. The woman seemed to understand, for she stood and turned to leave.

"We had no idea when we left the island what we would find. For all our lives, we were taught that those designated as Warriors of Destiny would be gods made anew on earth."

"Are you disappointed to find we are more human than godlike?" Thea asked. What a failure they must be to these faithful people who worshipped their ancestors for so long!

"In truth, I am in awe of you, of all of you," Aislinn said. "You have inherited a great power that you had no idea about and that could make you more than you are."

"And what are we now?" Thea asked.

"People who are trying to do the right thing for the rest of humanity. In spite of a lack of knowledge. In spite of a lack of faith. You have accepted this burden and you keep going even while you struggle with the power you have."

Thea looked at the woman now and noticed the silvery glow pulsing faintly around her. Even her eyes had taken on the color of the moon. Had she some power flowing through her veins as well?

"You felt the other part of your power this day. Each of the bloodlines has a power that can help and can hurt. It is the balance that you must seek."

Did she know? Did she know that Thea had killed today?

"Aye, I know the choice you made and the price you pay even now," Aislinn whispered. "Others have had to face that same choice. And you may yet again. But do not let it break your spirit, Sunblood. There is yet much for you to do."

The seer walked away then, leaving Thea to the solitude she'd sought when she was no longer needed. A tingle teased her then. An awareness of . . . Tolan. She stood and looked about but did not see or hear him. Was he within the earth as he had done before? Pressing her hand to the soil, she tried to sense him.

It was only when she looked off in the distance that she realized where he was. And she found a horse and went to him.

Thea lifted the latch and entered quietly, not knowing what she would find inside. Oh, Tolan was there now, but in what condition she knew not. She used her power to bring some light to the cottage so she could find her way around it. Her visit here had been brief and had only involved this chamber. Glancing at the back, she knew she would find within that room.

And so she did.

He sat with his back to her, on the edge of a raised pallet. His shoulders hunched over and an air of desolation filled him. His grief was so strong that the aura that outlined him was dulled somehow. This usually vibrant, strong man who moved among the villagers with ease was now broken by sorrow. Thea walked to him and placed her hands on his shoulders.

And that was when she saw Kirwyn's body there on the pallet. She'd heard Tolan's cry when it happened, but she had not seen the boy's death. His body lay there as though he slept.

"He told Hugh he would be a pawn no more, Thea." Tolan's voice cracked as he said it. He reached up and touched her hand, sliding his fingers around hers. "He fought off the fireblood who had tormented him so."

'Twas then she saw Kirwyn's hand, a lump of mangled and melted flesh that would never heal now. How Kirwyn had managed to stay conscious was beyond her. That he fought with Hugh in the face of such agony spoke well of the boy's courage. Her tears fell freely then, mourning the young man's valiant refusal to be used against his father as a hostage.

All for naught.

All for naught.

Tolan tugged her to him, pulling her around to sit

on his lap there as he poured out his grief. His sobs were silent, but she heard them welling from deep within his soul. He wrapped his arms around her and she held him tightly.

She could have given him solace and relief, but somehow it was wrong not to let him grieve in this way. He needed to release the pain and honor his son's actions. Or there would be no time when he could forgive himself for the boy's death.

They sat there in silence for some time after the tears ceased and she waited for some sign that he was ready to talk. Finally, he lifted his head and kissed her.

"I tried to save him, to bring him back to life," he admitted. "I thought if I took him into the earth, to where new life is beginning, he could absorb some of it and be alive again." He rubbed his hand across his eyes and laughed bitterly. "But my gift for bringing fertility and life to the lands does not extend to my son."

"If I could, Tolan," she began. The thought had crossed her mind as well, since the sun gave life. Mayhap if she laid hands on him and gave him some of her life's force, it would bring him back?

"Nay," he said, shaking his head. "We have played gods too much, Thea, and interfered when we should not have. This is the price I pay for my arrogance. This terrible price . . ." His voice shook then and he stopped.

After a few minutes of quiet, she slid from his lap and knelt there at Kirwyn's side, praying for his soul and for forgiveness. It gave her some comfort to use the words and prayers with which she'd been raised.

"I would bury him next to his mother so that she might watch over his soul," Tolan whispered then.

"A good place for a boy to be," she said. Her barrenness did not mean she could not understand a mother's love. "May I clean him?"

Tolan did not answer, but he moved aside for her to get closer. She went and gathered a bucket of water and some cloths from a trunk. It took some time, but with Tolan's help, she washed Kirwyn, removed his bloody clothing, and dressed him in a pair of breeches and a tunic that Tolan found there.

They said nothing, but Thea found herself softly humming the melody she'd heard Linne sing to her babe as she prepared him to be buried. Tears fell as she finished, wrapping him in a blanket and stepping back so Tolan could take him.

It wasn't right. A father should not bury his son. If only they had . . . If only they had not . . . She tried to be strong for him when she wanted to sob in sorrow.

"Would you want a blessing prayed for him before you take him, Tolan? I could seek out Father Ander or Corann if you wish."

"Aye," he said in a toneless voice.

She left him there to grieve alone while she rode back to the camp the others had set up. But when she returned, it was not with only the two priests.

Tolan felt them coming and walked out of the cottage. Instead of bringing only the two priests, as he had when he left Thea in the woods, she returned with everyone. The priests, the Warriors, the soldiers, the others—all who had witnessed his betrayal of their quest and his greatest failure. And yet he did not feel their censure as he surely deserved. He felt their sympathy and their grief at Kirwyn's death.

Father Ander and Corann, followed by Aislinn, entered the house after asking his permission, to give a blessing there. The rest stood beside him and at his back waiting for it to be done.

There had been such loss among them, this day and during their previous battles, and no one was untouched by grief. And yet they fought on and now they stood here accepting him and Thea after their weakness. What a fool he'd been to think they could somehow outsmart this great evil by themselves!

The priests and Aislinn came back out and walked over to him. Aislinn did not hesitate; she approached him and pulled him close in a hug, offering him words of sympathy. She was but the first, as every person there—be they man or woman—came and said something comforting. Even the other Warriors had offered their support before stepping away.

"Do you wish us to take him to the graveyard?" Father Ander asked. "We could see to it in the morning."

"Nay," Tolan said. "I will take him now." The priest nodded and stepped out of his way.

Entering the house once more, he placed the last fold of blanket around his son's face and lifted him into his arms. Carrying him outside, he nodded to Thea and then entered the earth. He traveled along the road and paths that Kirwyn had walked, through the village and finally to the entrance of the graveyard on the edge of the village. Rising from the ground, he walked to the row where Corliss had been laid to rest and he stood there for a few minutes, holding his son for the last time.

Tolan asked the soil to open and it did. Finally, because every second of holding him made it more difficult to part from him, he knelt down and laid his son in the grave. Though he could have moved the earth to cover Kirwyn with his thoughts, he did it with his hands, scooping the loose soil into place and pressing it down securely around the boy. When it was done, he stood and walked away.

He did not look back and chose to make his way through the village where he'd lived all his life. Passing the cottages of kith and kin, Tolan knew he would never return here. And if he and the others were not successful, this place might be destroyed along with countless other places in this world.

Resolved that his son had not died in vain, Tolan walked to the north road and then traveled back to Durrington. He needed to find Thea.

Thea watched as everyone else left and made their way back to the camp near the circle. Their response to her plea gave her hope in this time of terrible grief and loss.

Tolan had left some time ago, but she waited there at the cottage for him. She cleaned the bedchamber and straightened up as best she could. Realizing that it could be some time, she heated water and found the herbs that they'd brought with them . . . two days ago?

Her life had been in such chaos these last days, she'd lost track of it all.

And truly, it mattered not what day it was as long as she was with him. She would treasure every moment because she knew it could not last. Sitting on a stool before the hearth, she sipped the tea and let it soothe her.

If they survived what was coming, if they were able to return here to Durrington or to Amesbury, she could not remain with Tolan. More than ever, he would need sons and she could not give them to him. She would step aside, disavow their marriage, for it was completely irregular and could never be defended, to give him the chance at a family.

It was the only thing she could do for him now.

"You are thinking so hard I can hear your thoughts rumbling around in your head," he said from the doorway.

"Is it done, then?" she asked. She reached for the metal cup sitting at the edge of the hearth and handed it to him.

"Aye."

One sad word to mark the end of his son's life. She heard the hint of desolation in his voice in that one word. It reinforced the decision she'd made.

He stood in silence at her side, drinking from his cup. He reached over and pulled her closer to him. She savored his strength and his warmth for a few minutes. When they finished their tea, she moved to take his cup, but he stopped her. He took hers and his and dropped them to the ground. Wrapping his arms around her, he leaned his face to hers and kissed her softly.

"So, tell me what made your thoughts so dark that you lost your glow," he said. "Is it Kirwyn?"

"He is a part of it, Tolan," she said, releasing him and stepping back . . . or trying to. He would not let her put any distance between them. "I want you to know that when this is done, when all of it is done, I will release you."

"Release me?" He frowned and shook his head. "From what?"

"From our marriage," she explained. "'Twill be crucial for you to have—"

He stopped her then, placing his hand over her mouth and shaking his head. "'Twill be crucial for me to have you at my side. Always, Thea. I cannot seek justice for Kirwyn's death without you, and I will not live without you when we have claimed it."

"We could not save your son," she said sadly.

"You risked your life and your immortal soul to help me save my son. You risked everything because I asked it of you, my love. I will not let you go. Not now, not ever."

He would not hear anything she said then, and her heart soared when she realized he would not allow her to leave him. No matter what happened. No matter what came. They would face it together. When he kissed her then, he reminded her of the love he felt for her that not even grief and loss could diminish or destroy.

Thea told him that the others had asked to meet at

the stones in the morn. A decision would be needed about seeing it closed and the stones hidden away from view once more. The other two times, the circles had disappeared on their own, but this time was so different.

They spent the rest of the night wrapped in each other's embrace, talking quietly about what was to come. They would offer their help in undoing the terrible thing they'd done when they released Chaela from her prison. For, as William and Brienne had told her, they were stronger together and could not succeed without each other.

The sun shone bright on the lands the next morning, giving Thea hope that they might just succeed after all.

CHAPTER 25

Tolan and Thea approached the standing stones once more, and though he struggled not to look, he gazed over at the place where his son had died. It all poured through his memory in a moment or two and he shuddered at it. The feel of Thea's hand taking his reminded him that they would seek justice for his son and the countless others who'd died fighting this evil.

They found the priests standing outside the perimeter of the embankment in a group. From their expressions and words, they were discussing the very thing he and Thea had talked about all night. Of course, with their experience and knowledge, the others would know more about what could and should happen now that all this had been exposed.

"Tolan. Elethea," Corann said with a nod. Whispers of "Sunblood" and "Earthblood" floated through the group from those who could not address them by name. "The stones are still here."

"Since the two before disappeared after they were sealed," Aislinn began, "we know not if these will."

"I feel nothing from this entire place," Tolan admitted. "I do not believe it will go away on its own."

The first two gateways had been sealed, keeping their power to imprison the goddess strong and vibrant. This third one was empty and dead, without the power that the gods had imbued it with to keep in evil.

"You can bury it? Bury all this?" Father Ander asked, looking around at the width and breadth of the place.

"I think it should all be buried. Deep. So that none can find them again."

"We agree," William said, leading the other Warriors and Roger to where they stood.

"If we are to find that fourth circle and, gods willing, imprison her once more, should this gateway remain open?" Brienne asked. "Is there a way to close this portal so it cannot be used again?"

Tolan shrugged. He knew less about this part of it than any of them. "Thea suggested that since my ancestor created it, I could . . ." He searched for a word to describe it.

"Increate it? Take it out of existence?" Aislinn suggested. "Corann, what think you?"

"Since it was made by the gods and you were given his powers, I think it is possible."

"I want to try," Tolan said. "Then"—he pointed around the area—"I will bury the stones back in the embankment and the circle back under the earth."

"The thicket will return to hide it all once more?" Thea asked.

"Nay. Nothing will grow in this place forever."

His words settled over them as he considered how he might manage to increate such a thing.

"And how can we help you?" Soren said, walking to his side. "We must make certain it can never be used again."

"We must all do what we do best," Corann said. "We will pray and lay blessings and spells down on the area. You of the bloodlines must concentrate and support Tolan with your powers. Roger, you and the others must stand guard and make certain we are not disturbed."

"If everyone is in agreement, let us see to this so that we may make plans for our next step."

"There is a problem." Aislinn's soft voice carried much weight, so no one moved. "We have not received the prophecy. We know not where to go other than to follow the evil one's trail."

"Which may not lead us where we must go," Corann added.

"Where have you found these prophecies before?" Thea asked. "Do they come from praying or other worship? Pray do not say from sacrifice!"

"Nay! We do not sacrifice in that way to the gods, Thea," Corann said strongly. "Though some have given their lives freely to the gods in this endeavor, they have not demanded such blood in eons." Thea was no doubt thinking about the vision she'd seen. From the expression on Ran's face, she, too, remembered her own.

"We have found them within the circle," Aislinn explained. "But we"—she nodded to the other priests there gathered—"we have not dared to enter it yet."

"It is dead, Aislinn. You might feel her remnants, but she and whatever kept her there are gone," Tolan said. "Come, walk with me now." He held out his hand to the young woman and she took it, walking at his side.

When they reached the embankment, she began to tremble. The voices of the other priests joined in unison, murmuring some prayer as they crossed that first boundary. With each stride closer to the stones, he felt the resistance growing within her until he finally halted about four yards from the circle.

"Can you do this, Aislinn? Must you?" he asked her quietly.

"Go ahead of me, Tolan. I need a moment or two."

He nodded and led the others into the circle.

Brisbois was unnerved by the circle. Aislinn could feel his discomfort, which seemed more than hers for some reason. She watched him fidget and shift his stance several times and knew something was wrong.

"You need not be at my side," Aislinn said. "Roger and the soldiers have us protected, and the only ones here are our people."

His usual response would have been a belligerent

grumble and nothing else, so when he nodded and stepped back, it surprised her. As she looked around, she noticed that not everyone entered the circle easily. Some of the other priests yet lingered along the outside, struggling to make themselves enter such a place.

Aislinn moved from one stone to the next, examining the outside surfaces for any clue or marks. She walked the entire circle and found nothing. Glancing inside, she could see the blood-covered altar there and suspected that she must go within and touch it to find the prophecy they needed.

Then the stone on which her hand lay grew warm. She looked at the one standing opposite and saw that it was not marked by a bloodline symbol, but with that of the moon. Her mark burned then.

"Have you dreamed of him yet, little priestess?" a woman asked from behind her. Aislinn turned and found a strange woman there.

"What did you say?" Aislinn asked the woman. She did not look familiar, and yet she did in some way. "Do I know you?"

The woman smiled at her and nodded, holding out her hand to Aislinn. Feeling no fear, Aislinn took hold of it. . . .

The field was empty. No one stood within the stones now. The woman was gone, too, leaving Aislinn alone there.

The gaping chasm in the center of the circle was gone. Each stone glowed in its own way—a different color surrounding each one. The colors of the gods. The colors of the auras carried by the bloodlines. Blue and orange. Green and gold. Gray and turquoise. Looking across the circle, Aislinn saw the silvery one opposite of this closest red one.

She touched the stone and it grew warm beneath her hands. Gazing up, she saw the mark of Epona glowing there. The goddess of animals. The protector of horses. Her own mark seared deeper into her skin, dancing and moving like something alive.

Aislinn noticed that the woman was dressed more finely than anyone who traveled with them was. Her long black hair and blues eyes shone as though lit from within. Long ribbons of red twisted through her hair, and red jewels sparkled in rings on her fingers and necklaces around her neck.

"Who are you?" Aislinn asked, facing her.

The woman began to walk around the stone there, leading Aislinn in circling it seven times.

"One who watches you. Can you see them now?" the woman said, now once more at her side.

Aislinn had begun to shake her head when something moved on the stone. High above her head, etchings appeared, moving across and around the surface of it, like dancing flowers in the wind.

"Look closely, priestess. The words should be easy for one who sees them."

The shapes stopped then and arranged themselves in lines of words before Aislinn.

Praise be! This was the needed prophecy here carved on the stone. Aislinn spoke the words to herself first, knowing she must remember them to share them with the others.

The last ones gather to stand, Seven and One to close the circle. One of the Most Revered will lead the leader and step by step, stone by stone, the Six will triumph, the Seventh conquered.

She repeated the words again aloud.

"Praise be!" Corann shouted. "Praise be the gods have revealed their words to us!"

"A message of some hope," Father Ander added. "We do have another chance!"

Aislinn turned, confused to find herself standing within the circle and surrounded by the other priests and Warriors.

"What happened?" she asked, looking for the woman who had led her to this stone. The woman outlined in red like the stone of Epona. The woman who now stood before it, smiling at her.

"Daughter of the moon, Aislinn of Cork, you are beloved of the gods and blessed. Lead them," the woman whispered.

No one else seemed to hear or see her. She began to fade, becoming the stone, but in that instant before she did, the woman tossed something to her. "Find him there."

And she was gone.

"You dropped something, Aislinn," Enyd said, picking up a small object from the ground there.

A small horse. Like the other one she'd found in Orkney. Visions of a tall, muscular man with black hair and blues eyes came to mind as she gripped the horse in her hand.

Find him there.

"I know where the final circle is," she said to them. "I know where we must go."

Silence reigned at her words. Corann walked to her and took her hand. "What did you see, Aislinn? You stood there staring at the stone and mumbling. We dared not interfere."

"The final circle is—"

Corann squeezed her hand then, stopping her from speaking. "You must not, lady. Marcus said you could never return there."

"Lady?" William asked. "You called her lady, Corann. What means this?"

"You knew this, Corann." Aislinn met the older man's gaze and saw the truth. "You have known all along?"

"Nay, Aislinn. I knew you were special and came to us for that reason. Marcus only told me when he left to face down the goddess's minion. He knew he would not return to us and bade me see to your protection."

Aislinn glanced around and knew they waited on her answer, to know her story of how she came to live with the priests all those years ago. But for now, all they must know was their destination. She looked at the Warriors before her. "The final circle, the one that can conquer the goddess once more as your ancestors did eons ago, is across the sea in Ireland. The first place where the gods sought refuge on their long journey."

It took some time before the excitement of hearing the prophecy, words of hope truly, and learning their destination to calm down. Tolan watched the expressions of that hope and anticipation along with confusion and surprise on the faces there. Not having been there to witness the other prophecies received, he had no idea if this was normal or not.

"What will you do, Tolan?" Thea was at his side.

He'd thought of little else this last hour while the priests searched, and Aislinn found, the words needed to guide them forward. "I will undo what I did in the opposite order that I first acted."

"So, the chasm first and the stones next?" Thea asked.

"Aye, and then I will level this land, bury the stones, and raise the embankment."

"How can I help you?" she asked.

Just seeing the love in her gaze and knowing she would always be with him was enough. But he did not have to tell her that. "Stand with me. Belenus is the god of life and order," he said. "I think your power will make this easier."

He'd fought each stone in the circle into place and now he realized that the strong spells holding them beneath the ground had been a warning to him. One he ignored. One he, they, paid for.

It took some time to clear everyone from within the stones, but once they were away, he nodded to Thea. The other bloodlines stood at their side, offering whatever they could to his effort.

Staring at the abyss there in the center, Tolan knew he could not break through it, not even now when its purpose was done. So, instead, he thought one word, in the ancient language of the Church, as Father Ander taught him.

Increatus.

He said it in his thoughts several times before making it a chant as all his prayers to the gods were. Over and over, he sang it to himself and then aloud. He felt the power in his blood rise and the word took on its own power, echoing around the circle and into the abyss.

Increatus. Increatus. Increatus.

The ground beneath them shook and rolled. The stones trembled in their places and then the chasm began to . . . shrink. The walls vibrated as though they would break, but instead they tightened and tightened until they pulled in on themselves and closed before his eyes. Soon, nothing was there but the ground. The center of the circle was now unmarked and closed.

Increated.

The Warriors moved out of the circle and Tolan entered the earth, pulling each stone down and anchoring it with another chant. The one to close. It took less effort to return these to their original places deep under the ground than it had to raise them.

The only stone he did not allow to remain in the condition in which he'd found it was the altar stone. Tolan rose as a being of granite and crushed the altar into small pieces, pushing each of them deep into the soil. Finally, he smoothed the ground over the whole area and turned his attention to the stones on the ridge.

One for each day of the year. They were the easiest

and he moved quickly through the embankment, pulling them down until they were covered once more. With only a thought, he leveled the raised slope back to what it had been on his arrival there.

In just a few hours, the entire area of Durrington appeared to be nothing out of the usual in the landscape here. Tolan left with Thea at his side, knowing that these stones would never rise again.

William de Brus, it turned out, was a master at planning and strategy even in the absence of the warblood. He had his men packing and readying supplies by midday. Discussions about how to get to Ireland and all manner of other things continued through that day and into the next.

They needed supplies and more men to fill their ranks, and William and Roger and the others still left who'd sworn to William's cause made great progress in preparing for this last journey. No one spoke of what would happen or how they would find the circle. Or of the last remaining bloodline. For those things, they needed Aislinn and Corann's counsel and neither of them was speaking on it.

So it took another sennight before they left Amesbury and traveled south and west to the coast and to their ships. And soon, Tolan and Thea watched the land of their birth fade into the distance.

The Aftermath

It took Hugh a fortnight to find her hiding place.

And another sennight to see her recovered from her eons-long ordeal. And none of it was what he'd expected.

Chasing her trail, he'd driven his men hard to the west, slowed by the craggy heights of ancient mountains when they arrived in the west and crossed into Wales. Mist-filled glens and caves abounded there and were the stuff of legends. A dragon would not be unusual, he thought as they rode through yet another decimated village.

Those sacrificed by him and his ancestors were to appease and honor her and did nothing to relieve her hunger for human flesh. And that hunger was now being satisfied, for every burned village and hamlet that they traveled through was completely emptied of people. Not a single bone or body was found anywhere.

She was devouring them whole.

A prickling of fear tickled along his spine as they reached her hiding place. They had never spoken about many things in their encounters, and though they had done many things, Hugh had never seen her in human form. A human body could not have survived in that desolate place, but a dragon had.

Come to me, Hugh.

He heard her voice within his thoughts from high up on the mountainside and nodded at Eudes. Strange how differently she sounded now that she was no longer in the abyss.

Bring me sacrifices, my loyal one. Men. Vigorous men.

His mind was flooded with images then and he shuddered at what he saw. She would take them, take their life's blood and force and burn them to ashes.

"My lord?" Eudes asked, coming to his side. "Are you well?"

Hugh had not realized his expression was showing his horror. It would not do to have anyone think he was anything but pleased to satisfy the goddess's commands. So he lifted his gauntleted arm and backhanded his half brother across the face, knocking him from his horse and forcing the breath from him as he landed.

"Do not question me, Eudes. I am anxious to meet the goddess above. Bring along five, nay, ten, of the men."

It took some time for them to climb up the mountain. Their horses were too large for the narrow, rocky path, so they walked up. The cave was hidden in a crevasse in the side of the mountain and he paused there.

"Come in, Hugh," she said aloud. Her voice, human now, sounded . . . old.

Hugh removed his helmet and gauntlets and walked into the cave first. Though no torches could be seen, there was enough light for him to see and once he looked, he wished he had not.

The light came from fires that had burning bodies as their fuel. The smell nearly knocked him to his knees as he turned a corner and reached a larger inner chamber. Piles of bodies burned in the huge cavern. And in the middle of it all stood an old woman. The fiery orange glow around her body was the only way he knew it was surely Chaela.

Clothed in a few pieces of fabric that once was a garment of some kind, her dried and dying skin hung in folds around her. Her hair, a long gray mass of twisted, filthy locks, hung around her face and to the floor. It dragged around her with each step she took toward him. And when she raised her hand to touch his face, he fought with all his strength not to pull away in revulsion from the curled, centuries-long fingernails.

"Hugh, my beloved," she whispered in a cackling voice. "I need—"

"Eudes!" he called out with a pause. "Send in the first one."

The man stumbled into the chamber and Hugh went to him. Pushing his thoughts into the man, he ordered him to the goddess's side.

Hugh did not look at first. The horrible sounds of her smacking her lips in anticipation was too much for even him. The gurgling sounds and then sexual ones disgusted him and he tried to overpower his errant reactions.

She was Chaela, the Destroyer. The goddess of chaos and fire. The goddess who controlled his life and his destiny. She was everything he'd wanted and waited for and planned for. And she was . . . gorging on the man's face even while she rode his cock. Once she pulled his seed from him, she used her fire to burn him up. In minutes, there was no trace of him.

"Another," she whispered.

He noticed, though he tried not to see anything more, that with each one, once he'd spilled his seed and she'd fed on his carcass, she grew younger and stronger in appearance. Her voice grew less raspy and more vibrant. After the seventh man was dead, he dared a look at her.

Voluptuous breasts pressed against the strips of cloth, barely covering the large dark nipples or the triangle of curls between her legs. Wide hips and muscular legs held her victims in place as she ravaged them now. Her body filled out and womanly curves now replaced the rotting folds of skin. And her hair, black as night, hung in waves down her back.

His body reacted to the sight of her now.

"One more, Hugh," she whispered as she approached him now, fully human, fully woman. Her hand slid down the front of his and cupped his half-aroused prick, bringing it to a full stand. "Then we will have our time. I have waited so long," she said, walking around him, her hand never leaving his cock. "As have you." She laughed, a deep throaty sexual sound that stirred what he thought impossible within him.

He called the last man and this time he watched as she sucked the man's cock and then rode him. Hugh's body ached and throbbed now with need for her. And desire. He began undressing as she pleasured the man to death, his screams echoing through the cavern. By the time she'd wrung the last scream from the dying man's throat and the last drop of seed from his engorged flesh, Hugh stood naked before her, holding his own risen flesh, pumping it as she watched him now.

"Come to me, Hugh. I have waited so long for this."

Hugh did not care that she lay covered in the blood of her now-dead lovers. He stumbled and fell to his knees in his haste to reach her and she laughed in a new voice.

She was young now, no older than his traitorous daughter, with a body that aroused him further. No trace of crone remained. No trace of decay. Only Chaela.

She watched as he half crawled across the slippery floor of the cave to reach her. She spread her legs apart, exposing her cleft to him.

"You are mine now, Hugh de Gifford," she said, grabbing his hair and pulling him to her. She pushed his face against the glistening curls and then deeper until he dared to lick her.

"Worship me, Hugh. Then I will show you the true glories of the fire."

And he did, he worshipped her with his mouth and tongue and hands and cock. She drove him relentlessly, allowing him no rest, bringing his body back to arousal and then emptying him over and over for hours. Only then did she fulfill her other promise.

As the flames surrounded him, as he became part of her, as she forced her fire deep within his flesh and his soul, the screams were both of agony and ecstasy, of ungodly pain and immeasurable pleasure. Of dying and being remade and barely surviving only to have it done again and again.

Days later, when they emerged from the cave together, Eudes stood waiting as he'd been ordered. None would meet Hugh's gaze or dare to look on the goddess who stood at his side. He was certain of only one thing—his belief that he would give anything to serve his goddess and to enjoy the benefits of his loyal service to Chaela.

In spite of the searing pain in the blistering and constantly burning skin on his back and even though he knew she chose to let him remain damaged so that she could inflict agony on him whenever she wished, he would be there on his knees before her and do her bidding forever.

Whatever she commanded, he would do.

Whatever she needed, he would provide.

Whomever must die, he would kill.

For Chaela the Destroyer was his master in all things and he would do whatever he must to protect her. Even though it meant killing his daughter and every other one of the Warriors who were the only threats to her.

The Warriors of Destiny would finally meet theirs in Ireland. And he would be the bringer of their doom.

Don't miss where
the adventures all began in
the first Novel of the Stone Circles,

RISING FIRE

Available now from Signet Eclipse
wherever books and e-books are sold.

When the threat is revealed, the sleepers awaken,
A Warrior seeks the truth
while Fire burns away the deception.
Begin in the East, then North, then South, then West . . .
Find the true gate among the rest.

Late winter, AD 1286
Yester, Scotland

With the morning's cool mist long burned away by the strong rays of the midday sun, Brienne waited until the villagers were all seeing to their daily chores and tasks before deciding that this was the day.

And it was—she could feel it in her bones and in her blood. Something called to her, and some growing urge within her pushed her feet toward the place where she would find out the truth about what lived inside her. There had been tiny glimpses at what it might be, times when fire seemed to answer to her, but she would attempt something this day that she had not dared before.

Taking a deep breath, she lifted the latch and tugged the heavy door open a crack. It creaked on its hinges as she eased it open only wide enough for her to slip inside. Then, after stepping inside the smithy's dark cottage, Brienne closed the door behind her, wanting no interruptions. Since her father was off on an errand, she expected none. Entering into the small building that served as his workshop, she circled the fire pit and tossed in more wood, watching as the existing fire licked at the new pieces and then consumed them. She leaned over and pressed down on the bellows that fed air to the fire, encouraging it to spread and grow hotter and hotter with each breath of air that blew from the pump.

The flames flared higher before her and she could not resist the urge to look deeper into them. Brienne tried to fight their call, tried to fight the strength of it, but lost the battle. She inhaled slowly, trying now to control the fear that simmered in her belly while she moved closer to the fire's heat. As it called to her, icy tendrils slid along her skin in spite of the heat in the smithy. Shivering and sweating at the same time, she lifted trembling hands from her side and held them out.

Not knowing how to do what she planned, Brienne stretched her fingers, wiggling them, and watched as the flames did the same. Then she flexed each finger separately, and single bursts of flame followed each movement. When she twisted her hands, the reaction of the fire was overwhelming.

Each flame danced before her, swirling and dipping this way and that before joining the others in the growing swarm of heat and light. Even when she dropped her hands and closed her eyes, they remained vivid and shifting in her mind.

They danced for her—*they danced for me!*—moving in every direction when she simply thought it, and the sound of their movements surrounded her. Holding her arms out over the fire, she wiggled her fingers over the hearth and laughed as the flames writhed and swirled in answer to her gesture. This was not new to her. She'd done this many times before.

What she planned to do next was different and daring.

Moving her hands in a gathering motion, Brienne pulled the flames together and then spread them out until they filled the space before her, no longer limited to the fire pit and no longer dependent on wood or peat to fuel them. Staring into them, she searched for the center of the brightness and heat and waited.

"Mine."

She strained to keep her eyes on the fire and listened as the whispers came from the heart of it again.

"Come to me."

A shudder coursed through her body, and the fear overwhelmed her as the whispered words surrounded her, enticing her, entreating and tempting her. The back of her neck tingled, and her skin burned as the heat of the flames—nay, the flames themselves—encircled her. Keeping her body still, she waited to hear more, waited to recognize the voice or to learn who called to her through the fire. From deep within her soul, she drew the strength she needed to regain control over the flames and, standing within their embrace, she listened and waited to hear more.

"Daughter of my blood."

Brienne laughed aloud, feeling the power course through her, stronger and stronger each moment. The voice, the words, the flames at her command all confirmed her suspicion that she could control the fire. After hours or minutes—she knew not which—of her standing untouched within the flames, they began to sway and spark around her. As she gathered them once more under her control, they parted for her to move away.

When the voice disappeared completely, when she knew that presence was gone, her fear heightened. The heat began to burn her skin, so she tamped down the flames, guiding them back to the hearth of the smithy, easing them back into the coals of burning wood there so that they would be ready for her father's use. A smile teased the corners of her mouth as inappropriate pride flooded her.

She had done it!

Each time she dared, her power over the fire seemed to grow. And grow stronger. But this day, this time, she had stepped within them without dire consequences. Next time she would—

"Brienne."

She jumped at the interruption and spun around to face the door to the small building. Her father stood there, staring at her. Had he seen her move the fire? From the blank expression on her father's face, she could not tell. Pressing her now-sweating palms on her gown and adjusting her veil back into place, she waited for his reaction.

He closed the door quickly behind himself and checked the shutters, just as she had before attempting to call forth the ability to command the flames. But she'd not barred the door, so he could have seen everything she'd done. Would the flames follow her commands if another were present, or was this something she could do only in secret?

Brienne watched as concern and wariness entered his gaze. Leaving some tools near the doorway, he walked slowly toward his hearth, glancing between it and her several times.

"Are you injured? Are you burned?" he asked as he took one hand of hers and then the other in his larger ones, searching for signs of damage. Then he met her gaze. "How is this possible? What have you done?"

His suspicious, accusatory tone hurt her, but Brienne understood that he was worried about her. She stepped away from him and away from the constant draw of the flames before answering.

"I . . . ," she stammered, not truly knowing how to explain it all to him. Brienne glanced at him, imploring him to understand.

"Come here, lass," he said softly, opening his strong arms to her as he always did.

Embraced by him, she felt safe . . . for the moment. These feelings, these powers, these changes that grew stronger and stronger with each passing day frightened her. There was no one she could speak with about them. No one who could understand or accept that she was more like her true father than anyone had guessed. Even though Gavin the blacksmith had raised her and loved her as his own, she was not.

She shuddered at the thought of her true father, and Gavin responded by hugging her even tighter. The tears gathered in her eyes as she kept silent.

"I will keep ye safe, Brienne," he promised. His words and warm breath tickled her ear, and she nodded, accepting his pledge even if it were not the truth.

"I know you will, Father," she said, nodding her head and granting herself another moment of comfort before moving out of his embrace. "I have so many questions."

As always, her words stopped him. Gavin hated her questions. He hated the reminder that she was not his, that there was another who could step in at any time and take her. And though years had passed since any interest had been shown, all it would take was the untoward word and unguarded action to draw the wrong attention.

"I fear there is little I can add to what you've heard from your mother or ken already, lass. The lord had you brought here to us when you were but days old, giving you into our care. He gave no explanation, no instructions other than to care for you, and he has not interfered since that day," he said. Staring off into the corner, Brienne knew he was thinking on that long-ago day. Turning back to her, he shrugged. "We never had the courage to ask his reasons or why he gave you to us for fear he would take you away."

Brienne smiled at his admission. She knew of no one in Yester Village or in the area who would question Lord Hugh—or anyone who had survived questioning him. A shiver traced a path of icy sparks along her spine. She'd never even had the courage to approach him before, but now, now that she was discovering these powers and understanding he was the only person who could answer her questions, she might.

"Do not!" her father warned, taking hold of her arm and drawing her close. "Do not even think about speaking to him on such"—he glanced at the fires now banked low in his hearth—"such matters as these."

The fear gazing back at her from his eyes should have been enough to steer her from such a path. The whispered warning should have been sufficient to caution anyone not a bairn or a fool. The need that grew ever deeper and stronger within her pushed her in that dangerous direction. The desire to know her origins and the extent of these strange powers that inhabited her never diminished.

Words drifted to her in that silent moment, and she shivered. The power in them tempted her and called to her deepest longings.

Mine. Come to me.

Daughter of my blood.

Brienne, who had belonged to no one, who could call none family or kin, longed to be part of something. And this whispered invitation called to that deep need within her. She tried to shake off the fear and the temptation, but it all settled within her, keeping her blood heated and that unspoken need stoked. Gavin's sad expression called her back to this cottage and this moment.

"Nay, you are right, Father. 'Twould be foolish to speak to him," Brienne assured him, nodding her head.

Gavin kissed her on the top of her head, just as he always had when reassuring her, and released her from his arms.

ABOUT THE AUTHOR

Terri Brisbin is the *USA Today* bestselling author of the Novels of the Stone Circles series, featuring *Raging Sea* and *Rising Fire*. A three-time RWA RITA® finalist, Terri has sold more than two million copies of her historical and paranormal romance novels, novellas, and short stories in more than twenty languages in twenty-five countries around the world since 1998. She lives in New Jersey with her husband. She has three sons and three daughters-in-law and is a dental hygienist.

CONNECT ONLINE

terribrisbin.com
facebook.com/terribrisbin
facebook.com/pages/terribrisbinauthor

From *USA Today* bestselling author

Terri Brisbin

Rising Fire
A Novel of the Stone Circles

Lovely and innocent Brienne of Yester has always been able to manipulate fire, but when her powers suddenly surge, the simple life she once knew explodes.

Handsome, fearless, and commanding William de Brus has been summoned by the king to investigate a nobleman rumored to have powers linked to the fabled fire goddess. When he chances upon Brienne, his desire for her is immediate. But as his mystical quest unfolds, William realizes that she is at the center of it—for Brienne possesses the very power he has been sent to vanquish....

"A richly imagined, spellbinding romantic fantasy."
—*New York Times* bestselling author Lara Adrian

Available wherever books are sold or at
penguin.com

S0609

From *USA Today* bestselling author

Terri Brisbin

Raging Sea
A Novel of the Stone Circles

Eons ago, seven ancient deities trapped the goddess of chaos under a ring of stones. But now, in the darkest days of the 13th century, Chaela threatens to escape, leaving the fate of all humanity in the hands of two young lovers...

After an accident at sea, Ran Sveinsdottir, the daughter of a wealthy Orkney trader, discovers powers she never knew she had. Those powers have drawn her into a battle between two warring factions: the Warriors of Destiny, who she knows in her heart to be noble, and a menacing army holding her father captive. Her hope for survival is in the hands of Soren—the man she once loved, the man who betrayed her, and the only man she can trust in a raging battle against evil.

Available wherever books are sold or at
penguin.com